The Black Rider
and Other Stories

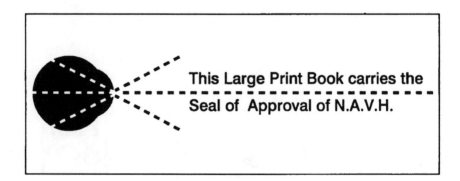

This Large Print Book carries the
Seal of Approval of N.A.V.H.

The Black Rider and Other Stories

Edited and with a Foreword and Headnotes by Jon Tuska

MAX BRAND™

G.K. Hall & Co.
Thorndike, Maine

Acknowledgments for previously published material appear on pages 345–346.

Published in 1996 by arrangement with
University of Nebraska Press.

G.K. Hall Large Print Western Collection.

The text of this Large Print edition is unabridged.
Other aspects of the book may vary from the original edition.

Set in 16 pt. Century Schoolbook by Minnie B. Raven.

Printed in the United States on permanent paper.

Library of Congress Cataloging in Publication Data

Brand, Max, 1892–1944.
   The black rider and other stories / Max Brand ; edited and with a foreword and headnotes by Jon Tuska.
     p.   cm.
Contents: The black rider — The dream of Macdonald — Partners — The power of prayer.
   ISBN 0-7838-1844-0 (lg. print : hc)
   1. West (U.S.) — Social life and customs — Fiction.
2. Western stories.   3. Large type books.   I. Tuska, Jon.
II. Title.
[PS3511.A87A6   1996g]
813'.52—dc20   96-19216

Contents

AUG 1996

Foreword

Max Brand is the best-known pen name of Frederick Faust, creator of Dr. Kildare, Destry, and many other fictional characters popular with readers and viewers worldwide. Faust wrote for a variety of audiences in many genres under numerous pseudonyms. His enormous output, totaling approximately thirty million words or the equivalent of 530 ordinary books, covered nearly every field: crime, fantasy, historical romance, espionage, Westerns, science fiction, adventure, animal stories, love, war, and fashionable society, big business and big medicine. Eighty motion pictures have been based on his work along with many radio and television programs. For good measure he also published four volumes of poetry. Perhaps no other author has reached more people in more different ways.

Born in Seattle in 1892, orphaned early, Faust grew up in the rural San Joaquin Valley of California. At Berkeley he became a student rebel and one-man literary movement, contributing prodigiously to all campus publications. Denied a degree because of unconventional conduct, he embarked on a series of adventures culminating in New York

City where, after a period of near starvation, he received simultaneous recognition as a serious poet and successful popular-prose writer. Later, he traveled widely, making his home in New York, then in Florence, and finally in Los Angeles.

Once the United States entered the Second World War, Faust abandoned his lucrative writing career and his work as a screenwriter to serve as a war correspondent with the infantry in Italy, despite his fifty-one years and a bad heart. He was killed during a night attack on a hilltop village held by the German army. New books based on magazine serials or unpublished manuscripts or restored versions continue to appear so that, alive or dead, he has averaged a new book every four months for seventy-five years. In the United States alone nine publishers now issue his work. Beyond this, some work by him is newly reprinted every week of every year in one or another format somewhere in the world. Yet, only recently have the full dimensions of this extraordinarily versatile and prolific writer come to be recognized and his stature as a protean literary figure in the 20th Century acknowledged. His popularity continues to grow throughout the world.

The stories I have collected for this book do not appear in chronological order. The organizing principle, instead, is the expansiveness of Faust's imagination when it comes to the

Western story as a form of literary art and the fecundity with which he would vary his themes, examining problems and dilemmas of the human condition from numerous disparate viewpoints. In another sense these stories fit together as episodes in a great saga, very much after the fashion of Homer in the Books of *Odyssey*. No matter how much editors or his agent might tell Faust that he was writing stories that were too character-driven, he could never really change the way he wrote. In order to write, he was fond of saying, I must be able to dream. As early as 1921, writing as George Owen Baxter, Faust had commented about Free Range Lanning in "Iron Dust" that Lanning "had at least picked up that dangerous equipment of fiction which enables a man to dodge reality and live in his dreams."

Brave words! Yet, beyond this, and maybe precisely because of the truth in them, much that happens in a Western story by Frederick Faust depends upon an interplay between dream and reality. There will come a time, probably well into the next century, when a reëvaluation will become necessary of those who contributed most to the eternal relevance of the Western story in this century. In this reëvaluation unquestionably Zane Grey and Frederick Faust will be elevated while popular icons of this century such as Owen Wister, judged solely in terms of their actual artistic contributions to the wealth and treasure of world literature, may find their reputations diminished. In such a reëvaluation Faust, in common with Jack London, may be seen as a purveyor of visceral fiction of great emotional power and profound impact that does not recede with time.

The stories collected here, early or late, have all been restored where necessary by comparing the author's manuscripts with the published versions. They are set in that land Faust called the mountain desert, a place for him as timeless and magical as the plains of Troy in the hexameters of his beloved Homer and as vivid as the worlds Shakespeare's vibrant imagery projected outward from the bare stages of the Globe. Faust was not so much mapping a geographical region in his Western stories as he was exploring the dark and bright corridors of the human soul — that expanse which is without measure, as Heraclitus said. For Faust, as for his reader, this experience is much as he described it in 1926 for Oliver Tay in what became *The Border Bandit* (Harper, 1947): ". . . He was seeing himself for the very first time; and, just as his eye could wander through the unfathomed leagues of the stars which were strewn across the universe at night, so he could turn his glance inward and probe the vastness of new-found self. All new!" In these explorations of the inner world Faust's fiction can be seen to embody a basic principle of the Western story, that quality which makes the Western story so vitally rewarding in world literature, the experience of personal renewal, an affirmation of hope through courage, the potential that exists in each human being for redemption.

The Black Rider

The Black Rider" was Faust's original title for this short novel. It first appeared in *Western Story Magazine* (1/3/25) under the Max Brand byline. Although until now it has never been reprinted, it did serve as the basis for *The Cavalier* (Tiffany-Stahl Productions, 1928), a motion picture directed by Irvin Willat starring Richard Talmadge and Barbara Bedford. This black and white film was made utilizing the early Photophone process that included on the track sound effects and a musical score composed by Hugo Riesenfeld. The theme song was "My Cavalier," with the music by Riesenfeld and lyrics by R. Meredith Willson, perhaps best known for his 1957 Broadway musical, "The Music Man." For some reason that only Hollywood screenwriters could ever hope to explain, Taki's ethnic heritage was changed in the film from Navajo to Aztec.

"The Black Rider" is an excellent example of a Western story by Faust in which most of the conversations between various characters intimate a subtext that is deeper and far more meaningful than what they would seem to be saying. The setting here is Spanish California at the time when the eastern colonies of this country were still ruled by Great Britain. Lucia d'Arquista is a splendid heroine and, notwithstanding the title, this is very much her story and her confrontation with her own soul. Indeed, the Black Rider in a way is only a metaphor for that divine force Vergil once sought to capture within an image both awesome and sinister: *numina magna deum.*

I "Beginning the Journey"

If *Señor* Francisco Torreño had been a poor man, the bride of his son would have been put on a swift horse and carried the fifty miles to the ranch in a single day, a day of a little fatigue, perhaps, but of much merriment, much light-hearted joyousness. However, *Señor* Torreño was not poor. The beasts which he slaughtered every year for their hides and their tallow would have fed whole cities. Sometimes he sold those hides to English ships which had rounded the Horn and sailed far and far north up the western coast of the Americas. But he preferred to sell to the Spaniards. They did not come so often. They offered lower prices. But Torreño was a patriot. Moreover, he was above counting his pence, or even his pesos. He counted his cattle by the square league. He counted his sheep by the flocks.

To such a man it would have been impossible, it would have been ludicrous to mount the betrothed of his only son and gallop her heedlessly over the hills and through the valleys to the great house. Instead, there were preparations to be made.

The same ambassador who negotiated the marriage with the noble and rich d'Arquista family in Toledo had instructions. If the affair terminated favorably, to post to Paris out of Spain with all the speed of which horseflesh was capable, and from the same coach builder who supplied the equipages of Madame Pompadour to order a splendid carriage. About the carriage *Señor* Torreño mentioned every detail, except the price.

Chiefly he insisted that the exterior of the wagon should be gilded with plenty of gold leaf and that in particular the arms of the Torreño family — that is to say, an armored knight with sword in hand stamping upon a dying dragon — should appear on either side of the vehicle.

All of this was done. The sailing of the *Señorita* Lucia d'Arquista was postponed until the carriage was completed and had been shipped on a fleet-winged merchantman for the New World. And, when the lady herself arrived, she was ensconced in that enormous vehicle as in a portable house. For it was hardly less in size!

Twelve chosen horses from the estate of Torreño drew that carriage. They had been selected because they were all of a color and a size — that is to say, they were all glossy black without a single white hair to mar their coats, and their shining black hides set off the silver-mounted harness with which they were decked. In the front seat, lofty as the lookout on a ship, was the driver, a functionary of importance, shouting his orders to the six postilions who, with difficulty, managed the dancing horses, for these were more accustomed to bearing saddles than pulling at collars.

In the van of the carriage rode a compact body of six men from the household of Torreño, mounted upon cream-colored steeds. Six more formed the immediate bodyguard around the coach itself. And, finally, there was a train in the rear. These were composed, last of all, of ten fierce warriors, well trained in Indian conflicts, skillful to follow trails or to take scalps, experts with musket and pistol and knife. In front of this rear guard, but still at a considerable distance from the coach, journeyed the domestics who were needed. For, at every halt, and on account of the wretched condition of the road, the carriage was sure to get into difficulties every three or four miles, and a tent was hastily pitched, and a folding cot placed in it so that the *señorita* might repose herself in it if she chose. There was a round dozen of these servants and, besides the animals they bestrode, there were fully twenty pack-mules which bore the necessities for the journey.

In this manner it will be seen how Torreño transformed a fifty-mile canter into a campaign. There were some three score and ten horses and mules; there were almost as many men. And the cavalcade stretched splendidly over many and many a rod of ground. There was a great jingling of little silver and golden bells. And the dust cloud flew into a great flag of flying cloud from beneath the many hoofs as they mounted each hilltop, and settled in a heavy, stifling fog around them as they lurched down into every hollow. They marched eight hours a day, and their average was hardly more than two miles an hour, counting the halts, and weary, slow labor up the many slopes. Therefore it was a march of fully three days.

All of this had been foreseen by the omniscient Torreño. Accordingly, he had built three lodgings at the end of the three separate days' riding. Some flimsy structure, you would say, some fabric of wood and canvas? No, no! Such tawdry stuff was not for Torreño! He sent his 'dobe brickmakers and his builders ahead to the sites months before. He sent them not by the dozen, but by the score. They erected three spreading, solid buildings. They cleared the ground around them. They constructed commodious sleeping apartments. And the foresters of Torreño brought down from the foothills of the snow-topped Sierras young pines and firs and planted them again around the various halting places, planted them in little groups, so that they made groves of shade, for the season of her arrival was a season of summer heat. And where in the world is the sun more burningly hot than in the great West of the Americas?

Shall it be said that these immense labors strained the powers of the rich Torreño? Not in the least! For the servants of the great man he numbered by whole villages and towns — Indians who had learned to live only to labor, and to labor only for their Spanish masters. He had almost forgotten the commands he had given until, riding down to the port, he had passed through the lodges one by one and, with the view of each, the heart of Torreño had swelled with pride. For the glory of his riches had never grown strange to Don Francisco. His father had been a moneylender in Barcelona who had raised his son in abject penury and left him, at his death, a more than modest competence. Don Francisco had loaned it forth again, at a huge interest, to a certain impoverished grandee, a descendant of one of those early conquistadores who considered the vast West of North America as their back yard. The grandee had been unable to pay interest. In short, in a year Don Francisco foreclosed and got for the larger half of his money — a whole kingdom of land. He sailed out to explore his possessions. For days he rode across it, league after league, winding up valleys with rich bottom lands, climbing well-faced mesas, struggling over endless successions of hills.

"What will grow here?" he asked in despair.

"Grass, *señor*, you see!"

They pointed out to him sun-cured grasses.

"But what will eat this stuff?"

"It is the finest food in the world for either cattle or horses," he was told.

He did not believe, at first. It was a principle with him never to believe except under the compulsion of his own eyes; but, when he extended his rides through the neighboring estates, he indeed found cattle, hordes of them — little, lean-bodied, wild-eyed creatures as fleet as antelope, as savage as tigers. They, indeed, could drink water once in three days and pick a living on the plains. So Don Francisco, half in despair, bought a quantity of them — they could be had almost for the asking — and turned them loose on his lands. He gave other attention to the bottom grounds and farmed them with care and at the end of ten years his farm land was rich, to be sure, but the cattle had multiplied by miracle until they swarmed everywhere. Each one was not worth a great deal — nothing in comparison with the sleek, grass-fed beeves which he remembered in old Spain; but they were numbered, as has been said, by the square league. They needed no care. They grew fat where goats would have starved. They multiplied like rabbits. In short, it took ten years for Don Francisco to awaken to the truth; then he got up one morning and found himself richer than his richest dreams of wealth. He went back to Spain, bought a palace in Madrid, hired a small army of servants, dazzled the eyes of the city and, as a result, got him a wife of his own choosing, high-born, magnificent, loving his money, despising him. She bore him this one son, Don Carlos, and then died of a broken heart among the arid hills of America, yearning ever for the stir and the bustle and the whispers of Madrid. In the meantime, Don Francisco grew richer and richer. He began to buy his own ships and employ his own captains to transport the hides and the tallow back to Europe. He sent expeditions northward along the coast an incredible distance into the frozen regions, and they brought back furs by the sale of which alone he could have made himself the richest man in Barcelona. But he no longer thought of Barcelona. He thought of the world as his stage. When he thought of kingdoms and of kings, he thought of his own wide lands, and of himself in the next breath.

Such was *Señor* Don Francisco Torreño.

Now he had brought back from Spain another lovely girl, this time to become the wife of his son, Don Carlos. Men had told him that she was not only a d'Arquista, but that she was also the loveliest girl in all of Spain; and, although he had not believed the last, when he saw her now, swaying and tilting in the lumbering carriage like a very flower, he could not but agree that she was worthy to be a queen.

And was not that, in fact, the destiny for

which he was shaping her? In the end he found that he could give her the highest compliment which it was in his power to bestow on any woman — she was worthy to be the wife of the son of Francisco Torreño!

As for Don Carlos, he was in a seventh heaven, an ecstasy of delight. He could not keep his eyes from touching on his bride to be and, every time they rested on her, he could not help smiling and twirling the ends of his little mustaches into dagger points. He went to his father.

"Ah, sir," he said. "Where can I find words in the world to tell you of my gratitude? In all the kingdoms you have found the one lady of my heart."

Torreño was pleased, but he would have scorned to show his pleasure.

"Bah!" he said. "You are young; therefore you are a fool. Remember that she is a woman, and every woman is a confederacy of danger in your household. When the married man locks his door, he has not closed out from his house his deadliest foe!"

"I shall not believe that there is evil in her!" said the youth. He clapped his hand upon the hilt of his rapier. He had been to Milan and to Paris to learn the proper use of that weapon and, though some parts of his education might be at fault, in sword play he had been admitted a master even by the Spaniards, who fight by rule book like mathematicians, and even by the French who fight like dreadful angels of grace. "And," said Don Carlos, "if another man were to suggest such a thing, I should . . . cut his throat!"

His father was pleased again. He loved violence in his boy, just as he loved his elegance. In all things, Don Carlos was his ideal of what a young man should be, just as he himself was what his ideal of what a man of sixty should be.

"You throat-cutters," said Don Francisco, sneeringly. "Powder and lead are the only things!"

So saying, he snatched a pistol from the holster beside his saddle and, jerking it up level with his eye, fired. He had intended to shave the long plume which fluttered from the hat of one of his postilions. As a matter-of-fact, the ball knocked the hat off the head of the poor fellow, and even grazed his skull, so that he screamed with terror and clapped both hands to the top of his head.

"Indians!" shouted the driver.

"Indians!" echoed the rear guard and the front.

Instantly they faced out and held their carbines at the ready. Don Francisco was convulsed with laughter. He rolled back and forth in his saddle and waved his pistol in the air, helpless with excess of mirth.

"Ah," he groaned in his joy, "did you see the face of the fool, Carlos? Did you see?"

But Carlos was already at the side of the carriage, comforting his lady and assuring her that it was only a jest of his father's. She had not uttered an outcry, but she sat stiff and straight in the carriage and looked at her fiancé with a very strange expression in her eyes — a strange, level glance that went through and through the soul of Don Carlos like the cold steel of a rapier — and out again at a twitch.

"Ah," she said without a smile, "was that a joke? What if the man had been killed?"

"Why, there are a thousand others to take his place," explained Don Carlos carefully.

"I see," she said.

And that was all. But at that moment he would have given a very great deal if she had smiled even a very small smile.

II "The Flute Player"

In the confusion that followed the explosion of the gun, the carriage, as a matter of course, had come to a halt. It had stopped in the center of a deep hollow where the road, pounded repeatedly by the great wheels of the carts which brought the hides down to the seaport town, had been scored with great ruts, and the surface cut away to the undercrop of rocks. Against one of these the rear wheels were wedged and, when the postilions tried to start the coach, they failed. They could not, at once, get the team to work together, partly, perhaps, because they were talking to one another — a rapid muttering running back and forth along the line of the drivers.

In the meantime, *Señorita* Lucia stood up and beckoned to her cavalier. He was in the midst of a rapture which he was pouring forth to his father.

"She is like a bird, sir," he was saying. "She is full of music. There is nothing about her that is not delightful!"

"Bah!" said the father, concealing his happiness as usual with a scowl. "Take care that she does not prove a sparrow-hawk, and you the sparrow!"

"When I hear her voice, my heart stops. Her eyes take hold on my soul like a strong hand. I could wish for only one thing . . . that she would smile more often! Do you think that she is happy? That she will be happy?"

His father turned short around in his saddle.

"Is she a fool?" he asked. "Can she not see that this is my land? And that all that we are to journey through is my land? Are not the cattle mine, the trees mine, everything but the sky itself mine? Did she not eat from silver dishes yesterday? Does she not eat from golden dishes today? And yet you ask if she is happy? Carlos, that is the question of a madman!"

"But she seems thoughtful."

"All women," said his father, "think while they are young. There is a need for that. They use their brains until they have caught a husband. After that, their minds go to sleep. It is better so. Rather an unfaithful wife than a thinking wife! Such creatures give a man no rest. And in our homes we should have peace!"

So said the great Torreño, and then nodded. Since he cared for the opinion of no one else in the world, he found a great delight in agreeing with himself.

It was at this moment that the son saw his lady beckoning to him. He drove in the spurs so deep, in his haste, that the tortured horse leaped straight up into the air. But as well to have striven to unseat a centaur as to dispos-

26

sess this master of the saddle. Presently Don Carlos drew rein beside the coach, his horse sliding to a halt upon braced legs. But to the dismay of the gallant Don Carlos, he found that *Señorita* Lucia was not even looking at him. She was raising one hand as though for silence. Her head was lifted and there was an expression of perfect concentration on her face.

"Will you tell them to be quiet?" she asked him.

"Idiots!" cried he. "Fools! Will you be still? Will you be barking like wild dogs?"

He stormed up and down the line of the postilions. Each was transformed to stone, looking sullenly down upon the ground. He came back to Lucia smiling like a happy child. There was not a sound, now, except the heavy panting of the horses. The dust cloud rose and floated away on the slow wind. The sun beat steadily, burningly down upon them. It dried the sweat on the flanks of the horses as fast as it formed and left powderings of salt.

"Now," said the girl, "you can hear it quite clearly! I thought I heard before . . . now I am sure!"

Don Carlos listened in turn, pointed the eye of his mind, so to speak, in the direction to which she pointed, and then he made out, very far and faint, very thin but very clear, like a star ray on a dark black night, the sound of a whistled music which floated to them through the air, now drowned by a stir of the wind, now coming again.

"That is a great flute player . . . that is a true musician!" said the lady.

He gaped at her for a moment. Something that his father had said was recurring to his not over-alert brain. Indeed, this was very like the hawk which knew what duller fowl could not. How had she been able to pick up that liquid, tiny sound through the jingling, stamping, creaking, shouting of the caravan?

It made her seem tall — though she was very small. It made her eye like the eye of an eagle, though it was only of the mildest blue.

He was filled with awe, and with astonishment. He had never felt such an emotion before, not even in the presence of his father, of whom he was terribly afraid.

"Who is it?" asked the girl. "It must be a man famous in this part of the country."

He could not tell her. He shouted to his father. But Don Francisco could not say who it might be. Neither did any of the others in the train have a guess to venture.

"I shall ride off to find him," said Don Carlos. "I shall be back in a moment."

"No," said the girl. "I shall go myself."

Among the led horses, of which there were half a dozen or more, there were two always kept saddled and ready for her in case she should choose to change from the carriage. She had not shown the slightest inclination

28

to leave that lumbering vehicle before. Now, therefore, everyone watched with the greatest attention, and the silent eagerness of born horsemen, while she dismounted from the coach and stood before the two horses. One was a bay, beautiful as a picture, but a useless creature except for a gift of soft gaits. The other was a roan, ugly in color, but chosen because of its rare and eager spirit, combined with perfect manners, and a mouth as sensitive as the mouth of a human being.

"Let us see," said Don Francisco when those horses were selected for her special use, "if she can tell a horse from a horse. If she can do that, she can be happy in this wild country even if she were the bride of a beggar!"

Now he rode close up.

"There is a right one and a wrong one," he said.

He took a ring from his finger. There was an emerald in it.

"You shall have this, my child, if you prove yourself wise!"

She gave him a steady glance, once again without a smile. Then she turned back to the others and regarded their heads.

"Not their heads only," entreated Don Carlos, anxious that she might make a good impression upon his father. And of the two heads that of the bay was far the more beautiful. "Look at the whole body . . . the legs . . . the bone . . . the hard muscle, Lucia!"

She shrugged her shoulders. "I shall ride this one," she said, and laid her hand on the nose of the roan.

There was a little shout from the whole cavalcade. For she had run the gantlet unscathed! But Don Francisco was almost scowling on her as he gave her the ring. And he muttered to his son: "A hawk! A hawk! Poor Carlos!"

Don Carlos did not quite follow the meaning that might be hidden away under this. He was too delighted by her victory. And, in another moment, she was galloping away at his side across the hills.

It was even farther than he had guessed, but the music led them across two ranges of the little rolling hills, and on the second range they saw their man seated cross-legged under a tree, with the flute at his lips and his agile fingers dancing over it.

He was a tall man with a white band of cloth around his long, black hair to keep it away from his face, and clean white trousers which extended to his heels. There was a sash around his waist. Altogether he was a romantic figure in such a setting among the olive-drab hills.

"Look!" said Don Carlos, as they drew rein.

At their approach, the musician had jumped up and whistled sharply. And at once the sheep which were feeding in that pasture land came running toward him, a rush of gray white which pooled around his feet, bleating and babbling.

The Indian, as he arose, was revealed as a tall man, slender-waisted, broad shouldered — with the form of an athlete and the air of a gravely reserved thinker.

"He looks," said the girl, "like a hero."

"He?" said Don Carlos. "He is only an Indian."

"He is not like the others," she said, looking thoughtfully at her fiancé.

"The others are mere root grubbers, ditch diggers," said the son of the lord of the land, shrugging his shoulders. "This fellow is different . . . yes. You can tell that he is a Navajo by that band around his hair and his white trousers. The Navajos *are* different. Most of them are men. But no Navajo with an ounce of blood in his veins would be herding sheep for a white man. This man is probably an outcast, a coward, perhaps a fool, certainly a knave!"

She gave Don Carlos one look, a long one; she gave the Indian another glance, a short one.

"I don't agree with you," she said.

"Why not, Lucia?"

"Because he is a musician. That's one thing. And besides. . . ."

"Besides what?"

"I don't know," she said, and added: "Talk to him, Carlos!"

This was pronounced so shortly that Don Carlos stared a little, for he had never in his life received commands except from his father who, after all, was a sort of deity of another order. However, when he looked to the girl, he found her smiling so frankly that he quite forgot he had received an order.

Now he reined his horse closer. The Indian had folded his hands and addressed his gaze to the distant mountains, lofty, naked rock faces, spotted richly with color all dim and blended behind a veiling mist.

"Tell me, fellow," said Don Carlos, "what is your name?"

He had asked the question, of course, in Spanish, and the Indian returned to him a dull, unintelligent stare.

"I shall ask him in Navajo," said Don Carlos to the girl. "He has probably come here only newly. Otherwise he would have understood such a simple question. These Navajos, besides, are not such fools, you know."

He said to the Indian, in a broad, quick guttural: "What is your name? Quickly, because we cannot stay here. What is your name and what made you learn the flute?"

Not a whit of intelligence glimmered in the steady black eyes of the other. Don Carlos flushed.

"The oaf dares to keep silence!" he said. "I shall give him a lesson that will be written in his skin the rest of his life!"

And he raised a riding whip. At the same instant, into the hand of the Indian came a long and heavy knife. He did not hold it by the hilt, but balanced it loosely in the palm of his hand, the knife blade exending over the fingers, so that it was plain he intended to throw it, and there was something in his unmoved air which gave assurance that his weapon would not miss the target. Don Carlos, with a gasp of rage and astonishment, whirled his horse away.

"The scoundrel!" he cried. "We'll silence that flute, by heaven! Turn your face, Lucia!"

"Carlos!" she cried, riding straight between him and his intended target. "Do you mean to pistol him in cold blood?"

"Cold blood?" cried he. "I tell you, Lucia, if we did not keep these desert rats down, they would eat through our walls and knife us in our sleep. They'd swarm over the whole land. There is only one way to treat an Indian . . . like a mad dog!"

Her expression, for the moment, reminded him of that of the Navajo — it was the blank of one who veils a thought.

"Here comes your father," she said. "Perhaps he will speak for *Señor* Torreño."

Torreño, in fact, had followed the two at a slow gait, not close enough to interfere with their privacy, but at a sufficient distance to keep his eye upon them, as though he dared not risk the safety of the two human beings who meant the most to him in the world.

III "Taki"

He had no sooner come up when his son explained everything that had happened in the following way:

"I asked this Indian dog for his name in Spanish and in Navajo. He dared to remain silent."

"So?" said Torreño. "A Navajo, however, is not a dog, but a man . . . or half a man." He said gently to the tall Indian: "*Amigo,* do you know me?"

Instantly the other made answer in perfect Spanish, smooth, close-clipped, the truest Castilian: "You are my master, *señor!* You are *Señor* Torreño."

Torreño turned to the girl with a broad grin on his face, as much as to say: "This you see is another matter when the right man speaks!"

He added to the Indian. "And now your name?"

"I am Taki, the son of. . . ."

"That is enough. So, Taki, you have drawn a knife upon my son?"

"A knife?" said Taki blankly. "I cannot remember that!"

The girl broke into ringing laughter, a small,

34

sweet voice in the vast silence of those hills. The music of it softened the hard heart of Torreño.

"I should have had him flayed alive," said he. "But since he has amused you, dear girl, I shall forgive him."

"Flayed alive?" murmured the girl. "Are such things possible here?"

"In this country," said Torreño, "one must be a king or a slave; and to be a king one must be a tyrant. I, *señorita,* am a tyrant, partly because it is necessary, partly because it pleases me to be one. Where I am, there is no other word, except for the sake of conversation."

He said this with a grave, sharp glance at her, which could not avoid giving the words a certain meaning. Whether she understood or not, however, could not be seen, for again her face wore an expression as grave and as unreadable as the Indian's. Torreño turned back to the culprit.

"You have drawn a knife upon my son . . . who is my flesh, who is me! Would you strike steel into my arm?"

"Heaven forbid, *señor.*"

"This Don Carlos is more than my arm. He is part of my heart. He is that part of me which will live after my death. To touch him is to touch me."

He added aside to the girl: "That is rather neatly spoken, child, is it not?"

"A pretty speech," said she without emotion.

"*Señor*, my master," said the Indian.

"Well?" queried Torreño.

"I have a horse, *señor*."

"You are rich, then? But what of the horse?"

"He is mine. He is my slave."

"Ah?"

"When I whistle, he comes. When I speak, he lifts his ears. I need no bridle to control him."

"This fellow," said Torreño, "talks like a man of sense . . . if I could only understand what he is striking at!"

This was spoken, like the rest of his asides, in French. And the Navajo instantly answered for himself, in the purest French of Paris, where alone French was pure.

"I mean that the horse is my slave, *señor*."

"By the heavens!" broke out Torreño. "The fellow speaks French, also. Better French than I use myself!"

"Wait, wait!" said the girl in a hurried voice, raising her hand to stop interruptions, and staring fixedly at the Indian. "He has something more to say."

"Aye," said Torreño, nodding. "The horse is your slave."

"Because he will do these things," said the Indian, "and because he is fleeter than the horses, even, which you ride, *señor* . . ."

"What! That's a broad lie, Taki!"

At this, the other stiffened a little.

"Nevertheless," he said, "it is true! It is a fleeter horse than any of those you ride. And it is also my slave. But, *señor*, though I value him more than gold, it is because his speed is all for me. His strength is all mine. No other man can sit on his back! To them, he is a devil."

"You are right, Taki. That is something I can understand!"

"If he were a horse for any man to ride, I should not care. There would be a price upon him. But me he serves for love! Therefore he is priceless."

"Very well . . . very well! And what has this to do with the knife you drew on my son, the *Señor* Don Carlos Torreño? By the heavens, Taki, tell me that!"

"If a man were to take a whip to that horse of mine, *señor*, should I not be happy if he used his heels?"

Passion had been swelling in the face, in the throat of Torreño. Now it relaxed a little.

"I begin to understand! I begin to understand! You, Taki, will have only one master?"

"*Señor*, you have spoken!"

"Not even if I assign you to another by express command?"

"Not even then, *señor*."

"God!" thundered the Spaniard. "There is a hangman and a rope for disobedient slaves!"

"*Señor*," said Taki, "death is half a second; but every day of slavery is a century of hell!"

"Ten thousand devils!" said Torreño. "He talks like a fool."

"Or a philosopher," said the girl, "and still more . . . like a brave man!"

"But are you not," said Torreño, "at this moment in my service?"

"For another fortnight, only."

"What?"

"It is true."

"Taki, are you mad?"

"No, *señor.*"

"I employ no man except when he is bought or hired for life."

"To me, however, you made an exception."

"In what manner? Have I ever seen you before?"

"There was a crossing of a river," said the other. "A dozen men were riding after one Indian. They shot his horse. He swam the river. They followed, swimming their horses. He killed the first man ashore with his knife, took his horse, and rode on. But the horse was tired. The others behind him gained. He was not ten minutes from death by fire, *señor,* when he saw you and your party and rode to you and . . ."

"I remember, I remember!" cried Torreño, clapping his hands together. "It is all as clear as the ringing of a bell! I remember it all! You came to us with Pedro Marva and his hired fighters raging and foaming behind you. I put in between. They were very hot, but not so hot that they did not know me. Ha?"

"They knew you, *señor,*" said the Indian gravely.

Don Carlos was gaping at this story; but *Señorita* Lucia flushed and bit her lip.

"They knew me," went on Torreño, "and when I told them that they could not have the man . . . because his riding pleased me . . . they turned around and went off, cursing. However, I paid Marva for his dead man . . . and all was well!"

"It's true . . . it is very true," said the Indian.

"You paid for the life of a man? A white man?" asked the girl.

"All things have a price . . . in this country," said the Spaniard.

She did not answer, but she looked around her on the bald, vast sweep of plain and mountain. She looked up, and there were tiny, circling dots which ruled the sky — the buzzards. And she shuddered a very little.

"But how," said the Spaniard, "are you to be in my service only a fortnight longer? I remember it all. You were to serve me until you had paid for the price of the man. And twelve hundred pesos could not be worked out in ten lives of a shepherd. How have you made the money?"

"There are more than eleven hundred pesos," said the Navajo, "already in the hands of your treasurer. He has kept the account. I have the rest to pay in soon."

"Rascal!" said the Spaniard. "You have not been in my service for six months."

"*Señor*, there are ways of making money, even for a poor shepherd."

"Who leaves his sheep?"

"Only at night, when a friend will come to watch them."

"Ah? Ah? You are a worker by night, Taki? And what do you find at night?"

"There was a great rider of the roads. There was a Captain Sandoval. . . ."

"He was killed three months ago. What of him? I was away."

"There was a reward on his head."

"Of five hundred pesos. Yes."

"The reward was paid to me, *señor*."

"The devil fly off with me! The terrible Sandoval . . . and one Indian killed him? How in the name of heaven?"

The Indian turned. His hand flashed back and forward. A line of light left it and went out in the trunk of a narrow sapling, which shivered with the shock. There stood the knife, buried to the hilt in the hard wood.

"Name of heaven!" whispered Don Carlos, and touched his heart, as though just there he felt the resistless death slide in.

"Ah?" said Torreño. "It was in that way?"

"It was in that way."

"And he did not touch you?"

"His pistol bullet just touched my hair, *señor*."

"That accounts for five hundred pesos only."

"There was another . . . a friend of Sandoval. Some said it was his younger brother, and he was a greater man; there were six hundred pesos on his head. That money became mine."

"Now I remember that it was said an Indian killed poor Juan Sandoval. But it was you, Taki? I am growing old . . . things happen on this place and I do not know of them! Still, Taki, that leaves a hundred pieces of silver. How have you saved them?"

"There are the dice, *señor*."

"A head hunter, a gambler . . ." began Don Carlos.

"And a musician," said the girl. "In what way did you learn to play the flute, Taki?"

"*Señor* Arreto, a great Spaniard, came to fight against my people. I was wounded and captured. But in the fighting he watched me and thought I was worth keeping . . . as a slave. He took me back to Europe with him. It was amusing, *señorita,* to see the poor Indian learn to dance, to play the flute, to bow and to talk like a real man. So I was taught. I went with him among fine people. When people talked of his journeys, he pointed to me. It proved that he was a great hunter. Imagine, *señorita,* a hunter come back from India with a tamed tiger in his company to follow at his heels like a dog!"

This ironical speech was so delivered that

neither Torreño nor his rather dull son quite caught the point of it, but the girl smiled faintly.

"And so you learned to play the flute?"

"Yes, *señorita*. My day was divided in three parts. There was the fencing master, the dancing master, the music master. In the afternoons I was taken forth and shown to the people. Everyone wished to hear me play the flute. Now and then a brave lady who was not too proud, permitted me to dance with her. And twice bravos were hired to fight with me and prove what I had learned from the fencing masters."

"And . . . ?"

"I killed them both, *señorita*."

"Then what followed?"

"When *Señor* Arreto died, he gave me my liberty. I took my little money and bought a certain fine horse which I had seen. The price was low, because the horse was a tiger and would not be tamed. But I, who *had* been tamed, understood how to manage him. With that horse I returned to this country."

"One instant, Taki," broke in Don Carlos, raising his hand and delighted to make a point. "If you are a master of the sword, why would you hunt your head . . . with a knife?"

"The teeth which God gives us," said the Indian, bowing, "are better than false ones for eating, *señor*."

"What do you think of him?" asked Torreño of the girl.

"He is enchanting!" she whispered back.

"An enchanting liar!" he said. "There never was an Indian in the world who could manage a weapon so formal as a sword. Shall I prove it?"

"If it can be done!"

"Ride back," said Torreño to his son, "and bring two foils. Quickly."

There was no need for the last word. All commands of Torreño implied the necessity for speed, and Don Carlos was instantly rushing back at the full flight of his horse toward that waiting caravan.

The girl drew closer to Torreño.

"For the little time that remains for him to serve you," she said, "let me have this man for a servant!"

"He will not be alive in ten minutes," said Torreño. "You will see that he handles the sword like a fool. And when that happens, I intend to shoot that liar down like the dog that he is. No Indian can kill a white, even a villainous white, and remain a good Indian!"

She grew pale, started to speak; then changed her mind and said simply: "But if he fences well?"

"That is impossible!"

"But?"

"Then he is yours, but give the dog a muzzle!"

IV "A Wager that Taki Wins"

Don Carlos came back at full speed, as he had gone, and he brought with him two foils in their scabbards, with leather covers over the hilts. Torreño took them, unbuckled the flaps which secured the hilts, and drew forth the blades. One by one, he whipped them through the air until they sang.

"Most people," he said to the girl, "use for their foils dull iron things, or poor steel that bends to nothing after a strong touch or two. But these are of the finest old Spanish steel, specially made for my boy in order that he might have exercise."

Her face lighted a little. "You love to fence, then, *señor?*"

"I? Love it? The devil take it. One good broad sword is worth a dozen such great darning needles, I say, or a saber at least. I have seen a Pole use a saber that it would have done your eyes good to watch him, but this stamping and parading and retreating and advancing and sweating, and bowing and scraping . . . bah! It makes me laugh to see it! When one good pistol bullet would put an end to it all!"

The light which had flickered into her eyes went out again.

44

"Here, Carlos," he said to his son. "Take one of these."

"For what, sir?" asked the son.

"Taki says that he's a fencer. If he can touch you . . . well, he is! If he cannot . . . he is a dead Indian!"

He drew out a huge horse pistol as he spoke and flourished it.

"Do you hear me, Taki?"

"Yes."

"Do you agree?"

"It is to see if I have lied about the fencing lessons," said the Navajo. "It is very just!"

"*¡Señor!*" cried the girl. "You do not mean it!"

"Peace, Lucia," said Torreño, bending his brows upon her. "Peace, child. Do not question the workings of my mind. You are a bright little thing, Lucia. But do not trot your wits over the same trail that I follow. For that is dangerous, and I would not abide it. I live alone, my girl. I live alone, I promise you. I open my purposes to whom I please. And to those who do not please me, I keep them closed. And so . . . for that!"

The girl had turned white. But she kept her eyes on the ground, while poor Don Carlos looked upon her in an agony, aching to comfort her or to speak a word to her, but not daring to move or to speak. He merely accepted the foil from the hand of his father and automatically stood on guard.

"Now, let me see," said Torreño, with a serene brow, as if he had already forgotten the manner in which he had trod roughshod over the girl, "let me see you work for your life, Taki, for your life. Liars are usually interesting people . . . but not when they're Indians. A truthful Indian or a dead one is my motto. Come! Engage!"

The blades crossed as he spoke, and Don Carlos, impatient to have the dirty work over with, with a curl of fine disdain on his lip as he faced his humble opponent, put the other's blade sharply aside and, continuing his point in the same motion, lunged full home. That is to say, he drove straight at the heart of the Indian, and the latter opposed no guard, yet managed to escape the button of the Spaniard by a supple bending of his body.

"You see?" said Torreño to the girl. "The fool knows nothing of the sword. The knife is as far as his brute heart can aspire."

"He is a musician, *señor*," said the girl. "This ring you have given me against . . . his service to me . . . that he wins!"

The other gaped at her. "Win, Lucia? Win? Are you mad? No, he is as good as dead already!"

"Nevertheless," she said, "though I ask your pardon for denying you, he is a fine fencer. See!"

Don Carlos, angered by the first lack of fortune, pressed hotly in, following lunge with thrust and thrust with lunge. But the Indian, still parrying only a little, escaped the point still by constantly retreating and by the deftness of his footwork.

"Any fool can run away from trouble," said Don Francisco. "Taki, Taki, I wish to see fencing, not a foot race. Stand to him. . . ."

He had not finished off his oath at his leisure when Taki stopped, indeed seemed to flick aside the blade of Don Carlos, and instantly dipped his own blade at Don Carlos. Then he leaped back and lowered his foil.

"A touch!" cried the girl. "He has won!"

"Seven thousand devils!" groaned Torreño. "Carlos . . . idiot . . . have you allowed him . . . ?"

"I hardly felt it . . . I am sure it was not a touch," panted Don Carlos. "It could not have been a touch!"

"I saw his foil bend as the button touched you, Carlos," said the girl coldly.

"He did not feel it . . . I did not see it!" exclaimed the tyrant. "It was *not* a touch! Engage!"

Don Carlos made a strange gesture to the girl, as though disclaiming this lack of sportsmanship. Then he hurried to cross swords with Taki. The latter showed not the slightest disappointment or excitement. But he was a little more gravely watchful as he engaged. Neither was Don Carlos so impetuous. He had been foolishly hasty before. He summoned all of his care at this moment, and he was not only the product of the finest teaching in the world, but he was a credit to that teaching.

But to the amazement of them all, Taki now stood his ground without flinching, putting aside the lunges and the thrusts of Don Carlos with the most consummate ease and at the same time, so fluid were his own movements, that he was able to talk, slowly, but without panting.

"I am forbidden to retreat, *señor*," he said to Don Carlos. "Therefore you will forgive me if I stand my ground for an instant before you. As for the last touch, it was upon your belt, and it was for that reason that you did not feel it, I have no doubt. The next time, with ten thousand pardons, I shall try to lodge the button against your throat . . . against the hollow of your throat, *señor*, if I can be so fortunate, for the sake of making that touch an unmistakable one! You will forgive me for it, *señor*?"

"Why, curse you," said Don Carlos through his teeth as he worked, "that time will never come!"

"Look!" said the girl. "Look!"

It was, indeed, a strange sight to watch the Indian. A slight wind had come up and blew his long hair back from his head, showing that lean face to greater advantage. And there was still the same quiet, thoughtful expression in his eyes. His head canted a little to one side, as though his opponent were at a distance. His look was rather that of a gunner than a swordsman. Only, from time to time, his foil was a wall of the most solid steel against which the assaults of Don Carlos clashed noisily but could not break through.

Then: "*Señor* a thousand, ten thousand pardons, as they say in Paris. But . . . there is a necessity."

And he attacked. For an instant Don Carlos bore up against the attack like a swimmer against a turning tide. Then he was borne back while his father shouted in a rage.

"Is this the result of the money I have spent on you? Oh, fool! Oh, dolt! I wish to heaven that the Indian's point was unbated! I wish it were through your heart! I have a lump, a clod for a son! Oh, what a shame this is to me! It is an Indian, not a gentleman who stands before you, Carlos! Are you sleeping? And if. . . ."

His voice broke off short. The button of the Navajo at that instant lodged against the throat of Carlos with such force that the strong blade of the foil doubled up like a supple switch in his hand. Carlos dropped his sword, caught at his throat, and then sank gasping to the ground.

It was Taki who raised him first. But he received across the body a slashing stroke from the riding whip of Torreño, who instantly flung himself from his horse and caught his son in his arms.

"Carlos!" he cried. "Is it well with you? You

are not hurt? I shall kill him if your skin is so much as broken! If. . . ."

Carlos recovered speech with a groan.

"He is the finest fencer in the world. Father, this is no Indian. Or else he is a devil disguised!" He added: "Let him alone. Don't harm him. I had rather know that last trick than have a million pesos!"

"You have had the finest blades in Milan and Paris to teach you. You come home to me to take lessons from a Navajo? You have my flesh and my blood in you. Otherwise, Carlos, I should call you a fool outright. Lucia, that man is yours!"

He mounted his horse and rode furiously away.

"He will never forgive me!" said Don Carlos sadly, still fingering his throat. "As for you, Taki," he said, turning a black scowl upon the Indian, "I'll teach you to curse this day!"

The Indian smiled. And there was more scorn in that smile than in a torrent of wordy abuse. Don Carlos stormed like a leashed dog.

"You redskinned snake," he cried.

"*Señor,*" said the Indian, "I belong now to the lady; and as her servant I dare not submit to such words. Our swords were bated, *señor.* But I have a second knife which is not."

"Carlos," said the girl, "don't speak with him again. Taki, you must leave the sheep where they are. You must follow us. You have a horse which you love too much to keep far away from you. Where is it now?"

"Waiting, *señorita*."

"Bring, it then."

He whistled high and shrill as the scream of a hawk; and then, as they waited, they heard a rush of hoofs, and a shining bay stallion whipped into view. He came up with the wind and the sun rippling in his mane and in his tail. At the side of Taki he paused, tossing up his head and snorting at the strangers.

"Saddle and bridle him," said the girl, "if you can. He is a glorious thing, Taki. I have never seen such a beauty . . . not in the king's stables!"

"He is saddled," said Taki, throwing a blanket over the back of the stallion and securing it with a single cinch. And, fastening a light halter of thin rawhide over his head: "He is bridled," he added.

"Then come after us," said the girl. "You have a fortnight of service remaining, Taki. That fortnight belongs to me!"

V "Beginning a Fortnight of Service"

The apartment of Lucia in the rest house, which the cavalcade reached, was like that in which she had spent her first night after leaving the ship, except that it was, perhaps, a little more complete. She herself went about restlessly examining everything. But she said not a word. It was her aunt, the pale and patient lady who had chaperoned her niece to this far land, who broke forth into eulogy and into wonder.

"It is like a scene from some biblical story, Lucia," she declared, "illustrated in the concrete! What a wonderful and strange country this is!"

"A wonderful and strange Francisco Torreño," said the girl without emotion.

Her own chambers consisted of a large room at a corner of the house, with two small, deep windows cut through each wall; in those casement recesses were small climbing vines whose roots extended to the outside of the wall, where they were sunk in pots of rich, wet soil. There were chairs and couches, crudely made but cushioned to softness and everywhere — on chairs, on couches, on the floor beneath their feet — were fine sheepskins washed to a dazzling whiteness, and combed until they were light as a mist before the face of the moon. To the side of this chamber in one direction were two small bed-chambers, each well-nigh filled with gigantic four-posters, one for Lucia and one for her aunt, Anna d'Arquista. On the other side of her reception room were two other apartments to correspond with the sleeping rooms. One was the bath; the other was a small chapel. In the making of the bath alone a very world of labor had been expended, for in digging the foundation for the house, the builders had struck a solid rock, dark green like sea water. This had been chiseled out to an appropriate depth and little steps cut in the side, so that the lady Lucia might walk down into her bath. The remainder of the floor of the bathroom was paved with great slabs of red limestone, soft and yet porous, delicate to the touch of a bared foot. And there was a red sandstone bench made of three large pieces of stone, roughly shaped but with a polished sitting surface. Into this room the servants were now bringing the heated water — an endless chain of dark-faced Indian women with earthen jars of water poised on their shoulders pacing gracefully in, each with a white flash of the eye as she passed the *Señorita* Lucia d'Ar-quista, seeing in her, indeed, the future em-press who would control their destinies.

There are few who do not care to make their

first impression an agreeable one, particularly to those who are socially their inferiors. But the *señorita* was one of the few. If there were kindness, gentleness in her heart, she carefully disguised it. If she looked at that passing line, it was in a detached, impersonal manner, as one might look at a painting.

And each of the serving women went on with downcast glance fixed upon the brown heels of the one who went before. And the bath was gradually filled, each earthen jar discharging a crystal stream of heated water into the bath where it was turned instantly into pale green.

Last of all came two young girls, olive-skinned, solemn-eyed, graceful as young trees in a wind as they walked, strong as panthers, beautiful as evening. They passed into the room of the bath. They took from small, wooden boxes handfuls of a powder which they dropped into the quivering surface of the water; instantly a delicate fragrance stole through the chambers, not to be identified, languorously sweet as the perfume which a warm and lazy spring wind gathers from a whole field of mingled wild flowers. Then they came back before Lucia. They were sent by the master, they said, and they were to prepare the *señorita* for the bath, if it was her pleasure.

She spoke not to them but to her aunt in quick French: "You see, *madame,* that one does not live in this country; one is to be carried through life by slaves!"

She turned her back and went to the door of the little chapel.

"Hush, Lucia!" said Anna d'Arquista in the same language. "Hush, child. One cannot tell what ears will hear you."

"Ah, yes," said the girl, without turning to answer, "you feel it, also. Even the empty air has ears and is spying on us! But look, *madame*, how this man who does not know a prayer has fitted up a chapel for me!"

It was complete. There was a jeweled crucifix. There was a little gilded Madonna holding a child whose tiny hand was raised to teach. There was a tall, pointed window filled with stained glass beyond price. On the floor before the Madonna was the skin of a great mountain lion. A strange prayer rug!

Anna d'Arquista came to look.

"All this," she said, "for a single night's resting place! What a miracle of wealth, what a king this Torreño is! And who knows, Lucia? There may be a religious reverence in his heart, also!"

"A religious fiddlesticks," said Lucia. "If a man has jewels, he shows them, does he not? All that he cares for in this place is the cost of making it. Look in the bath! How many hand strokes to make it . . . for this one evening only, perhaps!"

"It is wonderful, Lucia."

"Aye," said the girl, turning suddenly and

throwing out her hands, "and beautiful, too! If one may be a queen, even over barbarians, why not?"

She went toward her bedroom and the two attendants followed, with stony faces. And poor Anna d'Arquista sank into a chair and laid her head in her hands, and wept. For she loved her niece with all her heart, having mothered her, or tried to, for ten years. But where was all this swelling discontent in the girl pointing? To disaster, she felt, but disaster of what sort she hardly knew. It was a wretched business, she felt, and had always felt since the moment Lucia had been sold to this stranger from a strange land, sold not because the head of the d'Arquista family lacked money or lacked power, but because he was avaricious of more.

A curtain had been drawn across the bedroom door. Behind it she could hear voices — that of Lucia, like a small crystal bell, and then the soft, husky tones of the half-breed girls. They came out. The masks of stone had fallen from the attendants. They were smiling. Their happy eyes watched over their mistress as she walked a little before them, wrapped in a robe of blue silk, delicately brocaded. They entered the bath, the curtain was drawn; and then out to Anna d'Arquista floated noises of splashing water, and laughter sweet as the singing of birds — laughter from three throats!

Oh, to be young, thought Anna d'Arquista.

What a miracle! What a miracle of grace and gracious power!

And to be beautiful! What virtue of a saint could balance against that gift? Aye, what could be surer of heaven itself, in the end? She pressed her cold thin hands over her heart, because the ache in it made her faint.

Then, stealthily, she slipped into the chapel. She kneeled on the tawny lion skin. She rested her forehead against the altar of red limestone, and she prayed, or tried to pray. Afterward, she went back into the room, but time had hurried past her more quickly than she knew. That bath was ended; Lucia had been dressed; all the weariness of the day had been smoothed from her face; her eyes were filled with a reckless light.

"Find Taki," she said. "Send him to me."

They were gone instantly, hurrying to the door; then, as it closed behind them, the scurry of their running feet was faintly heard as they raced, to be first in filling this command of their new mistress.

"They are sweet children," said Lucia.

Such a child to speak with love and with pity of children! And yet, to be sure, there was always something old in her niece. There was always a power of knowledge which made even Anna d'Arquista feel sometimes like a foolish infant.

Another step came to the door and a hand knocked once.

"That is Taki," said the girl, her face brightening. "You have heard me tell about him. You have not seen him yet. When he comes in, watch his steps. They are like a tiger's! As swift, as strong, as noiseless. He is a dreadful creature, Aunt Anna!"

She called: "Come!"

The door opened; Taki glided in before them. There he stood in front of the closed door, his arms folded across his breast, his eyes upon the floor submissively — but it was the submission of a trained lion which passes through attitudes that have no meaning in its heart.

"Look!" Lucia whispered. "He is magnificent, is he not?"

"And terrible," breathed the other.

He seemed larger, indeed, than he had before. Among the open hills he fitted more easily into the picture. Here he seemed inches taller, stronger. Where his arms were folded, the muscles bulged beneath the sleeves of his shirt.

"You have come quickly, Taki," she said.

"I have been waiting," he said.

"You knew that I would send?"

"Yes, mistress."

She paused a moment, thoughtfully.

"That word, Taki," she said, "comes awkwardly from you, I think."

"I have been a free man . . . mistress," he said.

"Do you think that my service will be very

58

hard?" she asked him.

"Ah," he said, with a stern smile touching his lips, "even to be the slave of a man is a knife in the heart of a slave!"

She started at this.

"I think," she said to Anna d'Arquista, "that the rascal is impertinent!"

"Hush! Peace!" gasped out Anna d'Arquista. "If you rouse him, he will murder us both, crash through the wall, and escape!"

Lucia d'Arquista laughed, but she shivered, also, and seemed to find that thrill of dread not unpleasant.

"And to serve a woman, any woman," she said, "is infinitely worse than to serve the worst of men?"

He remained silent.

"Did you hear me, Taki?"

He said at last: "Why should I speak when your answer is already in your own mind?"

And his eyes, for the first time, flashed up from the floor and looked into her own, not with a fleeting glance, but steadily, quietly.

VI "Lucia's Servant Interviewed"

It made the lady frown; then it made her flush. As for Aunt Anna, she was covered with terror.

"You are terribly unwise, my dear!" she whispered to her niece.

But Lucia merely waved such fears aside with a graceful gesture.

"You don't understand," she said. "And I think that I do . . . a little."

This rather mysterious speech there was no time to explain.

"How long," said Lucia, "were you in Europe?"

"A year and two months, *madame.*"

"A year and two months?" echoed Lucia.

Then she leaned back in her chair and began to smile like one who has solved a difficulty. She nodded at him again.

"One can easily see," she said, "how you could afford to spend so long a time on your studies."

He regarded her rather anxiously, but did not speak.

"A year and two months," said Lucia, "completed your liberal education. Well, well, it is delightful to hear of such natural talents! There are some men who labor all their lives to learn how to fence, and even then they succeed only poorly. I remember that my father, even when he was quite an old man, used to spend an hour every day with the professor. He still takes fencing lessons twice a week! And I have a brother who has dreamed of nothing since he was a boy except to manage a rapier. But you, Taki, in the course of a year and two months, have reached such a point of skill that neither my father nor my brother could compare with you. I have seen them; I am sure that *Señor* Don Carlos Torreño fences as well as they do. And indeed, Don Carlos has made it the greatest work of his life . . . his fencing, I mean! It shows a very real and a very rare talent, Taki, that you have been able to learn so much in a short year and two months. You must have practiced very hard constantly!"

He was still watching her with a shade of anxiety; but he answered: "I was constantly at work, *señorita.*"

"But I forget! I forget! In that time you had also your lessons in dancing, in which I suppose you progressed as well as you did in fencing? Perhaps . . . even better?"

"I became a very stupid and very poor dancer, *señorita.*"

She laughed at him. "Will you tell me that when you confess that the ladies would dance with you?"

"They were curious, *señorita,* to see the poor

barbarian act like a civilized man."

"Nonsense," she exclaimed, with the surety of absolute knowledge. "No woman would make herself appear ridiculous for the sake of curiosity. Not in such circles."

His face was covered instantly with his habitual mask.

"However, the dancing and the fencing is not all. By no means. There is the singular purity of your French, Taki. Most strange that one should pick up so perfect an accent in a single year. I, for instance, have worked half my life like a slave to learn that language. And still, any child could excel me! Indeed, Taki, you are very apt. You shame my father, my brother, Don Carlos, and me; you excel us so very far, Taki."

He answered neither word nor look but still stared past her with a sort of bland indifference.

"But I have forgotten the most important thing of all!" she exclaimed, "and the surest proof that you are a genius, Taki. You were able to master the flute in a single year . . . master it to a perfect smoothness. In a single year . . . that difficult instrument. In a single year, Taki, to become a master flute player, a dangerous and polished fencer, a dancer of grace at least; in a single year you have equipped yourself also with the very French of Paris. What additional study was there required to add Spanish to that list, for I see that you speak it with great precision. And," she added with a sudden change of voice, and speaking in excellent English: "What other languages are you a master of beside your own Navajo?"

"Of none, *señorita*," he answered, and then caught himself and bit his lip.

"You answer me in Spanish," she said, "but you understand the question I put in English."

"When I was a boy," said Taki, "I knew a trader who was from the colony of Virginia. I learned English from him."

She merely smiled, her eyes bright and hard as she examined him.

"Admirable, Taki," she said. "In all things you are excellent, in all things! Perhaps when you were a boy you also knew a missionary who taught you French, a generous soldier who instructed you in fencing, a kind Spaniard who schooled you in Spanish grammar, and some dapper dancing master who went among the Navajos to teach them ballroom steps in their spare moments! So you had received the basis of your knowledge and the year in Paris was merely to add the perfect finish to what you already knew!"

He did not reply, standing tall and stiff before her. There was no trace of emotion in him, except that the muscles of his folded arms swelled and rippled.

"That is all," she said. "You may go now!"

He vanished instantly.

"Lucia, Lucia!" said her aunt. "I would never have dreamed of it. But you seemed to have proved that he has told us a great series of lies! Of course in one year he never could have accomplished what he claims."

Lucia was walking up and down the room, a faint smile on her lips. She did not answer at once.

"But the first thing is to tell *Señor* Torreño!" said Anna d'Arquista.

"Do you know what the *señor* would do?" asked the girl.

"Punish him, of course."

"Punish him by stripping him naked, giving him a start of a hundred paces, and then loosing the hounds after him! I heard him tell how he occasionally disciplines unfaithful servants."

"He is a stern man, indeed!" said the elderly lady.

"If he were not so rich, he would not be called merely stern!"

"Lucia, what are you saying?"

"What I think."

"Oh, my dear, how dreadful!"

"To say what I think?"

"No, but I mean. . . ."

"That I should not think? Yes, that is right. I should close my eyes. I should learn how to smile blindly. That would be the best, of course. It is sinful to see that he who is to be my father-in-law is brutal, savage, conceited, narrow."

"Lucia!"

"And it is a greater sin to guess that the gallant Don Carlos is a mere fool!"

"Ah, Lucia, God forgive me for listening to you! Child, child, what are you saying?"

"Nothing, nothing, of course! Nothing that should be remembered. I am preparing myself to be blind and deaf the rest of my life." She added sharply: "Because of this marriage, how many new estates will my father be able to buy, Aunt Anna? Can you guess that?"

Aunt Anna turned gray with horror and with dread. And her niece turned the subject.

"No," she said, "I shall give poor Taki a better start than *Señor* Torreño would give him. By this time the bay stallion has whipped him away toward the mountains faster than any wolf could run! Well, I trust that he rides well and fast and far. He is a strange man, Aunt Anna. Did you see the shadow over those black eyes of his when I showed him that I understood? Not a muscle of his face changed . . . except once!"

"Ah, Lucia, he may do some terrible thing if you do not warn the *Señor* Torreño. I fear that this Taki has come with us for some purpose that is not good . . . now that he is gone, I begin to be terribly afraid of him. When he was here, well, it was as though the skin of the mountain lion had come to life and the great beast lay crouched in the chapel, watching us with burning eyes. Chills and shudders went through me while Taki was in the room, here!"

"And through me," said the girl; but she smiled.

"What will you do now?"

"Wait another five minutes."

"And then? Tell the *señor?*"

Lucia, instead of answering, dropped into a chair and began to study the changing light through the windows. The sky beyond was turning to a deeper blue as the sunset time came nearer. The minutes passed with Aunt Anna turning in her mind all that her niece had actually said and all that she had inferred. She dared not carry what she guessed to an actual conclusion. All that she knew was that her mind was full of confusion and dread of what would come of this unhappy marriage.

Lucia rose presently.

"It is time," she said. "He should be two leagues away by this time. If he is not. . . ."

There was a little bronze bell standing on a polished table in the corner of the room. She struck it with the padded mallet which lay beside it, and one of her two attendants appeared at once.

"Find Taki," she commanded.

In two minutes the messenger appeared again.

"He is here," she said. "Shall I bring him in?"

"He is here?" breathed the girl.

"In the patio."

She slipped to the window and looked out. There stood Taki, the ruddy light from the west in his face, his expression as woodenly impassive as ever.

"Tell him," she said, "to wait there."

The servant bowed and left.

"Oh, Lucia?" breathed the other.

"I have told him that I know he is a liar," said Lucia. "And since he dares to stay . . . what Torreño does to him is on his own head. But what can his purpose be in remaining? What is in his barbarous mind, Aunt Anna?"

"God alone can read their thoughts . . . these solemn Indians!" said Anna d'Arquista. "Perhaps he intends to murder us all while we're asleep and carry . . . our scalps . . . ah! You must send to *Señor* Torreño at once!"

"Yet," murmured the girl, "what a dull place this would be with the wild man gone! What a dull place. Hush! What is that?"

A thin thread of whistling, carrying a weird strain of music, floated into the room from the court. Anna d'Arquista hurried to the window and saw Taki, the Indian, sitting on a low stone bench with the flute at his lips.

"Do you hear? Do you hear?" asked Lucia in great excitement.

"It is beautifully played . . . yes!"

"But the words . . . the words!"

"What are they?"

"It is an old Scotch ballad. Listen!"
She began to sing:

"Ye highlands and ye lowlands,
Oh, where hae ye been?
They hae slain the Earl of Murray
And they laid him on the green.
"Now wae be to ye, Huntly,
And wharefore did ye sae?
I bade ye bring him wi' you
And forbade ye him to slay!"

There the music of the flute stopped.

"It is his message! It is his message!" breathed the girl.

"Lucia, what under heaven do you mean? What message in the playing of a flute?"

"But the words of the old song, Aunt Anna! Don't you see? He puts himself in my hands!"

"Lucia, go instantly to *Señor* Torreño!"

"Not for a million pesos!"

"Then I. . . ."

"Aunt Anna, if you betray him, I shall never forgive you. Never!"

VII "Guadalmo"

In the meantime, as the dusk settled, there began through the house a great bustle. Servants ran here and there. Beyond the court, men were seen putting up tents. Everywhere were voices of command, and scurrying feet. It would have been a simple thing for Lucia to call her maids and ask her question of them. But she preferred to go to the window and speak through it to the Indian. He rose and came before her instantly.

"Someone has come, Taki. Run and learn who it is."

"It is the *Señor* Hernandez Guadalmo. He has come to take shelter here with my master."

"How could you know all of this, Taki, without leaving this little court?"

"No man other than *Señor* Guadalmo would travel with so great a train. Besides, I have heard them speak his name as they ran about."

"He is some great man, then, traveling with such a train?"

"He is a friend of the governor. He has monopolies. He is very rich."

"Does he not carry his own tents then?"

"Those are his tents they are putting up yonder. But *Señor* Guadalmo prefers to sleep behind strong walls, *señorita*."

"Why is that? Is he afraid of the night air?"

Taki smiled a little, a very little — more with his eyes than with his lips.

"The night air is sometimes very bad. Men go to sleep strong and very well. They are dead when they waken."

"Taki! Is there some frightful plague here in California?"

"Yes, *señorita*."

"What are the symptoms of it?"

"The instant they are seen, the man is already dead."

"You speak of the men. Does it never touch the women?"

"Rarely, *señorita*."

"This is very strange. What are the symptoms, then?"

"They are different," said Taki. "Sometimes the man who was strong and well goes to sleep and is found in the morning with a great cut across his throat. Sometimes there is no outward mark, but his body is swollen. . . ."

"Do you mean throat-cutting and poison, Taki?"

"But the symptom that is usually found," said Taki, without answering her less obliquely, "is the handle of a knife standing over the man's breast, with the blade fixed in his heart."

She frowned at him seriously. "It is a murderous country, then? Why?"

"The law is far away."

"And this Guadalmo is very much afraid?"

"Very, *señorita.*"

"Is he a coward?"

"He is a famous fighter . . . a very brave man. In Spain his name was famous."

"Guadalmo, the duelist! Is it he?"

"It is, *señorita!*"

"I have heard that he feared nothing . . . not even God, or the devil."

"There was a time when he did not. He would ride alone a thousand miles."

"What changed him?"

"There is one man who follows him. Five times he has tried to get the life of *Señor* Guadalmo. And five times he has nearly succeeded. Therefore, *Señor* Guadalmo has surrounded himself with great warriors. They would sooner get out their swords than take off their hats. They had rather fight than eat. These men protect him."

"Who is this man who follows Guadalmo?"

"No one can tell. It is a mystery. Some people say that it is the devil himself who has come for *Señor* Guadalmo, because no man would dare to face him."

"That is nonsense!"

"There are others who believe that it is merely the brother of a man *Señor* Guadalmo killed."

"Tell me of that."

"A hundred long marches to the East, *señorita,* there are many cities."

"The English colonies. I know."

"A trader came from them. He was called John Gidden. He had a ship which he commanded, and he traded here for hides. *Señor* Guadalmo and he dined together one day, and quarreled over some little thing. But when the wine had died in them, *Señor* Guadalmo sent for Gidden and told him he was sorry and asked him to come to his house. *Señor* Gidden came. In the night they quarreled again. They fought, and with swords. *Señor* Gidden was killed."

"If it was fair fight, Taki. . . ."

"It was fair fight, *señorita*. This *Señor* Gidden was one who lived by the sea. He had strong hands and a fearless heart. But the only weapons he knew were a cutlass and a pistol. A rapier was strange to him. However, he fought *Señor* Guadalmo, the great duelist, with a rapier. Therefore, being a fool, he was killed."

"That has an ugly sound, Taki."

"If he had not been a fool, he would have fought with a cutlass or with a saber."

"Perhaps he was not allowed?"

Taki made a gesture.

"As for that, I cannot tell. But he was killed; and afterward a letter came to *Señor* Guadalmo from the brother of this *Señor* Gidden, saying that he was coming to find Guadalmo and to kill him. And, after that, five times a masked man has set on *Señor* Guadalmo, as I have said, and five times *Señor* Guadalmo's life has been saved by a miracle. Therefore, he loves strong walls around him when he sleeps at night, and he has come this evening to beg a shelter from *Señor* Torreño."

"This is a strange story, Taki. However, I wish also to tell you that it has given me a thought. You are a fighting man, Taki."

"I, *señorita?* Among the Navajos I was a chief and a warrior. But the poor Indian is a child among the white men. His hand may be strong, but his wits are weak."

She chuckled. "However," she said, "since there is this plague in the land, I feel that I need a guard and, while you are with me, you must be my protector, Taki."

"The *señorita* has commanded," said Taki, his eye as blank as ever. "I pray to the Great Spirit that my hand may be strong for her."

"You speak sadly, Taki."

"Ah," said Taki, "how can the guard of fighting men help us when there are other dangers which fighting men cannot face?"

"That sounds like a riddle. What dangers, Taki?"

"I have spoken too much," said Taki. "I am not the guard who can help the *señorita.*"

"What guard should I have, then?"

"A father confessor," said the Indian calmly.

"A priest! And what would he do for me?"

"He would listen to the troubles which are in your heart, *señorita!*"

She had almost invited the blow but, when it came, it shocked her. She stiffened a little and drew back from the window.

"Your tongue," she said, "runs faster than your horse!"

At that he made her a ceremonious bow. Certainly the lessons of the dancing master had not been entirely thrown away upon Taki. As for the girl, she did not pause to wonder over his grace but she turned in anger to her Aunt Anna and saw, from her grave, sad face, that she had overheard everything.

"I shall go instantly to *Señor* Torreño," said the girl, "and tell him what I suspect of Taki."

Aunt Anna d'Arquista merely shook her head.

"I think you will not, Lucia," she said. "I pray God may rule us for the best!"

She seemed so close to tears that Lucia dared not speak again, for the moment. She stormed into her room and there she flung herself down on her bed. Her face was burning. And cold little pangs of shame shot through her heart.

She had thought that she controlled her tragedy so well that not a human being in the world could ever have guessed at it. But here was a wild Indian who had looked through her at a glance and, in a moment, had read all her secrets. She wanted to destroy him utterly. And yet, after a time, she found herself sitting up, musing, and almost smiling.

"He is a clever rascal," said the girl to herself. "And if I were in a great need, he could help me!"

She was called for the night meal after this, and met the guest, Guadalmo. He was a tall, wide-shouldered man of about forty, with a grim face and a gray head that might have been ten years older; but his body was still young and supple — the body of the professional duelist. He bore traces of his encounters — a ragged scar in his right cheek and another which crossed one eye and kept it half closed so that he bore, continually, a quizzical, penetrating expression. He had donned his most magnificent clothes for this occasion. He wore, above all, old-fashioned lace cuffs and a great lace collar worth a fortune in skill and labor. It made an odd setting for his forbidding features.

He was a courtly man as well as a warrior, however. And he entertained the girl with talk of Paris and the French court, full of little cuts and thrusts of gossip. He was one of those who can speak with an easy familiarity of the great men of the world and seem to bring their presences into the room. Don Carlos listened to him, agape with delight.

"Tomorrow," said Don Carlos, "I shall beg

five minutes of your time to teach me some clever thrust. I have been shamed by an Indian today, with the foils. I must have some revenge on him!"

Guadalmo raised his brows. "An Indian," he said, "who fences?"

"The skill of a fiend incarnate," said Torreño, breaking in. "I should give a great deal to see you cross blades with him, *señor!*"

Señor Guadalmo smiled.

"For Indians," he said, "I keep a whip . . . and bullets. I advise you, my dear friends, to do the same."

Here a door behind Guadalmo swung silently open, but he knew it by the soft sighing of the draft, and leaped violently to his feet, setting all the dishes on the table in a great jangle. He had a pistol in his hand as he whirled, but he saw behind him only an empty threshold, dimly lighted.

"*¡Señor! ¡Señor!*" cried the host. "One would think that you feared the Black Rider even in the midst of my household!"

"Set a man to watch the door," asked Guadalmo, reseating himself, but still with a pale face. "I have a profound respect for your household and your management of it, *Señor* Torreño. But when one has to do with the devil . . . one needs caution . . . caution . . . and again, caution!"

The effect of that fright was still ghastly in his face, but with an inward struggle he forced a smile to his lips again.

He took up a glass of white wine in which the imaged light of a candle flame was trembling; and the tremor, the girl noted, was not in the flame of the candle, but in the hand of Guadalmo. She observed and she wondered. And when a breath of air through the open window set the draperies behind her shivering and whispering, she trembled in turn, as though the ghost of the Black Rider were behind her chair!

VIII "The Black Rider"

Who is the Black Rider? It was the commanding question in the mind of the girl when she went out into the patio beneath the stars with the others. From the little white tent city around the main house, all the retainers of Don Francisco were waxing merry and raising songs from time to time and, at the end of each day's work, the followers of the worthy don received due portions of that colorless brandy which the Mexican Indian loves and which burns the brain of the white man like a blue flame. But even their singing was subdued, for Don Francisco hated all loud noise except that of his own strong voice.

Obviously no questions about the Black Rider could be asked while *Señor* Guadalmo was himself present; but after an uneasy moment he bade the rest good night and withdrew to his appointed quarters for sleep; so he said. But during an interval which followed, they could hear the stir of men.

"Guadalmo is filling the house with his guards," said Torreño. "Look! Even under his window!"

They saw two stalwarts, each with sword and carbine, take post beneath the windows of Guadalmo's room. There they remained, huge black specters.

"*I* have an idea!" said the girl. "The Black Rider is one of *Señor* Guadalmo's men with a grudge against him!"

Torreño chuckled in the bottom of his thick throat.

"My dear," he said, "that is child's talk. You do not know Guadalmo and his men! He has picked up the neatest set of murderers that ever wore sword and pistol since the beginning of time! There is not a one of them that does not owe his escape from the gallows to his master. They live by him; they would be hung except for him and his influence with the governor. They know it and they would fight for him as for themselves. He is their safety; he is their charm against death! Those two men yonder . . . I can tell the one by the feather in his hat, the other by the limp in his walk. The tall man used to cut throats in Naples; Guadalmo smuggled him aboard his ship and made off with him. The other was a soldier in the Low Countries, a gambler who made up for his losses on the highway. He fled to Guadalmo also. So they are here. They will watch over him more tenderly than they will watch over their own souls!"

"But this Black Rider, has he never appeared except to *Señor* Guadalmo?"

"Some dozen times," said Don Carlos. "He knows, it appears, whenever some solitary traveler sets out with a large sum of money. Then the Black Rider appears. Usually he sweeps up from behind on a horse swifter than the wind, it is said. The animal is sheathed in a light caparison of black silk. There is a hood of thin black silk covering the Rider, too. That is how he gets his name. He stops his man, rakes his purse, and is gone. Sometimes they were brave and resisted, at the first. A bullet in the leg or through the shoulder always ended the fight. The Black Rider does not kill. He does not have to. He can see in the dark, it seems, and he shoots with such a nice aim that he could kill a bat on the wing at midnight!"

That was all the explanation she received concerning the Black Rider. After his first few captures, the mere terror of his presence had proved enough to paralyze all resistance. Men were benumbed with fear when he approached.

At last Lucia stood up to go to her room; and, as she turned, it seemed to her that there was a movement in the far corner of the patio.

"In the name of heaven, *Señor* Torreño!" she breathed.

The shadow stirred. A man stood upright.

"Carlos . . . fool . . . your pistol!" growled out Torreño.

"It is I . . . Taki!" said the shadow.

"Tie the red-face to a post and have him whipped!" commanded Torreño. "Have you turned into a spy, Taki?"

"It is the command of the *señorita,*" said the Indian. "I am to stay close to her to protect her in case of harm."

"Seven thousand devils!" thundered the other. "Am I not guard enough for her, and in my own house? Lucia, what madness is this?"

"Only *Señor* Torreño," she said, "because he was given to me, and I did not know what other work to give him."

"Well," said Torreño, "you must not be afraid of the ghosts you make with your own hands. But for half of a second, I looked at him and thought . . . the Black Rider!"

"Is the Black Rider so large a man?"

"Larger, it is said. A very giant! A span taller than this Taki of yours. Good night!"

Don Carlos went with her to the door of her room; Taki was three paces to the rear.

"Dear Lucia," he said, as they paused there, "now that you have seen my father and his country, do you think that you can be happy among us and our rude people?"

She looked up to him with a little twisted smile. "Ah, Carlos," she said, "I should be afraid to say no to the son of Don Francisco!"

And she hurried on into the room with Anna d'Arquista. Don Carlos turned to speak to Taki, but that man of the silent foot had already disappeared. There was no definite quarters assigned to the Indian. He was left to shift for himself, and the place he had chosen was in a nook behind a hedge. There, from a blanket roll, he provided himself with what he wanted, which was chiefly a mask of black silk, fitting closely over his face, a pistol, and a rapier. Provided with these, he made his way back toward the house, moving swiftly but with caution and going, wherever possible, in the gloom beneath the trees, for the moon was up, now, and the open places were silvered with faint light. He came to the wall of the big, squat house and moved around it until a form loomed in front of him.

A short-barreled musket was instantly thrust against his breast. Yet the voice of the guard was muffled, for fear lest he needlessly disturb the slumber of his master.

"Who is this?" he asked.

"I am the new man."

"I know of no new man."

The footfalls of the other sentinel, who kept guard around the corner of the wall, paused at the end of his beat. In a moment he would be back and in view of them. Taki drew in his breath and tensed his muscles.

"I have ridden all afternoon up from the harbor."

"Ah?"

"You are Giovanni?"

"Yes."

"I have brought you a message."

"From whom?"

"Naples."

"¡Diablo!" breathed the other. "Are you from Naples?"

And he lowered the muzzle of his gun a trifle. In that instant Taki struck the other with bone-crushing force on the base of the jaw, and he slumped gently forward on his face. Taki stepped over him.

"Giovanni?" he heard the other guard murmur as he approached the corner of the wall.

And then the second man turned the corner and came full against Taki. He had no time to cry out. The left hand of the Indian, like a steel-clawed panther's foot, was fixed instantly on his throat. And as his breath stopped, he snatched a knife from his belt. But Taki struck with the hilt of his rapier, and the guard turned limp in his grip.

After that, in a single minute of swift work, as one familiar with such things, he gagged them with their own garments and bound them back to back. Then he flattened himself against the wall and looked around him.

All was quiet in the house; only from the distance came an amiable, musical hum of voices from the tents; a reassuring sound of men at peace with one another and with the world. And Taki's teeth glinted white as he smiled at the moon. Then he turned, adjusted the silken mask, laid a hand on the sill of the open window, and drew himself softly into the room.

Señor Don Hernandez Guadalmo slept but

lightly; and even that silken smooth entrance of the Indian's had roused him. Now, as Taki turned from the window, he faced Guadalmo, who was sitting bolt upright in his bed, but so paralyzed with nightmare horror that he could not move his hand. Before he recovered, he had clapped a pistol to his head.

"Don Hernandez, son of a dog," he said, "for the sixth time we have met."

"God receive my soul!" murmured the wretched man.

"The devil will receive it," said the other. "But not from this room. You must step out with me, *señor!*"

"If you have murder to do, do it here! But first, let me see your face!"

"Before you die, you shall see it, I promise. And if I fail, you may use your discretion upon me. Here, *Señor* Guadalmo, is your favorite sword. I make free to borrow it. Now, step before me through that window. If you cry out, if you attempt to run, I send a bullet through your back . . . or an ounce of lead to mingle with your brains, my friend!"

"What reward is there in the end?"

"A chance to fight with me fairly, point to point, sword to sword, and die like a murderer, as you deserve, but also like a gentleman."

Guadalmo fairly trembled with joy. "Is it true?"

"On the honor of one whose faith has never been broken."

"I go as to a feast!" said the duelist. He paused only to draw on a few garments. Then he slipped through the window before Taki and was rejoined by him on the ground.

"The guards?" he queried in a whisper.

Taki pointed to a tangled heap of shadow at the corner of the wall. "They will not notice your going, *señor*."

"You have confederates who have done this?"

"Confederates? Yes, my two hands. Walk straight ahead, *señor*. I shall remain just half a pace behind you."

"My friend, the Black Rider," said Guadalmo, "this promises to be a notable and happy night."

And he walked straight forward down the slope and into the hollow beneath.

IX "Flashing Blades"

Here," said the Indian, "we will be very comfortable."

Guadalmo paused. He found himself in a little level-bottomed clearing surrounded by the squat forms of oak trees, each with a dim, black pattern printed beneath it on the brown grass.

The moon was bright. A cool sea wind stirred across the hollow and brought to it the indescribable freshness of salt water. And from the highlands came the additional scent of the evergreens.

Guadalmo cast off the light cloak from his shoulders.

"I am ready, *señor,*" he said.

"Your sword," replied the other, and presented it to him by tossing it lightly through the air. Guadalmo caught it with considerable dexterity and made the blade whistle in the air.

"Now God be praised. *Señor,* the Black Rider," he said, "I see that I have to do with a gentleman and not with a cutthroat."

"Be assured, friend," said the Indian dryly, "that if I were a throat cutter, yours would have been slashed at our first meeting. This is to be a fair fight with equal weapons."

"However, you still carry a pistol at your belt."

The Indian tossed that weapon behind him and into the shrubbery.

"We are now even forces."

There was a ring of joy in the throat of Guadalmo.

"Fool," he said, "you are no better than a dead man! If you dare to stand up to me for ten breaths, I promise you a swift road to heaven. But as for equal forces . . . if I am hard-pressed, I have only to shout, and a dozen men will come for me."

Taki started, then shook his head as though to reassure himself.

"I have thought of that, of course," he said calmly, "but I think that I know you too well. For you had rather die, Guadalmo, than have men know that you cried out for help against a single man!"

"Come, come!" exclaimed the Spaniard. "The time flies. If the bound guards are found and I am missed, there will be a noise at once!"

"That is true. ¡Señor, on guard!"

Their blades whipped up in a formal salute; continuing the same motion, Guadalmo passed on into a murderous lunge. Only a backward stroke saved Taki from that treacherous move.

"Ah, murderer!" he breathed. "This is your beginning!"

"Save your breath for your work. You shall have plenty of it!" said Guadalmo, and attacked instantly.

He came in with the reckless abandon of one accustomed to looking upon his narrow rapier as a secure wall of steel against his enemy's point. And the blade of Taki met his with a continual harsh clattering. Neither would give back. They pressed on to half sword length.

"Ha!" cried the Spaniard through his teeth, and delivered an upward thrust at the throat against which there seemed no possible ward.

But Taki found one. With his bare hand he knocked aside the darting weapon. He stepped in with the same movement and crushed Guadalmo against his breast. The hug of the bear could not have been more paralyzing.

"I am a dead man! God receive me!" gasped out Guadalmo as the point of the shortened sword appeared at his throat.

"With that stroke, *señor,*" said Taki, "you killed Antonio Cadoral in Padua. Tonight it has failed you. What else have you left?"

He cast the helpless man away.

"Breathe again, Guadalmo," he said. "Now, *señor,* your utmost skill."

"Devil!" groaned Guadalmo. "You have only a minute to live!"

And he attacked not recklessly, but with the utmost deadliness of finesse, working as though a picture were being drawn by the point of his weapon. It became a play of double

88

lightning, the two blades flashing in the moonshine.

But the minute passed and Taki still lived, and without giving ground. He began to talk again as they worked, as one who held his task lightly.

"*Señor* Guadalmo, there is a grove near Toledo where a gallant gentleman, Juan Jaratta, met you without seconds. You killed him with foul play . . . a sudden thrust when by mutual agreement you had lowered your swords to take a breath."

"It is false!" snarled out Guadalmo. "Besides, there was no human eye near to take note of such a thing."

"I, however, was nearby, and watched."

"You are the devil, then!"

"As you please. But beware, Guadalmo! For the sake of Jaratta, I am about to touch you over the heart!"

"I defy you!"

The rapier in the hand of Taki darted out as the hummingbird darts toward the deep mouth of a flower — and as the hummingbird stops dead in mid flight and then shoots forward again, a mere flash of rainbow color and sheen, so the blade of Taki paused and drove beneath the parry of Guadalmo and the keen point pricked him on the breast.

"Damnation!" gasped out Guadalmo, and quickly leaped backward with all his power.

He began to perspire with the weakness not

of exhaustion, but of despair and fear.

"We have only begun," said Taki. "There was in Nice, on a time, a young gentleman from the American colonies of England. He had loaned you money, Guadalmo, and when your time came to repay it, you found a quarrel with him and met him outside the city on a broad green lawn. There were great flowers planted around the lawn. As the dawn grew clear, you could see their colors . . . golden-yellow, bronze, and deepest scarlet. Do you remember?"

"If I remember, you shall soon forget. So!"

"A good thrust," said Taki, putting the stroke aside with a flick of his own blade. "And a favorite in Bologna. With it, in fact, you killed the poor gentleman. And, for his sake, another touch above the heart. . . ."

Who can escape the leap of the lightning? *Señor* Guadalmo was tense with dreadful anxiety, and yet he could not avoid the sudden flash of Taki's sword. And again there was a bee sting in the flesh above his heart. He felt a little warm trickle of blood run down inside his shirt — warm blood over a body that had turned to ice.

He gave ground. He looked wildly up the slope above the trees, where the roofs of the house of Torreño were faintly visible. There was succor, in ample scope, so near, so near! He thought of turning and fleeing toward it, but as he watched the tigerish smoothness of the advance of Taki, he knew that he would be overtaken in a single leap. There was no escape that way. He thought of crying out — but before the sound had left his lips, the inescapable mischief which played so brightly in the hand of the tall man would be buried in his heart! And the cold perspiration streamed down the face of Guadalmo. His body was dank with it.

"There are still others," said Taki. "You have covered your way with killings, damnable murders made legal. You have picked quarrels with young men who had scarcely left their fencing masters after a month of practice. But above all, there was one man who had never held a straight sword in his life. He was an honest sailor, Guadalmo. An honest man, do you hear me? A breath of his was worth more than your eternal soul. He was a kind, bluff man. All who knew him, loved him. He had behind him a young wife and two small children. Ah, Guadalmo, my friend, what a devil it would have taken to murder that honorable man? And yet there was such a demon in the world. There was such a murder done. All honorable! He was challenged and met with rapiers. He was forced to fight, he thought, to defend his honor. His honor against a rat, a snake, a wolf! Think of it, *Señor* Guadalmo. Can you conceive it?"

"Are you done?" snarled out Guadalmo, perceiving that the end was near. "Are you done whining? Yes, I killed him. And you are his brother? Hear me, friend. When the steel went through him, he screamed like a woman!"

Taki groaned. "He screamed with agony of sorrow because he thought of his wife and his family . . . with bewilderment that such a tiny needle of a weapon should have taken his life . . . but never with pain or with fear. For he was a lion, *Señor* Guadalmo! And it is for his sake that I am about to touch you for the third time, and this time, you are to die! Think of him, and how he lay in your patio, panting and gasping. He had messages which he begged you to send to his wife. He would forgive you, pray for you, if you would send them. Did you send them, Guadalmo? Did you send them? A word, only, to his widow or his orphans?"

"Bah!" gasped out the Spaniard, and lunged with all his force.

It was attacking a will-o'-the-wisp. He closed again with a shout of despair. Then a limber hand of steel closed around his sword. He felt a wrench that twisted his wrist far to one side. Out of his wet fingers the sword was drawn, and flipped high into the air, spinning over and over, brilliant against the moon, in its fall. And Guadalmo followed it with eyes of horror and of bewilderment.

He looked down at the leveled blade of his opponent. And then, from the rear of the clearing, a pistol spoke, a bullet hummed past and thudded heavily against the body of an oak tree, and into the open ran three men. There was a wild cry of rage from Taki. He leaped at Guadalmo with a final lunge, but the latter fell groveling upon the ground and missed death by a fraction of a second. Over him leaped Taki — no time for a second stroke.

Another bound brought him among the shadows of the trees — and he was gone, with a final volley whirring about him.

And, in the meantime, it seemed that a hundred voices had suddenly begun to shout at the same time, before him and behind him.

There was no pursuit on the part of the valiants, however. They did not care to follow the tiger into his lair among the crowded trees; they preferred to make a close guard around Guadalmo and shout for help. So Taki paused to drop the rapier into a shallow bed of leaves. He snatched the black mask from his face.

Just before him a body of six men broke in among the trees.

"Who is there?" they shouted to him.

"Taki," he said. And he joined in the hunt.

X "Trapped"

It was a matter not to be mentioned in the presence of *Señor* Torreño. It was well enough if some rascally brigand dared to hold up passers-by upon the great highway. But when they ventured into his very presence and there committed their villainies, it was high time that an end were put to these proceedings. *Señor* Torreño ordered his entire household to mount. He left at the house a mere guard of half a dozen men. With the rest, he scoured the country. And, conspicuous among the foremost riders was Taki, the Navajo, who distinguished himself by being the only man of the party who thought he saw a fugitive vanishing among the hills. However, they could not trace the vision of Taki, and therefore they eventually turned back to the house, gloomy and disgruntled. The lips of Torreño flowed curses faster than a well gives forth water. He damned the entire world in general and the Black Rider in particular. He began again with the Black Rider and went backward, damning the entire world. He would burn the entire region of California to a crisp, but in the end he would have this reckless manhunter who ventured upon his kill in the very lair of the Torreño himself!

The story of Guadalmo was simple and clear. He had been wakened from sleep by having a cord thrown around his body. Therefore, he awakened helpless. He was forced to dress in haste and climb down through the window, and so was taken to the hollow where he was eventually found. There he was about to be murdered, but he had managed to excite the pride of the Black Rider sufficiently to make the outlaw begin a single-handed duel in the course of which he was about to spit the Black Rider like a chicken, and so put an end to that sinister public plague, when they were broken in upon by fools who thought they were running to the rescue. It made no difference that the rescuers, according to what their eyes had told them, vowed that they did not notice any sword in the hand of Guadalmo. They were not believed to have seen what was before them. For, though it was conceivable that the great Guadalmo might be conquered in fight, it was notably ridiculous to conceive that he had been so overmastered that he was actually disarmed!

Señor Guadalmo, however, made light of the whole matter when they sat together to break their fast in the morning, after the futile manhunt had ended.

"Now that I have seen this ghost face to face, and noted the color of his eyes," said Guadalmo, "I assure you that there will soon be an end to him. Oh, fool, fool, fool that I was!"

He struck his palm across his forehead and sighed.

"What is wrong, Guadalmo?" asked his host.

"When I think that I might have put this monster out of the world with a mere touch . . . and that I allowed him to live! Alas, Torreño, I am covered with shame and with fury."

"Tell us, Guadalmo."

"No, no! It sickens me to think of it! Fool, fool that I was!"

"We must hear it, *señor.*"

"It was in this manner. We had closed. We were at hardly more than half sword distance. I threw him off balance with a strong parry and at the same instant I closed on him and took him by the throat. The dog lost heart at once. He dropped his sword and fell on his knees and babbled out a prayer for mercy! Mercy has ever been my besetting sin. I could not kill that wild beast even when I had him in that position."

Lady Anna d'Arquista fairly trembled with admiration. To think that at the same table with her sat a man who had been able to crush the famous Black Rider to his knees was enough to make her shudder. She said to her niece: "Did you ever see such a gallant and noble gentleman, Lucia?"

Lucia wasn't always graceful in her manners. Now she grunted as a man might have done, and a very rough man at that.

"He has a sick look," she said.

"Guadalmo?"

"He has had troubles enough to last him out the month," said the girl, nodding her head sagely.

"Of course, to be wakened by that fiend. . . ."

"A poor weak devil!" scoffed the girl. "Our great Guadalmo takes him by the throat and makes the devil beg!"

"You do not believe?"

"Of course I believe," said Lucia, yawning a little. "I believe anything that is amusing! There is little enough, at that!"

She could not be moved from this position. Guadalmo finished his recital in the midst of a silence which was a greater tribute than applause. He promised, however, that when he had a little spare time on his hands, he would hunt down this wretched road-haunter, this and cut him to shreds the very next time they encountered.

Here Lucia spoke aloud: "The next time, *señor,*" she said, "will surely be the last. It will be the seventh. And that number is surely fatal, is it not?"

To the surprise of everyone, *Señor* Guadalmo turned white and his face was glistening with perspiration.

"I pray heaven, *señorita,*" he said in a shaken voice, "that you are not a prophet."

"Ah, ah!" cried Lucia. "I mean, of course, that

the meeting will be fatal for him . . . for the Black Rider!"

It was too late to give the thought that turn in the mind of Guadalmo. He seemed stricken. He sat bowed in his chair, his head in his hand.

He said over and over: "There is a sort of fate in it, is there not? I meet him again and again . . . I alone. Six times he has encountered me . . . six times the breath of the devil has fanned my cheek. But all this is only a warning. The seventh time the devil will gather me in!"

He removed from the table presently and went from the room. All remained in an uneasy silence for a moment behind him, and at length Torreño himself murmured: "Who would have believed this of the great Guadalmo?"

His steward came in at that moment. He was full of excitement. He reported that, in a shallow bed of leaves in the forest, not far from the very spot where *Señor* Guadalmo had been found in close fight with the marauder, one of the peons had stumbled into a hidden sword and got a shrewd cut in the leg for his discovery. It was given to the steward, who instantly gave it, of course, to the master of the house. Could it be, by any chance, the weapon of the Black Rider, which had fallen from his hand? Torreño took the rapier and held it at arm's length.

"That is a rapier worthy of a gentleman, not a brigand," he said. "I'll swear that the Black Rider would rather have parted with so much flesh nearest his heart than to have lost this weapon. At least, we have one of the feathers of the crow, which is more than all the other hunters for him can say. But what if he comes back for it?"

Here there followed an impressive little silence, and into it ran the sound of a far-off flute:

> *"Ye highlands and ye lowlands,*
> *Oh, where hae ye been?*
> *They hae slain the Earl of Murray*
> *And hae laid him on the green.*
> *"Now wae be to thee, Huntly,*
> *And wharefore did ye sae?*
> *I bade ye bring him wi' you*
> *And forbade ye him to slay."*

Then *Señor* Torreño stood up. He sent for Guadalmo. He sent for half a dozen other of his most trusted men — and then changed his mind and took with him the same number of Guadalmo's practiced fighters.

"This hand to hand fighting and this dueling," he said, "is all very well. But I prefer a net which is sure of catching the bird."

The wounded servant limped along to show them the way; it was a perfect place. Low shrubbery enclosed a little hollow, and in that pool of leaves, stirred by only the strongest winds, the rapier had been found. Guadalmo and the rest instantly took cover among the shrubs. In the meantime orders were sent back for the rest of the train to be busy preparing the coach and packing up for the journey.

If the Black Rider were nearby, watching, he might venture down even now to secure his lost weapon!

But nothing came near them except the sound of the flute of Taki, the Navajo, as he wandered casually among the trees. He appeared, presently, from among them. He came to the pool of the dead leaves and scuffed through it. He turned, still with the flute at his lips, and went shuffling through the leaves again.

Then he stopped, lowered the flute, and frowned. Presently he leaned over and slipped his hand among the leaves. It seemed, indeed, as though he were searching for something. And what he wanted was not there! He dropped to his knees, then, and pocketing the flute, he was busy with both hands.

Suddenly the voice of Guadalmo rang loudly as he started up.

"Take him, my friends! This is the man we want!"

They started out of the shrubbery like six bloodhounds. Instantly they closed around the tall form of the Indian. He was still a head above the tallest man. He made no resistance.

He merely looked about him in a bewildered fashion as they laid hands upon him. Torreño came storming from his place. The Black Rider was a man of wit and invention, a dashing, clever fellow. This was no more than a red Indian and could not be the man.

"He has come here to hunt . . . for what?" asked Guadalmo. "For his lost sword, of course. Besides, I have heard his voice; I have seen his height and his form. It is the man, Torreño. My life on it! Another thing . . . give me hot water and a little scrubbing and you will see some of the red come from that skin! None but a white man could handle a sword as he handles his! I'll go a step farther, my friends. I'll give him a name . . . which is Gidden!"

So much surety turned the scales at once.

"Bring him instantly to the house," said Torreño. "We'll have a try with water at his hide."

"There is no need, *señor*," said the prisoner calmly. "I freely confess that I am Richard Gidden!"

Señor Guadalmo began to laugh. The lines of trouble disappeared from his face. Years of age seemed to have been stripped from him.

"Taki," he said, "would have given the hounds a run, but Richard Gidden will be found worthy of hanging. Is it not so, Torreño?"

XI "The Chase"

To this question, the master of those lands did not immediately return an answer. He looked about him with a vacant eye of thought over the brown hills and the dark patches of oak groves here and there, studded with a scattering of cattle. Then he turned to Guadalmo.

"This man is worthy of death," he said at length. "That is clear. He confesses it himself. Now, my friend, when I see a white man I am ready to give him a white man's death. But when I see a redskin, an Indian's death is a better thing for him. His skin is red. He calls himself Richard Gidden. It is an odd name. He is known to me only as Taki. And as Taki I swear he shall die!"

"And how?" asked Guadalmo, falling in readily enough with the viewpoint of the other. "For my part, I say, tie his hands behind his back and send a few ounce bullets through his head. That will make an end of him. However, there may be better ways. What way, *Señor* Torreño?"

"The dogs!" said Torreño. "I have traveled without them for this time only. But you have them with you constantly. The dogs, Guadalmo, and a fifty-pace start for him!"

"*Señor* Guadalmo," broke in Richard Gidden, "your life has been in my hands, and I have spared it. Remember!"

"My life in your hands?" snarled out the Spaniard. "You lie, you rat! Besides, my pack need a blooding. They have grown dull on the trail! The dogs, Torreño, the dogs! An Indian's death for a redskin."

And the first man to echo that cry among the followers of *Señor* Guadalmo was none other than Giovanni of Naples, with a bruised patch at the base of his jaw and a fury of rage in his heart. It was taken up; it swept to the house; it reached the ears even of the lady, Lucia. She could not understand, at first, but when she did, she went straight to Don Carlos. He was about to hurry to the manhunt, with gaiety in his face.

"Carlos," she said with a sort of stern eagerness, "if you wish my love and my respect, stop this hideous thing. He is a man, Carlos, not a beast. And they tell me he is a white man. God in heaven knows that I guessed that before I had heard him speak three words. For the sake of your soul . . . for my sake, Carlos, stop this hunt! And if. . . ."

Her voice was broken short by a loud clamor of deep-voiced hounds. She beckoned him away and turned to the house with her head bowed, her hands pressed over her ears. Don Carlos left her like a frightened boy who has seen a mystery. It had never occurred to him that it was wrong to hunt Indians with dogs. He had done it. His father had enjoyed that same wild sport. What there was in it of sin he could not see. And for the fact that the man was white, it was obvious that since he had chosen the disguise of a redskin, an Indian's death was only ironically proper to him. And yet, seeing the horror in the face of the girl, he comprehended dimly that there *was* both a crime and a sin here. Most of all, he was afraid of her. He would have faced anything rather than incur her displeasure. He would have faced his very father. And, a moment later, he did so.

The hounds were out, and Torreño was discussing their merits rather than the merits of the work which was before them. The admirable *Señor* Guadalmo had in person brought this pack from Germany. The base of their blood was the boar hound. But having been trained by the skillful hand of Guadalmo, they were soon accustomed to course far nobler game. Huge of shoulder and quarter, with great, square, muzzled heads and brows wrinkled with lion-like sagacity and fierceness, they possessed, in addition, long limbs and the tucked-up bellies of greyhounds which were token of their speed. There were a dozen in the original pack. Seven remained, but they were like seven tigers in ferocity and cunning. Already they sensed work to their liking, and raged on the leashes. Two servants held each dog — and each dog was worth the price of two peons! The entire household was gathered to watch the chase. It was now that Don Carlos encountered his father.

"*Señor,*" he said, "for the grace of heaven, do not hunt this man with the dogs!"

His father turned slowly upon him. He had been touched to the very core of the heart with rage by the invasion of his house the night before. Now he saw some chance to let loose the gathering thunder of his anger.

"The grace of heaven? The grace of heaven?" he echoed. "What do you know of the grace of heaven, boy?"

Don Carlos was stricken. He retreated a pace. His voice trembled a little as he added: "It is not I who ask, Father," he said. "It is Lucia!"

"It is Lucia!" mocked Torreño, putting a semi-awe into his own tones. "It is the peerless lady, Lucia. Now, boy, hear me and understand me. I have paid a price for that girl. And may my soul roast if the price was not high! There is one way she may make me a return for my money . . . and that is to be an obedient daughter. But as for what she wishes . . . damnation, Carlos, am I to be ruled by the whims of a girl and a fool? Am I to be ruled? I?"

His voice had raised at the end. Don Carlos was fairly quaking with fear.

Yet still he remembered the face of Lucia

and so he persisted for a moment.

"Alas, sir," he said. "If you had seen her as I saw her, when she begged me to. . . ."

"Begged?" said Torreño, breaking strongly in. "That is good! Teach her to beg. She is too apt to demand. As for this business, she knows nothing about it. A woman's gentleness would fill this land with red devils in a month. It is one of *my* servants, Carlos, who dared to enter *my* house and raised a hand against a guest of Francisco Torreño! I will see him torn to shreds! Do you hear me?"

"I hear you," said Don Carlos submissively.

"As for the girl, your wife to be," continued Torreño, a little appeased by the frightened face of his son, "she may weep today, frown tomorrow, and sulk the next day. Then give her a ring . . . a horse . . . or some other trinket. And she will forget. Here is time to learn a great thing in the management of women, my lad. Let them feel the whip now and then . . . the whip, Carlos!"

He rubbed his hands together and laughed loudly.

"Now, friends!" he called to the others. "Is all prepared? Look to the cinches of my saddle, Juan. Mind his heels, fool! *Señor* Guadalmo, this will be sport!"

"Unless he runs away from the dogs," said Guadalmo with a discontented face. "The surest way is a bullet through the head. Let the dogs have him afterward, if you choose!"

He added in thunder: "Bring out Taki! Bring him out! Place him here!"

Fifty not over-long strides he advanced before the leashed pack and marked the spot by driving his heel into the ground. To that place they led out Richard Gidden, half naked. There was no doubt about the true color of his skin now. All his body had been dyed copper, but only about the face and hands had the stain been carefully renewed. The rest of him was many a shade lighter, and across his shoulders the white seemed fairly shining through.

He came forth with a firm step. He regarded the beasts who were to hunt him. He watched the mounting of the riders. Then he turned his glance before him, as though selecting the best course for his race. He was rather like an athlete contending for a great prize than one about to struggle hopelessly for life.

"Cast him loose!" commanded Torreño. "Stand fast, Taki, until you hear the word. Stand fast, or we send a dozen bullets through you. Now, lads, with the dogs. . . ."

The guards, who had surrounded the prisoner, now gave back in haste to open a channel through which the dogs might run at their prey. But by this time they were in a frenzy of eagerness. They reared to a man's height as they strained at the leashes.

"Unleash!" cried Torreño. "Halloo! Away!"

A horn blew; the dogs leaped off, giving

tongue; and Richard Gidden whirled to flee. But, as he whirled, he whistled once, a long, shrill note that cut through the air like the scream of a bagpipe. Then he fled down the slope toward the nearest hollow.

For fifty yards, with the fear of death winging his feet, he gained on the flying dogs, for the boar hound, after all, is a stout but clumsy runner. For a hundred yards he held them even. Then they began to gain steadily and surely. They crossed the hollow. They sped up the slope beyond with the hillside giving back their deep voices in thunder. They topped the first hill and lunged down into the gentle valley beyond. And now they were straining forward closer and closer to his heels. The leaders began to slaver. The note of the baying rose sharper and shorter as toward the kill. And the horsemen who swept at an easy canter in the rear shouted encouragement. Torreño was strangled with laughter; *Señor* Guadalmo, like a madman in his joy, yelled to the hounds and brandished his fist above his head.

By the time they reached the next hollow they would pull down the fugitive, beyond doubt. The morning sun shone on his limbs, burnished with perspiration; his body swayed, now, with the agony of his labor, and his head was flagging back with exhaustion.

And then a red flash left the thicket to the left, and a red bay stallion flaunted across the open straight at the fugitive. It was Guadalmo who first understood the meaning of the thing.

"Torreño!" he screamed. "Look! Look! His horse! Once on the back of that red devil, he is gone like the wind! Ride down the hounds. Get to him! Pistols and swords, my friends, if you love me! If he escapes today, we are but murdered men tomorrow!"

They heard him with a shout of rage, gave their horses the spur, and instantly they were among the pack and rushing fast upon the runner. But though they rode hard and recklessly down that slope like true cavaliers, their speed was nothing compared with the unburdened stallion. He came like a loose lightning flash, down the slope and into the hollow. Straight beside Taki he rushed, and swerving there, with hardly a hated gallop, they saw the fugitive fling himself at the bay, grapple the mane with one hand, take a long, winged leap as he was jerked forward by the running horse, and then rebound upward to his back.

But he was not yet free. The pursuit came hot behind him, and now their guns were out. But heavy horse pistols fired from the backs of running horses strike a target by chance rather than by skill. A dozen bullets combed the air about him as he lay flat on the back of the horse. But he guided the stallion by the touch of his hand to the left. Twenty paces before the pursuit he reached the next grove of oaks. And the voice of Guadalmo was a moan of desperation.

Through the open grove they pushed, bringing blood with every stroke of their spurs. The pack of boar hounds strained far, far to the rear now, setting up what seemed a foolish clamor. As well might they try to catch the wind as to overtake this fugitive. He was work for their masters. Too much work, indeed, even for them. For when they gained the open again, the red bay was racing over the next hilltop, and when they reached the next hilltop, he was entering a broken copse of oak in the hollow.

For another ten minutes they labored with curses and whip and spurs; but at the end of that time Richard Gidden had vanished from among the hills! The chase halted. All were silent. Torreño's brow was black as a thundercloud. The lips of Guadalmo were twitching in a passion which he dared not release in words for fear lest words alone would not suffice him. But the eye which he turned upon Torreño was the very soul of eloquence.

So they came back toward the house. The dogs followed on through the hills unregarded. Later, servants would pursue them a weary distance and bring them in once more. But they would bring no consolation to Torreño or to Guadalmo. Those captains rode with faces averted from one another and so regained their quarters. And the view of them as they came in with failure printed on their brows brought joy to one person only — and that was the *Señorita* Lucia. Anna d'Arquista had come running to her and found her in prayer at the foot of the altar in her little private chapel — passionate prayer, with her face pressed against the cold stone. She rose and ran to the window, and looking out, she cried: "God has heard me! God has heard me!"

XII "Lucia Faces the Master"

The son, *Señor* Don Carlos Torreño, had enjoyed the race after Taki — or Richard Gidden,
to give him his true name — as much as any
man. But when the red stallion appeared and
swept the fugitive away to safety, he was the
dreariest of all the party who turned back
toward the house — with the single exception
of *Señor* Guadalmo. The duelist was thinking
of death; Don Carlos was thinking of his lady;
it would have been hard to say which of the
two had the colder heart.

But, in the meantime, there was the bustle
of starting on that day's journey, and during
that time he was able to avoid the eye of Lucia.
And when the carriage was lumbering along
the road, at last, he was spared a face-to-face
encounter with the girl again. For Hernandez
Guadalmo had found it necessary to change
direction in which he was traveling and had
decided to accompany the cavalcade of Torreño. There was no doubt in the minds of the
others that he was moved by fear of Richard
Gidden. But such an opinion could not, of
course, be shown. The important thing was to
make the celebrated Guadalmo welcome, and
for that purpose both the elder and the

younger Torreño rode at his side.

It was a gloomy day's journey, and, at the close of it, when they reached the third rest house of Torreño, built for the comfort and for the honor of Lucia d'Arquista, Don Carlos realized by something in the glance which she cast upon him that the interview had been postponed — not dulled by the delay!

And she had hardly gone to her chambers when one of her serving maids came to him. She wished to see him, and at once. And poor Don Carlos girded up the loins of his resolution and prepared for trouble. It came almost the instant he was before her.

She sat beneath a window of her room with the dust of her journey still upon her clothes, tapping at the big stone flags upon the floor with a tapered riding whip. And while he talked, her glance went continually from the floor to his face to the floor; and every time she looked at him, he felt as though he had been struck by the lithe body of the whip itself!

"Carlos," she said, "this morning I begged a small favor of you, which was the life of a slave."

He sought his first refuge behind a quibble.

"It was no slave, after all," he said, "but a white man . . . Richard Gidden. I could have saved a hundred, a thousand Indians, Lucia. But this fellow, Gidden. . . ."

"What had he done?"

Don Carlos waxed warm with a simulated heat.

113

"You must remember, Lucia! He invaded my father's house, struck down his servants, took away a guest from his chamber. . . ."

"Tush!" said Lucia d'Arquista. "He came for a professional fighter . . . a man who murders according to a legal form . . . Hernandez Guadalmo. He is notorious! He bound two of the servants of that cutthroat. He entered the room of Guadalmo. Did he stab the villain to the heart to revenge the death of his murdered brother? No, no, Carlos. Like a gallant fellow, he took Guadalmo out from the house to a little distance; no matter what Guadalmo says, I know the truth and you have guessed it, too, and so have all the others. He challenged Guadalmo to a fair fight. And before the fight was ended, in came your father's men and saved Guadalmo. That is the only crime against Taki . . . I mean Richard Gidden. I asked that you save this man, Carlos!"

He bit his lip. He was ashamed of his own fear of her.

"Such a man does not need saving," he said with an attempt at lightness. "He saved himself, you see."

"He saved himself from the dogs," said the girl, her anger trembling in her voice now. "Oh, God, that such a thing should be! An honest Christian man hunted with dogs! To be torn to pieces like a wild beast."

"But he was not!" protested Carlos. "He was saved, Lucia. Surely you know that."

"Saved by you?" she asked bitterly.

"Lucia, hear reason. . . ."

"I wish to hear much reason. I wish to know, Carlos, why I needed to beg such a favor of you. Why were you not already working with all your might because you loathed such barbarism? Why were you not? Or was it because he had beaten you in a play of foils? Or in your heart, were you not hungering to see that manhunt?"

When the truth is told about us, it carries with it a sting that pierces through our utmost complacency. Don Carlos had been shaken already. Now he was crimson, and panting as he spoke.

"I could not stir my father. I talked until he was in a furious anger. I could not budge him from his purpose, Lucia!"

"Ah," she said, "if I had been a man, I should have taken my stand at the side of poor Richard Gidden. If the hounds were loosed at him, they should have taken me also!"

He threw out his hands in a gesture of wonder. "After all, he is the Black Rider . . . he is a highway robber, Lucia. You forget!"

"I forget nothing. What justice could he have in this country except from his own strength? He came here to revenge his brother. He fell into trouble. He was saved by your father . . . by accident, I may say. He went into slavery and took to the highway to repay a debt. Was that not like an honest man? He has repaid

115

the debt. Now he is free to turn his hand to Guadalmo. But you catch him and hunt him with dogs! Ah, it sickens me, Carlos! I only wondered if you would truly try to justify it. And I have heard you."

She turned her back on him and stared out the window. Don Carlos hesitated, turned two or three sentences in his mind, and then decided that the words would not do. He wanted, above all, to have the free blue sky above his head, and he fled at once. He had scarcely left the house when he encountered the last person he wished to meet — his father. Torreño stopped him.

"You have the face of a sick man, Carlos," he said.

"It is nothing," stammered Carlos.

"You are white; you are dripping with perspiration. What is it?"

"Nothing," said Carlos.

"Fool!" thundered Torreño. "Will you attempt to hide from *me?*"

The son surrendered on the spot. That ringing voice went through him like a sword.

"It is Lucia," he said faintly. "She is in a fury because of Gidden and the dogs."

"She is in a fury?" repeated Torreño. "She has complained to you?"

Don Carlos sighed and shook his head.

"I shall go to her myself," said Torreño.

Don Carlos caught his arm with an exclamation. "She is not herself . . . she does not

116

know what she says!" he pleaded.

"I shall bring her to herself," said the father roughly and, shaking himself loose, he went to the door of Lucia's chamber. She herself opened it to him. He stalked in and threw himself unceremoniously into a chair. She remained standing, looking calmly down at him. Her very calmness enraged him the more. For he loved to inspire fear.

"You have been talking with Carlos," he said sternly.

"He has gone tattling, I see."

"He has answered his father's questions, as a respectful son should."

"I have no doubt, *señor,* that he is a perfect son."

"You are scornful, Lucia. Now you must understand that in this country all is not done as it is done in Spain. In a rough land rough ways are needed."

"I think I understand. Men are hunted instead of boars. Why, *señor?* Because they are more helpless?"

Torreño writhed in his chair. His voice doubled its volume.

"What I order," he said, smiting his hands together, "is never questioned."

"Do you choose to be obeyed through fear only?" she asked him.

"Obedience is what I demand. The cause of it does not matter."

"*Señor,* I am as yet a free person. If I marry,

117

I shall swear obedience to your son." And she smiled. The smile maddened Torreño.

"Have a care, girl!" he cried to her. "That marriage has not yet taken place. If you return to Spain unwed. . . ."

"You threaten with a sword which has no point, *Señor* Torreño," she said. "I, also, have been thinking of Spain."

That answer brought Torreño stiffly out of his chair. He stared at her, bewildered. It came suddenly home to him that this was not mere sham — that this girl could indeed contemplate a petty life in old Spain rather than become the queen of the Torreño estate. It staggered him. It shamed him.

"Is that in your brain?" he said. "However, Lucia, you are not a free agent. The marriage has been contracted for. It shall be celebrated if I have to drag you to the altar with my own hands. And when the ceremony is ended, we shall see if you have not two masters instead of one. That is a thing which we shall see!"

He strode to the door and then turned back to her.

"To those who give me obedience, girl," he said, "I am gentle as a lamb. To those who cross me, I am a lion. Lucia, beware!"

With this, he left her, and she heard the beat of his heels and the jingling of his spurs as he went down the corridor. She went into the next room and found Anna d'Arquista crouched on a bench in the corner with a stricken face.

"You have heard everything?" asked Lucia.

"He spoke so loudly. . . ."

"Oh, I am glad that you have heard. That doesn't matter. You see, Aunt Anna, that I have fallen into the hands of hunters. If I cross this frog-faced devil, I suppose that he would set the dogs on me?" She began to laugh, savagely, without mirth.

"Lucia, poor child," moaned the spinster, "I have had a foreboding of evil to come. Let us pray God to bring you happiness in spite of all!"

"It is time to think and to plan," said Lucia. "It is time to remember that I am a d'Arquista. It is time to wish that I were a man!"

XIII "The Seventh Encounter!"

Prudence held some sway in even Francisco Torreño, however, and after supper he walked with the girl in the outer garden where they could hear the steady roar of distant water through a ravine, a sullen noise which seemed to come from the quivering ground beneath their feet.

"Now, Lucia," he said, "while we are alone, and without anger, let us talk over everything and admit that we have made mistakes . . . both of us. I was wrong in treating you as if you were without a brain and a will of your own. You were wrong in saying that you did not wish to marry Carlos. Shall we begin by admitting these things?"

"*Señor* Torreño," said the girl, "there is no need for sorrow. We have seen the truth about one another. You, *señor*, have no room on all of your lands for more than one person . . . and that is yourself, of course. I have the same need of room, *señor*. We could never be happy near one another."

Torreño felt the blind rage swell in his heart. But he controlled himself. He even managed to smile.

"You are still angry," he said. "Young people

120

remain angry longer than old ones do. Because anger is a childish passion, do you see? But, Lucia, how could your wishes conflict with mine? What is there which we mutually could desire? Will you have rich clothes and many of them? Whatever is made in China or Flanders and all the lands between is yours! Are you fond of jewels? I already have caskets heaped with them . . . trays piled deep as your fingers can clutch! But if you wish more, you shall have more. Are you a lover of hunting! The finest English runners shall be brought half the distance around the world and put in your stables . . . *your* stables, Lucia. Do you hear me? Perhaps you love hawking. We have some falcons already. You shall have more! Do you love rich fittings in a house? You may plate your walls with solid gold if you choose! What more is there that a woman can wish? I have known of some bold hearts among your sex who loved the water. Lucia, there are many waterways where the sea is quiet between the islands and the coast. Aye, Lucia, and if you wish to be alone and reign like a queen and never feel any power, you shall have one of those islands . . . the largest . . . for your own. It shall be stocked with cattle and with servants. You shall build a house there according to your will. You shall build ships and trade with them on the seven seas, if you desire.

"You see, child, that when you speak of

finding room on my estate, you may have as much as any prince . . . and more! And still, I shall never notice what you have taken!"

To this lordly tale the girl listened with a faint smile.

"There is one rock on which all of those plans would split," she said.

"And that?" asked Torreño.

"Don Carlos."

"Ah? What of him?"

"Which of us would rule him?"

Torreño's face grew dark with angry blood.

"He shall rule himself, *señorita*."

She waved her hand. "That is folly, *señor*. I can twist him around my finger; and your very breath makes his whole strong body tremble like a dead leaf! Which would prove the stronger with him? Which of us would he dread the most? Which would he prefer . . . that I should laugh at him or that you should rage at him? I cannot tell. But I feel, *señor*, that after a time I should be too strong for you. Therefore I advise you for your own sake. Break off this unhappy marriage."

There was enough of the fox in Torreño to appreciate craft in others. He looked at Lucia with a glint of appreciation in his eyes.

"If I were twenty years younger . . . yes, or ten . . . there would be no question of Carlos. I myself should marry you, Lucia!"

"There would be no peace in your house."

"For a year, for two years, no! But after that,

I would give you commands by mere glances and liftings of the finger! So! Your voice would never be heard except in answer to my questions. Ah, yes. It would be that way!"

"But since you are too old for this battle, do you think that Carlos has strength for it?"

"I shall teach him," said Torreño. "In the meantime, our grip is on you. You are in our cage. We have thrown the net over your head. Beat your wings, sing your song, but escape if you can, my dear! But you cannot. You belong to me; you belong to Carlos. There is the end! In a few months, a few years . . . what is a little time? . . . you will learn to curl up in your nest! All will be well!"

To this she made no answer, but she smiled at him in a way that made his heart fall.

"Tell me, Lucia," he said, "what manner of man could make you love him?"

She answered instantly: "One who could fill me with fear."

"And have you seen such a man in all the world?"

"One."

"And what was he?"

She was silent again, and Torreño stared at her in real bewilderment. But here their interview ended. Filled with a whimsical impulse, he went to Carlos and told him everything, word for word.

"Would you have her under these conditions?"

"I love her," said Carlos sadly. "And if love can breed love, she will come to care for me before the end!"

"Bah!" said the elder man. "The mailed fist is the thing for her!"

After that, the great Torreño gave little thought either to his son or to Lucia herself. He had before him what he felt to be more important matters, the details leading to the celebration of the marriage itself, which was to take place within three or four days after their arrival. And so, on the following day, they arrived at Casa Torreño itself.

It was like a child's dream of a castle. Through a shallow little valley a stream ran and pooled its waters in a spacious lake. Beside the lake was a village of white adobe houses; above the village the road wound to the flat top of a great hill, and on the plateau stood the house itself, built of hewn stone. And at one side, a great square tower arose against the sky.

"Why will you have such a fortress and such a dungeon keep for a house?" asked Lucia.

"So that all the people in the plains may look up to this in clear weather and see the top of the tower . . . you see that it is painted white? And so they know that the eye of their master is on them while they work, while they sleep!"

The instant they were in view over the top of the hills, a bell in the great house began to ring, and its larger voice was taken up by the jangle of other bells in the hollow where the village lay. People appeared, streaming from the Casa Torreño, and out of the village a gay-colored procession started up the road. Torreño looked triumphantly toward the girl, but her face was a blank. The next instant he had broken into curses. For the most inopportune interruption came to break up the solemnity of this occasion. At the last rest house there had been added to his train some couple of fleet greyhounds, and they had been brought along on the leash all day without finding anything to their liking in the way of game. But just at this instant their sharp voices were raised; Hernandez Guadalmo was heard loudly ordering them to be slipped, and in another instant half a dozen of the lean-bodied hunting dogs were straining across the hills after a flying hare. Behind them rushed Guadalmo and a few others of his immediate train; the followers of Torreño had far too much wit to leave the ranks at such a moment as this.

The diversion took much from the grandeur of the moment, but Hernandez Guadalmo gave no heed to that. He was as greedy a hunter of wild game as he was of man. It mattered not the size of the quarry. The hunt itself was the thing for which he lived. He followed the greyhounds over the first hills and through the next valley. He leaped his horse recklessly across the brook and plunged up the slope beyond, many a length ahead of his closest followers, for nothing they bestrode was comparable with his fine barb. Uphill, however, the hounds gained fast upon him. And the hare fled like a thing possessed of the fiend. It darted up the hill, gaining ground on the dogs at every enormous bound. It reached the more even country beyond, and here the dogs gained at each stride as the hare had gained uphill. And, with each second, the gap between Guadalmo and his men grew greater. He was at the heels of the flying dogs when he saw something stir among the next grove of oaks. A deer, he thought at first. It burst into full view — a bay horse of matchless beauty with flying black mane and tail as it swept toward him, and on its back a tall, familiar figure — Richard Gidden come for the seventh time against him.

The seventh time! If there were any special fate in numbers, one of them must surely fall on this day! And the courage of Guadalmo wavered. There even came into his mind the thought that back yonder among his followers there would be safety — if he turned and fled to them!

But at the thought of flight — and flight before so many witnesses — his soul was steeled to face the ordeal. He caught out a horse pistol from its holster beside the saddle. He brought down the pace of his horse to a hard gallop and, taking careful aim, he fired at the advancing rider.

But still Gidden closed. There was no gun in the hand of his foe. Only the naked blade of a rapier gleamed in the hand of Gidden as he rushed in. Plainly he had determined that Guadalmo should die in the same fashion that Gidden's brother had received a death wound from the hand of the Spaniard. He drove straight on at Guadalmo.

It seemed fate, not a mere mortal man, who bestrode that horse. Then Guadalmo threw the pistol away with an oath of fury and snatched out his own rapier. Holding it like a spear at arm's length before him, he spurred the barb at Gidden. They met in half a dozen lightning strides. There was a double flash of light. Then, as Gidden hurtled past and swept off in a great arch away from the Spaniard, Guadalmo threw out his arm and the sword dropped from his hand. Still he held the saddle for a moment with his head thrown back to the sky. He was like a man who sees an enraptured vision. Then he slumped sideways to the ground.

XIV "A Rescuer"

With song and with dance, with shouting and with music, they brought the cavalcade to the Casa Torreño. In all the great house there was only one sad heart, and that was the heart of Lucia d'Arquista. And she, sitting behind her window, looked down across the moonlit valley and saw the bright winding of the creek and the broad silver surface of the lake, darkened at the margin by the shadows of the trees. The air was crisp in these highlands, and a cool breeze blew to her, filled with strange, pungent odors unlike the meadow perfumes of old Spain. All was huge and strong and new in this country at the other end of the world. She was oppressed by its newness; she was oppressed by its size; and for one familiar glimpse of the old land she would have given ten years of life. Even the singing and the merriment in the house oppressed her more. And her last ally was stolen from her. Anna d'Arquista had been sympathetic enough until she saw the Casa Torreño itself. But after she had walked through it, hall after hall, garden after garden; after she had seen the artificial pools, the statues brought at fearful cost, the stables large and costly as a palace in themselves, her mind was changed.

"There are marriages for love," she had told her niece. "There are also marriages of state. The sons and the daughters of kings submit to them happily enough. Why cannot you, Lucia?"

And the girl made no answer; it was a thing not worth argument, she felt. And the willful blind cannot be made to see.

Torreño himself was quick to see the change in the girl's chaperone. He was at this minute closeted with her. Perhaps he was suggesting certain methods by which she could change the mind of Lucia. As for that, the girl cared nothing. Steel cannot be changed to lead even by magic.

Here the wind increased suddenly almost to a gale — then fell away to its former strength. It was as though a door had been opened and shut behind her. So she turned her head, carelessly. She saw nothing, at first, but just as she was moving back again the tail of her eye caught on a tall black figure against the wall, half obscured by the curtain. She whipped around upon him. But even before she saw his face, she had no doubt.

"*Señor* Gidden!" she breathed.

"It is I," said the Black Rider.

"You escaped from Guadalmo's men. I knew that you would! But how by magic did you ever reach this room? They have guards every-where."

"The same means by which I shall leave it. The hill is tunneled through from top to bottom and steps cut. It was done before the house was built . . . so long ago that even Torreño has forgotten them, I suppose. They brought me up to the cellar level. After that, I have been feeling my way until I reached you."

She was trembling with fear and with delight.

"Where shall I hide you? Where shall I put you, Richard Gidden, madman! They spy on me every step I make. They have listeners at every door!"

"They know that the bird will be out of the cage if they are not wary. But they are cautious too late. She is already gone!"

"*¡Señor!*" breathed the girl.

"What would you give, *señorita,* to be free from this house, and away on the sea?"

She paused.

"I am paying for every second of this talk," said Gidden a little sternly. "Speak to me as if I were your inner mind. Let there be nothing between us but honesty."

"I would give all my life!" said the girl suddenly. "You knew that or you would never have come. But I am lost. Not even a miracle could save me."

"Yankee hands and Yankee wits will accomplish that miracle," he said. "If you will trust yourself to me. Come to the window!"

He led her to the casement.

"Do you see the trees under that hill above the river? I have two horses there . . . my own and a strong black mare which *Señor* Torreño will miss out of his stable in the morning. They are saddled and bridled. In a few short hours they will take us to the sea. And in the port there is a Yankee ship loaded and waiting for a fair wind and a word from me. The wind has come. Do you feel it? There is only one thing that keeps the anchor of that skipper down and that is tidings from Richard Gidden. Will you come with me . . . down those same steps that I climbed to get to you?"

"If we are caught, you are a dead man, *señor*. I shall not go!"

"As well die now as later. They have marked me down. They are ten thousand to one. Sooner or later they are sure to take me if I stay in this land. Guadalmo's men have sworn to take me!"

"Then flee, Richard Gidden! Ride for the shore and the ship of your friend."

"And leave you here? I cannot! If they were an army, I should stay near you in the hope of seeing you once in a year . . . a single glimpse."

"Do you care so much, Richard?"

"I love you, Lucia."

"And I you, Richard, even when your skin

was red and you stood so tall and proud and disdainful before Torreño. I was afraid of you, afraid for you, and I knew that I could love you."

Like two shadows that the wind moved, they swayed together, whispering.

"But I never dreamed that such a wild joy could come to me."

"Now I fear nothing, Lucia. Nothing! I used to think when I sailed for this country that I had only one great purpose in my life, and that was to revenge the death of my poor brother. I was shipwrecked and lived among Indians. I felt that God kept me for that end alone. I was hunted for my life. And still I felt something predestined that would bring me on. But it was not to meet Guadalmo. It was to find you, my dear, and save you from the calf, Don Carlos, and the bull, his father. Save you and keep you and love you forever."

"Richard, if. . . ."

A footfall in the hall; she started back from him.

"It is my aunt!"

"It cannot be!"

The footfall approached, paused at the door, and then went on.

"Now," he said, "that is a warning. Are you ready?"

"One instant. My jewels, Richard. . . ."

"Let them be! Let them be! I am robbing Torreño of you. Let him keep the jewels. They will be a part repayment. I want you as you are, dear. Without a thing, without a penny. To be all mine!"

"If they see us as we go . . . if you are lost, Richard . . . I want to carry some weapon. They shall not have me back!"

"Hush, my dear. That is a sin. No harm shall come. Are you quite ready?"

"Yes."

"Is there one regret?"

"None in all the world!"

XV "Escape"

They slipped into the outer corridor. A door opened; a shaft — a soft yellow lamplight slipped down the wall. But the footsteps which sounded immediately went before them, almost as though leading the way. And the lovers looked at one another with suffused faces, with glistening eyes, thinking the same thought.

Now down the hall to the rear of the house. They reached a stairway at the back, narrow, swiftly turning, and down this Richard Gidden descended first, with the girl behind him, and as he climbed down he could feel the tremor of her breath behind him and sometimes catch a whispered word, so he knew that she was praying for their safety. But he needed no prayers to help him; he felt the strength of a lion in him.

They turned a sharp corner of the stairs — a servant, scampering up, crashed against Gidden and recoiled, staggering.

"In the name of heaven," he gasped out.

"Dog!" said Gidden sternly. "Are you a blind bat?"

The magnificence of his manner struck the other full of awe. He cowered against the wall.

"Alas, *señor,* on these steps . . . the servants only . . . I did not know. . . ."

Gidden brushed past him with the girl on his arm.

"He has stopped and is staring after us. He begins to suspect something," said Gidden. "The devil fly away with him. I should have stabbed him to the heart and gone on without a word!"

"No, no, Richard, only when your own life is in danger . . . swear that you will not harm a single human soul! If there is blood on this first day. . . ."

"The devil is loose!" murmured Gidden. "He has given an alarm. Did you have the hood over your face?"

There was a loud babbling of voices from the rear of the great house.

"I had the hood over it. He could not have guessed."

"He has guessed, nevertheless, Lucia. We can never reach the bottom of the hill by the hidden stairs before the whole household will be swarming like hornets."

"We are lost, then, Richard? Shall I turn back? Shall I hide you?"

"You could not hide me here if I were no larger than a grain of sand. Old Torreño would smell me out. Keep heart, Lucia. We walk straight forward and trust to blind chance!"

They entered the great hall. Yonder sat Don Carlos himself at a small table with a book in his hand, but with idle, sad eyes fixed straight before him.

"We are lost!" whispered the girl.

"Not yet. He knows my red face, not my white one. And you are hooded. He will think it strange but he is in a dream. Perhaps he will not even see. We must walk straight toward the big door, yonder. If I have to delay, run straight forward, dear. There are horses in the courtyard tethered at the rack. Take one and ride with all speed down the hill. I shall be after you in a trice . . . or else I shall be a dead man. Do you hear?"

"Yes!"

"And are you afraid?"

"No!"

"Then. . . ."

"*Señor, señor!*" broke in the voice of Don Carlos from the side.

"*Señor* Torreño!" said Gidden in his perfect Spanish and with a courteous intonation. To the girl: "Faster, my dear!"

"One moment!"

"On, on!" whispered Gidden. "I must stop here for an instant. Show no haste. Be slow and at ease. Sing a song softly. It will be better than a mask!"

He turned to Carlos.

"I have not your face in my mind, *señor*. Are you one of poor Don Hernandez's men?"

"I am, *señor*," said Gidden.

"Your name, then?"

"Christobal Paraña."

"Paraña? I have heard all the names of his men. I do not recall that one. Yet there is something familiar about your face. It is connected with some sinister recollection in my mind, sir."

"I shall explain to you whatever you wish when I return. The girl. . . ."

He gestured.

"*Señor!*" said Carlos sternly. "Stand where you are. I have the strangest thought in the world. You are Gidden!"

He was drawing his pistol as he spoke. Half of its silver-chased length was in view when Gidden caught his wrist with fingers of hot steel that crushed the flesh against the bone and made him drop the weapon. He himself tore the pistol out and with the heavy barrel of it struck poor Don Carlos to the floor and that in the view of half a dozen *mozos*. The servants raised a shout. Someone fired a gun. But Gidden was already out of the hall and down the white stone steps into the courtyard. There he saw Lucia mounted on a tall gelding, with the reins of another in her hand. Before her stood a cavalier of Guadalmo's troop, half frowning, half smiling. No doubt it was his very horse, by unlucky chance, that she had mounted.

He saw before him greater obstacles. There were a dozen armed men in that court. Two watched the gate steadfastly. Others were scattered here and there. It was plain that Torreño considered his house a garrisoned fort until that marriage was consummated.

"Don Carlos!" shouted Gidden as he raced out. "They are murdering Don Carlos! Help!"

That startling word brought a rush from the nearest men to the door, and there they crushed against the outcoming tide of those in pursuit of Gidden. Only one man had stayed by his place, and that was he who argued with Lucia. Gidden bounded on him like a tiger and struck him to the ground, then leaped into the saddle of the horse which Lucia held. He had one glimpse of her pale, set face, then they whirled and raced for the gateway.

Through that gateway they pressed at full speed and, out of the babble swelling confusedly behind them, they heard one great single voice — the voice of Don Carlos: "It is Gidden and the *Señorita* Lucia! Kill the man."

A gun exploded; but it must have been fired wildly, for not even the sound of the bullet came to them. Then they were rushing down the looping road which led to the base of the hill. Halfway down they looked back to Casa Torreño's stone face, pale in the moonlight, and a dark tangle of horsemen who spurred out from the gate. Then face forward, they goaded their horses and galloped for the stream. The stone bridge rang beneath the heavy hoofs. They tore up the valley toward that shadow of trees beneath the hills where the picked horses of Gidden waited for them.

Twenty riders stormed behind them, and the leaders were gaining when Gidden and the girl reached the covert. It seemed the ropes which tied the horses were strands of iron, refusing to be loosed. And the horses themselves were possessed of devils, dancing wildly, unwilling to be mounted. By sheer might of hand he raised the girl and put her into the saddle. Then into the saddle on the back of the bay. The brush was already crashing with the charge of Torreño's men as they started away on their fresh mounts.

They issued on the farther side. Through the trees, shadows among shadows, the horsemen of Torreño cursed and spurred and shouted. Don Carlos, pressing toward the front, was offering thousands and fresh thousands for the capture.

But the fugitives had beneath them, now, speed like the gallop of the wind. A long level lay before them, twisting around the shoulders of hills which stepped down into the valley, and over it they raced, with the clamor growing fainter behind them.

It was a black sea under the cold light of dawn that they saw at last. But rocking on the waters of the little harbor they saw the long body of a ship. To them it was like a promised land. On the hilltop above the beach they loosed the two horses. The black mare raced off with high head and flaring tail, but the bay horse followed his master curiously and watched as the pair with numbed, weary hands, gathered driftwood and kindled two fires.

"If they come . . . if Torreño comes before the boat?" she breathed, as they stood shivering beside the growing fires.

"Fate," said Gidden, "is against them. Look!"

From the side of the ship a boat had put off and was heading to the shore, swinging on with the rhythmic stroke of half a dozen men. It came closer. In the sheets stood a tall man, waving his hat, calling. And they hurried down to the edge of the water, where the wet sands yielded beneath their feet.

The bow cut the sand. The sailors leaped out, regardless of the icy water; but Gidden was already waist deep beside the gunwale, bearing the girl in his arms. And as she was lowered gently to a place, she heard a man in the bow saying in the unfamiliar English tongue: "Dick Gidden, we have cheated the devil and got you safe! But here are two birds instead of one!"

"It is the spring of the year," said Gidden.

The Dream of Macdonald

The story that follows first appeared in *Western Story Magazine* (4/7/23) under the title "'Sunset' Wins" by George Owen Baxter. Titles were, and still are, often changed by editors to make them seem more exciting or more appealing. When William F. Nolan included a severely abridged and rewritten version of this story in his edition of *The Best Western Stories of Max Brand* (Dodd, Mead, 1981), he claimed in his headnote that Faust's title for it had been "Macdonald's Dream." That surely could not have been the case since the title on Faust's original manuscript is the title that now has been restored.

It was a characteristic of Faust's style when using the genitive case in English that he preferred the French syntax to the Germanic construction of adding an "s" to indicate possession. There is also a subtle difference between Macdonald's possessing his dream and the dream of Macdonald since the alternative suggests that the dream is in possession of Macdonald. C.G. Jung made a comment in his Introduction to the Tibetan *Book of the Dead* that I would translate: "It is so much more immediate, more striking, more impressive and therefore more persuasive to behold how it occurs to me, than to observe, how I *produce* it." Faust knew precisely what was intended when he rendered the title for this story . . . "The Dream of Macdonald."

I " 'Red' Macdonald"

His father was a Macdonald of the old strain which once claimed the proud title of Lord of the Isles. His mother was a Connell of that family which had once owned Connell Castle. After that terrible slaughter of the Connells at the Boyne, those who were left of the race fled to the colonies. After the Macdonalds had followed Bonny Prince Charlie into England in that luckless year, 1715, the remnants of the proscribed race waited for vengeance among the Highlands, or else followed the Connells across the Atlantic.

The Connells were great black men, with hands which could crush flagons or break heads. The Macdonalds were red-headed giants, with heaven-blue eyes and a hunger for battle. But the passing of generations changed them. They became city dwellers, in part, and those who dwelt in cities shrank in stature and diminished in numbers. They became merchants, shrewd dealers, capable of sharp practice. They lived by their wits and not by the strength of their hands. They gave corporals and raw-handed sergeants to the war of the Revolution; to the Civil War, nearly four generations later, they gave majors and colonels and generals. Their minds were growing and their bodies were shrinking.

And so at last a Mary Connell, small, slim-throated, silken black of hair, wedded a Gordon Macdonald, with shadowy red hair and mild, patient, blue eyes. They were little people. He was a scant five feet and six inches in height, and yet he seemed big and burly when he stood by the side of his wife. What manner of children should they have? For five years there was no child at all, and then Mary died in giving birth to a son. He was born shrieking rage at the world, with his red hands doubled into fat balls of flesh, and his blue eyes staring up with the battle fury — he was born with red hair gleaming upon his head. His father looked down upon him in sadness and bewilderment. Surely this was no true son of his!

His wonder grew with the years. At thirteen, young Gordon Macdonald was taller than his father and heavier. He had great, long-fingered bony hands and huge wrists, from the latter of which the tendons stood out, as though begging for the muscles which were to come. And his joy was not in his books and his tutor. His pleasure was in the streets. When the door was locked upon him, he stole out of his bed at night and climbed down from the window of his room, like a young pirate, and went abroad in search of adventure. And he would come back again two days later with his clothes in rags, his face purpled and swollen with blows, and his knuckles raw. They sent him to a school famous for Latin and broken heads. He prostrated two masters within three months with nervous breakdowns, and he was expelled from the school weak, bruised, but triumphant.

"Force is the thing for him then," said his weary-minded parent. "Let us discipline his body and pray God that time may bring him mildness. Labor was the curse laid on Adam. Let his shoulders now feel its weight!"

So he was made an apprentice in a factory, at the ripe age of fifteen, to bow his six feet two of bones and sinews with heavy weights of iron and to callous his hands with the rough handles of sledge hammers. But though he came home at night staggering, he came home singing. And if he grew lean with the anguish of labor in the first month, he began to grow fat on it in the second. His father cut off his allowance. But on Saturday nights Gordon began to disappear; money rolled into his pockets, and he dressed like a dandy. Presently his father read in one paper of a rising young light heavyweight who was crushing old and experienced pugilists in the first and second rounds under the weight of a wild-cat onslaught; and in a second paper he saw a picture of this "Red Jack" and discovered that he was his own and only son!

After that he took his head between his

hands and prayed for guidance, and he received an inspiration to send his boy away from the wiles of the wicked city for a year and a day. So he signed Gordon Macdonald on a sailing ship bound for Australia. He bade his boy farewell, gave him a blessing, and died the next month, his mind shattered by a financial crash. But he had accomplished one thing at least with his son — Gordon Macdonald came back to Manhattan no more.

In the port of Sydney, far from his homeland, he celebrated his seventeenth birthday with a drunken carousal, and the next day he insulted the first mate, broke his jaw with a pile-driving jab, and was thrown into the hold in irons. He filed through his chains that night, went above, threw the watch into the sea, dived in after him, and swam ashore.

He was hotly pursued by the infuriated captain. The police were appealed to. He stole a horse to help him on his flight. He was cornered at the end of the seventh day, starved, but lion-like. With his bare hands he attacked six armed men. He smashed two ribs of one, the jaw of another, and fractured the skull of the third before he was brought down spouting crimson from a dozen bullet wounds.

The nursing he received was not tender, but he recovered with a speed that dazed the doctor. Then he was promptly clapped into prison for resisting arrest, for theft, and for assaulting the officers of the law.

For three months he pored upon the cross section of the world of crime which was presented to him in a wide, thick slab in the prison. Then, when he was weary of being immersed in the shadows of the world, he knocked down a guard, climbed a wall, tore a rifle from the hands of another guard, and stunned the fellow with a blow across the head, sprang down on the farther side, dodged away through a fusillade of bullets, reached the desert land, lived there like a hunted beast for six months, with a horse for a companion, a rifle for a wife, and a revolver for a chosen friend. At last he reached a seaport and took ship again on the free blue waters.

When the ship touched at Bombay, the hand of the law seized him again. He broke away the next night, reached the Himalayas after three months of wild adventure, plunged into the wastes of Tibet, joined a caravan which carried him into central Asia, came to St. Petersburg a year later, shipped to Brazil, rounded the Horn on a tramp freighter, and deserted at a Mexican port.

At the age of nineteen he rode across the border into Texas for the first time. He stood six feet two and a half inches in his bare feet. He weighed two hundred pounds stripped to the buff. He knew guns and fighting tricks, as a saint knows the Bible, and his whole soul ached every day to find some man or men capable of giving him battle which would ex-

147

ercise him to the uttermost of his gigantic strength.

But on his long pilgrimage he had learned a great truth: no matter how a man defies his fellows, he must not defy the law. For the law reaches ten thousand miles as easily as a man reaches across the table for a glass of water. And no matter if a man has a hand of iron, the law has fingers of steel.

Suppose the mind of a fox planted in the body of a Bengal tiger, a beast of royal power and a brain of devilish cunning. Such was Gordon Macdonald. He looked like a lion; he thought like a fox; and he fought like ten devils, shoulder to shoulder.

First he joined the Rangers, not for the glory of suppressing crime, but for the glory of the dangers to be dared in that wild service. He gained ten commendations in as many months for fearless work; in the eleventh month he was requested to resign. The Texas Rangers prefer to capture living criminals rather than dead ones.

So Gordon Macdonald resigned and rode again on his friendless way. He rode for ten years through a thousand adventures, and in ten years no man's eyes lighted to see him come, no woman smiled when he was near her, no child laughed and took his hand. The very dogs snarled at him and shrank from his path. But the Macdonald cared for none of these things. The spirit which rides on a thunderbolt does not hope for applause from the world it is about to strike. No more cared "Red" Macdonald. For he was tinglingly awake to one thing only, and that was the hope of battle. Speed, such as hides in the wrist of a cat, strength, such as waits in the paw of a grizzly, wisdom, such as lingers in the soul of a wolf — these were his treasures. Through all the years he fought his battles in such a way that the lie was first given to him by the other man, and the other man first drew his gun. Therefore the law passed him by unscathed. And all the years he followed, with a sort of rapturous intentness, a ghost of hope that some day he would meet a man who would be his equal, some giant of force, with the speed of a curling whiplash and the malignity of a demon. Some day he would come on the trail of a great devastator, an incarnate spirit of evil, and these men who now ceased talking and eyed him askance when he entered a room, these women who grew pale, as he passed, would come to him and fall on their knees and beg him to spare them. He carried that thought always in his heart of hearts, like a secret comfort.

Such was Gordon Macdonald at the age of thirty. He was as striking in face as in his big body. That arched and cruel nose, that long stern chin, that fiery hair, uncombable on his head, and, above all, his blue eyes stopped the thoughts and hearts of men. One felt the endless stirring impulse in him. To look in his eyes was like looking on the swift changes of color which run down the cooling iron toward the point. It was impossible to imagine this man sleeping. It was impossible to conceive this man for an instant inactive of mind, for he seemed to be created to forge wily schemes and plan cruel deeds.

He had crowded the events of a dozen ordinary lives into his short span of years. And still, insatiable of action, he kept on the trail which has only one ending. One might have judged that with such a career behind him, some of it would have been written in his face, but even in this he was deceptive. To be sure, when he frowned, a thousand lines and shadows appeared in his face; he might have been taken for a man of forty. But when he threw back his head and laughed — laughed with a savage satisfaction for work accomplished, or for danger in the prospect, he looked no more than a wild youth of twenty.

Such was the Macdonald in his thirtieth year. Such was the Macdonald when he saw Sunset, and at once he sensed that the fates had arranged the encounter.

II "Sunset"

The horse had his name from his color. When the brilliant colors at the end of the day begin to fade from the clouds, and when they are only shimmering with a rusty red, such was the tint of the hide of the horse, and yet the mane and tail and the four stockings of the stallion were jet black. It was that rich, strange color that first startled the Macdonald and held his mind. It was like the thick blood with light striking across it, he thought, and that grim simile stayed in his mind.

The thought struck an echo through his brain at once. There was something of fate in this meeting, he felt. A strange surety grew up in him that his destiny was inextricably entangled with Sunset. An equal surety came to him that that destiny was a gloomy thing. If he had that horse, evil would come of it, and yet the horse he must have!

He rode closer to the edge of the corral and examined the stallion more in detail. It was not color alone in which Sunset was glorious. He was one of those rare freaks of horseflesh in which size is combined with an exquisite proportion and fine working of details. It is rare to find a tall man who is not poorly put together, whose legs are not too long, or whose arms are not too lean; there are sure to be flaws and weaknesses when a man stands over six feet in height. And, rare as it is to find a big man who conforms to the Greek canons, it is rarer still to find a tall horse neither too long nor too short coupled with bone to support his bulk, but not lumpy and heavy in the joints, with a straight, strong back, with a neck neither too heavy nor too long and gaunt to balance comfortably a head which is apt to be as big as the head of a cart horse, or as ludicrously small as the head of a pony.

Sunset avoided all these possible defects. One knew at a glance that he would fit the standard. So exact, indeed, were his proportions that it might have seemed with the first survey that he was too lean and gangling of legs; but, when one drew closer and gave more professional attention to his survey, one noted the great depth of body where the girth ran, the wide, square quarters, rich in driving power, the flat and ample bone, the round hoofs, black as ink, the powerful sweep of the long shoulders, dimpled over and rippling with muscles like the tangled lashes of a thousand whips. He stood a scant inch under seventeen hands, but he was made with the scrupulous exactness of a fifteen-hand Thoroughbred, one of those incredible carvings of nature that dance like little kings and queens about the turf at a horse show, or take the jumps as though winged with fire.

And here were the same things drawn to scale and made gigantic. The great heart of the Macdonald contracted with yearning. He looked down with unspeakable disgust to the nag which bore him. Big-headed, long-eared, squat and shapeless of build, the gelding had only one commendable quality, and that was an immense strength which was capable of supporting even the solid bulk of the Macdonald, with a jog trot that might last from morning to night. But on such a steed he was a veritable slave. If he offended, a swift-riding posse might swoop down and overtake him in a half hour's run. No wonder that he did not violate the law when he was damned by slowness of movement. And what availed him all his prowess, if he could neither pursue nor flee? Were there not a score of men who had insulted him and then avoided the inevitable lightning flash of his revenge by springing upon the backs of neat-footed horses and darting away across the mountains?

He looked up to the ragged sides of those mountains. The rider of such a horse as Sunset could make his home among those peaks. From those impracticable heights he could sweep down like a hawk on the wing and take toll from the groveling men of the plains — strike — ravage — destroy — beat down enemies — award justice for past injuries — and

153

then away on wings again — wings strong enough to sweep him up the slopes and back to safety, while the sweating posse labored and puffed and cursed and moiled vainly in the dust far behind him!

No wonder that the Macdonald looked back from those distant heights to the stallion with a heart on fire with eagerness. The speed of an eagle, the strength of a lion, and the heart of a lamb. Yonder stood the giant horse nosing the hand of the man who was talking softly to him and stroking his sleek neck. The Macdonald dismounted. He stepped closer to the pair.

He had one gracious quality, and that was a soft and deep bass voice. He used it with more effect because in all his travels he had picked up no slang; he spoke the same pure tongue which he had learned in his boyhood.

"I wonder," he said to the stranger, "if you're the man who owns this horse?"

"Sunset?" The other turned, as though surprised that any one should have asked such a question. He was a tall and slenderly-built youth, with long tawny hair, a brown, weather-marked face with joyous gray eyes looking out at the Macdonald. "Yep," he said. "I own Sunset."

"Sunset?" echoed the Macdonald, and he looked back to the stallion. It was an appropriate name, and he said so. It was doubly appropriate now, as the big horse turned, and a wave of red light rippled along his flank, like a highlight traveling over bright silk.

At the deep and quiet sound of his voice, Sunset came closer, snorted softly his suspicion, then reached out with bright and mischievous eyes and nibbled at the brown back of the Macdonald's hand.

"Oh, he doesn't seem to be afraid, does he?" asked Macdonald of his companion in the profoundest wonder.

"Why should he be afraid?" asked the other, frowning. "He's been raised right and treated right. He don't connect with gents with clubs and spurs, like most of the horses around these here parts!"

The Macdonald looked over his shoulder and under his eyes, and his gelding flattened its ears and stared at the master with concentrated malice. Back to Sunset turned Gordon Macdonald. The teeth of the stallion had caught up a fold of skin on the back of his hand and pinched it very gently. Yet, as though he had committed a crime deserving punishment, the red horse started away, tossing and shaking his head. No rough curses followed him. He came back again slowly. Once more he sniffed at the stranger. Once more he came back and thrust out his beautiful head. Wonder of wonders, he permitted that great, strong hand of Macdonald to reach and touch his velvet muzzle. He permitted the tips of those terrible fingers to rub his forehead, to touch his silken ears, to stray along his throat. Nay, he grew so emboldened that he reached high. He caught the brim of Macdonald's hat. He twitched it off, and then, wheeling like a dog playing a game, half afraid and half delighted, he bolted across the field, whipping the hat from side to side and flashing his heels in the air.

"Hey!" yelled the owner. "Come back here, Sunset! Say, stranger, I'm mighty sorry that happened . . . looks like a good hat, too!"

He broke off in his apologies. Fifty dollars in gold had been paid the Mexican who first owned that sombrero. But now Macdonald was staring after a fleeing horse, like one enchanted by a dream of beauty. The long sweep of that gallop made him dizzy with delight. His stern lips parted to the tenderest of smiles. On the farther side of the field Sunset dropped the sombrero and dashed his hoofs upon it. In an instant it was a mass of rents and fragments. And behold, Macdonald turned to his companion a laughing face.

"He's like a big, happy dog!" he said.

The other stared upon him with no less surprise than if he had been convicted that instant of lunacy. And, indeed, there was something wild in this careless throwing away of a sombrero, dearer to a cowpuncher's heart than aught except his gun.

After the episode, Sunset picked up the hat

again and came back at full gallop, the fragments dangling from his teeth, his head thrust out, his ears flattened, his mane flying like the plumes above a Grecian helmet, swift as an arrow loosed from the string, the ground shivering under the impact of his beating hoofs. A red flash of danger he shot at them, then threw himself back and slid to a halt on stiffly braced legs, while his hoofs plowed up long strips of the turf. At the very feet of Macdonald he dropped the hat.

"Like he expected a lump of sugar for spoiling my hat!" said Macdonald and laughed again. "And look at this! He comes right back to my hand again! Man, man, there's only one horse in the world . . . only one horse in the world!"

"Come here, Sunset," said the master. "Come here, I say."

But Sunset only wavered toward his owner. Then he returned to the fascinating task of trying to catch a lock of Macdonald's fire red hair in his teeth. What it meant to Macdonald no man could know. Perhaps a mother feeling the tugging hands of an infant could understand how his heart ached with joy to see this magnificent dumb creature defy him without malice and tease him as though he were some harmless child.

"What have you done to Sunset?" growled the young owner. "Never saw him act up like that to any other man."

It was wine of purest delight to Macdonald.

"He doesn't take up with strangers, you say?" he asked greedily.

"Takes them with his heels, if he can!"

"Well," said Macdonald, "he's no common horse. He understands! He understands, eh, old boy?" He turned abruptly on the youth. "What's your name?"

"Rory Moore."

"Moore, is your horse for sale?"

"Nope."

"Moore, I've got five hundred dollars in my pocket."

"He's not for sale. Why, I raised him!"

"Look here, five hundred is quite a lot. It takes a long time for a cowpuncher to save that much." He put the amount in Moore's hand.

"No use talking, stranger!" declared Moore.

"Six hundred, then!"

"Not if you made it six thousand!"

"Moore, here's nine hundred and eighty dollars. It's yours. Give me the horse!"

"Not for nine thousand eight hundred!"

Moore recoiled a little, for the expression of Macdonald had changed. His lips had stiffened. His big body had trembled. There was even a change in the hand which had been stroking the neck of the stallion, for the horse suddenly drew back and sniffed suspiciously at the bony fingers. But if there had been a glimpse of danger in the face of Macdonald, he smoothed it away quickly enough and managed to smile.

"No way in the world that you'd give up that horse . . . couldn't be taken from you?"

"Not unless the luck was against me!"

"Luck?"

"I mean I've never backed down at dice for any man! And, in fact," Rory Moore was laughing at the thought, "I'd stake my life on my luck! Look here, I've got a pair of dice with me. Your nine hundred against Sunset . . . one roll."

Eagerly Macdonald reached for the little cubes, then drew his hand back with a groan.

"I never gamble," he said.

"What?" cried the other, as though the sun had vanished from the heavens. "Never gamble?"

"No." He turned, took one last, long look at Sunset, who had pressed his breast against the fence, as though eager to follow, and then stepped to his gelding.

"What name'll I remember you by?" asked Moore.

But Macdonald did not seem to hear. He had thrown himself into the saddle and spurred the gelding down the road toward town, whose roofs already pushed up above the trees.

III "The Pact"

But how a gold digger like you," said Macdonald, "could ever go broke, I don't see! You can make the cards do everything but talk, can't you? And I've watched you practice with the dice and call your throw nine times out of ten, even bouncing them against a wall!"

The gambler lifted his wan, lean face from his hands. Then he shrugged his shoulders.

"Yep," he said, "I can do that. And I had my big game planted, Macdonald. There was a fortune in sight . . . a hundred thousand, if there was a cent in that game! I had the cards stacked. Nothing better. Gent started betting against me. He had two aces and two jacks. My guns, how well I remember! I'd given him the ace of spades and the ace of hearts and the jack of spades and the jack of diamonds. He opened on the jacks, and I gave him the aces on the draw. The fifth card ought to have been the seven of clubs. I had three little deuces, but they looked big again' two pair. I figured him to be bluffing. He began to raise. I raised him right back. He began to sweat. I figured that he was sorry for his bluff, but thought that he could work it out. He saw me and raised me right back.

"Then I smeared in the rest of my chips . . . every cent I had was on that table . . . and he called. I showed my three deuces . . . I was reaching for the pot, and he laughed and put down two jacks and *three* aces on top of them. Yes, sir, it wasn't the seven of clubs that I'd given him . . . the first mistake I'd made in a hundred deals, and how I made it, I dunno! An ace full on jacks is what he hands me, and me with three measly deuces! That's how I'm busted, Macdonald!"

"Just change that name, will you?" said Macdonald.

"They don't know you here?"

"No, it's new country for me."

"Me, too, and bad country it is. What name d'you want? I call myself 'Jenkins!' "

"Call me nothing . . . call me Red, if you wish."

"All right. And, Red, you ain't fixed to stake me, are you?"

"What?"

The gambler shrank from him with a sickly smile.

"I meant to stake me to a couple of square meals, pal. I'm lined with vacancy, fact! Ain't eaten since I can remember!"

Macdonald rubbed his knuckles across his chin, and under his gaze Jenkins shuddered. His eyes widened. Plainly he knew a great deal indeed about the past of this slayer of men.

"Suppose I do stake you?"

"Why, then I'll sure pay you back, partner, the minute. . . ."

"Suppose I stake you to five hundred dollars?"

The jaw of Jenkins fell.

"Five hundred!" he whispered. "What you want of me, Mac? What can I do for you? You know I ain't any hand with a gat, or for. . . ."

The raised hand of Macdonald silenced him.

"I want you to gamble for me."

"Why I'd play my head off! You mean I'm to split with you after. . . ."

"Shut up," said Macdonald. "I want to think!"

He strode up and down the room for a time, and the rat-like, sharp eyes of Jenkins followed him guiltily back and forth. Presently he shrank back in his chair again, as the bulk of the other loomed before him, and Macdonald stood still, with his legs braced far apart.

"I want no split," he said. "If you win, you win, and you keep the coin you make!"

Jenkins swallowed with difficulty, and his haunted eyes clung to the face of Macdonald.

"There's a youngster who lives in an old house near the town. His name is Moore."

"Oh, yes, Rory Moore!"

"You know him?"

"All about him!"

"What do you know?"

"The Moores used to own most of this here country. Look across the street!"

162

Macdonald looked across to the lofty and gabled front of the hotel. It was a spacious building for such a small town, and it was set far back from the street in deep grounds, in which all the garden had perished except a scattering of shrubs.

"That used to be the Moore home," said Jenkins.

"Well?"

"Rory's father blew the whole wad of coin. He was a hot spender. Paris was his speed, that's all. Come back with a mighty small jingle in his purse and a funny accent. The kids got his empty purse, but they couldn't inherit the funny accent!" And Jenkins laughed with a malicious satisfaction. "If he wanted to throw his coin away, why wasn't poker right here in Texas as good as Monte Carlo? Down with a gent that don't patronize home folks, I say!" His thin lips writhed into a snarl of deathless malevolence.

"This youngster, Rory Moore . . . he likes to play pretty well?"

"And he usually wins. That's how he's made enough money to start his ranch. He's sure got luck with dice and cards. Well, you know what luck means!"

"You mean he's crooked?"

There was an expressive shrug of the shoulders.

"I think you are lying, Jenkins!"

The latter winced under the word, but he

recovered himself at once.

"I ain't *seen* him crook the cards," he confessed. "But he's a bad one . . . a fighter." He stopped short, watching Macdonald, in dread lest this imputation of blame to a fighter might offend the man of battle. But Macdonald was not thinking of himself.

"He's a fighter, you say? Neat with a gun, eh?"

"Quick and certain . . . which is what counts most!"

"Look here, Jenkins, would you have the nerve to sit in with Moore at a game and beat him?"

Jenkins turned white.

"What if I made a slip . . . and he seen? I'd be ready for planting, right there and *pronto!*"

"What if you didn't make a slip?"

"Then I'd clean him out!"

He twisted his bony hands together in glee at the prospect.

"Yes, he's the sort that would bet down to his last dollar," nodded Macdonald.

"He'd bet the boots he rides in," assented Jenkins. "And if he stuck by the game, a gent could clean him out of his ranch . . . out of everything! But what's the use of talking like that? I ain't got a stake to start a game, have I?" He fixed upon Macdonald the eyes of a ferret.

"Five hundred dollars, Jenkins. I'll stake you as high as that."

"And how do we split?"

"How do you think we should?"

"I dunno," whined Jenkins. "You furnish the cash, but I take the chances. And if he thinks I'm running up the cards on him, there'll be a gun play sure!"

"He has a horse. . . ."

"Sunset, you mean?" asked Jenkins.

"That's the name. Jenkins, I want that horse. When you break him, he'll stake Sunset. I want Sunset, but you can keep the cash!"

For a time they were both silent, the lips of Jenkins moving, and his eyes fixed so intently upon the distance, that he reminded Macdonald of one who bet his last cent on a horse race and sees the ponies battling desperately down the home stretch.

"A man has to die sometime," said Jenkins at last. "And ain't it better to die flush than broke?"

"There's no doubt about that!"

"I'll take you up, Red! Gimme that coin and I'll lay for him! I'll get him tonight. Say, Red, I been broke so long that this looks like a pile of money that you're giving me. Don't you want some sort of a receipt?"

But Macdonald, as he put the wallet back into his pocket, merely smiled. "No," he said. "I don't need a receipt."

"Sure you don't! Sure you don't!" murmured Jenkins, shivering violently, as another thought came to him. "I guess there ain't many west of the Mississippi that would try to beat you out of anything." His shivering ended in a crackling laugh. But in the meantime he had a pocket bulging with money, and his spirits would not stay down. Warmth was beginning to strike through all his body.

"One thing I never could make out about you, Red," he went on.

"What's that?"

"You can do about anything that any other man can do. But you always stay shut of cards. Don't seem to want to take chances that way. But you sure made a mistake, Red. With your nerve you get by fine. The trouble with me . . . the trouble with me is that I get to thinking of what might happen, if they should find me out in a pinch, and something sort of melts in me."

It was not often that Macdonald showed any delicacy of feeling, but now he turned away to hide the scorn which darkened on his face.

"Jenkins," he said, facing the other again, "has an honest gambler a chance of winning?"

"Honest gambler!" sneered Jenkins. "There ain't any such bird!"

"That's why I don't gamble," said Macdonald. "I haven't enough coin to throw away, and as for the other way of gambling, I hate a sure thing!"

"But look here," argued Jenkins, "do you think that *I'm* going to play square with Rory Moore?"

Macdonald scowled upon his confederate.

"I offered Moore twice the value of his horse," he explained. "He was a fool not to take it, and you're a worse fool, Jenkins, to ask questions!"

IV "The Dream"

Here ended the talk, of course. Macdonald left Jenkins and stalked across the street to the hotel. There he went at once to his bed and flung himself upon it. Since he had not closed his eyes in forty-eight hours, he could hardly prop them open long enough to finish his bedside cigarette, peering through the shadows of the room at the old photographs and pictures which hung along the walls. These might all be members of the clan of Moore — kinsmen, relations, supporters of the old power in the days when it was really great, and when this hotel was like a castle in the midst of a principality.

Such were the thoughts that formed vaguely in the mind of Macdonald before he threw his cigarette butt through the window, turned on his side, and was instantly asleep. It was a sleep filled with visions of uncertain misery for a time, but by degrees he passed into a dream of such pleasantness that he began to smile in his sleep.

For it seemed to Macdonald that he was mounted at last upon the great red beauty, Sunset, and that he was galloping over the mountain desert like a dry leaf soaring on a wind. A dizziness of joy swept into his brain, with the sway and swing of that galloping. And there was perfect accord between the red horse and himself. A pressure of his knee was as good as a twist of the reins, and his voice was both bit and spur.

In the meantime he came to a river twisting among the hills, a swift, straight stream, save where it now and then dodged the knees of a hill and plunged on again. Macdonald looked upon that river with a careful eye, but he could not remember having seen it before.

He went on up its bank, glorying in the brown rushing of the waters with streaks and riffles of yellow foam upon the surface. On either side the banks were being gouged away. Here and there trees were toppling on the edges of the banks, with half their foothold torn away. And even the hills of rock, which the stream dodged perforce, were rudely assaulted and carved by the currents.

And, just as this dashing and thundering torrent was different from other peaceful rivers full of quiet, of pauses, and stars, was not he, also, equally different from other men? Did he not bear down those who opposed him? A thousand crimes might be laid to his account, but who was strong enough or cunning enough to call him to a reckoning?

At length he came to a turn of the river, so that its main body was removed to some distance from him, as he drove on straight up the valley and, as the waters were withdrawn, it seemed to Macdonald that their voice was gathered in great, thick accents: "Turn back! Turn back! Turn back!" repeated over and over.

So startling was the clearness of that phrase that he shook his head and thundered out a fragment of a song to thrust the thought from his head; but, when he listened to the river again, it was calling as clearly as ever: "Turn back! Turn back! Turn back!"

He halted Sunset and looked about him. As he stared about him now, it seemed to Macdonald that he had indeed seen this river before. He had ridden that way, but he must have looked only casually about him. He could recall no single landmark, but he remembered the whole effect, as one remembers the sound of a human voice without being able to identify it with descriptive words.

Now he followed the stream again, as it dwindled swiftly. He crossed a fork, where another creek joined it. He went on, and in another half mile he was at the big spring which gave the river birth. A little farther on he came to the divide, a ragged crest which overlooked to the east a rich plain, dotted with trees, spotted here and there with houses, and in the distance the gathered roofs of a town with a few clusters of spires above it. And, as he paused, the wind blew to him faintly the lowing of cattle made musical with distance.

Another sound was forming behind him, the small voice of the creek, and again it seemed to be building words: "Turn back! Turn back! Turn back!"

Macdonald grew cold in his sleep. A heaviness of foreboding depressed him. But he reached for his guns, and they were all safe; they were all loaded. He looked again upon the plain below. It was bright with sun, spotted with shadow as before, and all was wrapped in a misty noonday of content and prosperity.

There could be nothing to fear in this, he told himself, and straightway he gave Sunset the rein. Down the slope they went in a wild gallop. They started across the fields with Sunset jumping the fences like a bird on the wing dipping over them. And so they came suddenly to a long avenue of black walnut trees, immense and wide-spreading, trees that interlaced their branches above the head of Macdonald.

He stopped Sunset. It was more than familiar, this long double file of trees. He had seen it before. He closed his eyes. He told himself that if he turned his head he would see a section behind him, where three trees had died, and where three smaller and younger trees had been planted. He turned his head; he looked; and, behold, it was exactly as he had guessed.

It was very mysterious. He had never seen

that plain before, he told himself, and yet here he was remembering an exact detail. Macdonald swallowed with difficulty. He looked hastily around him. But there was nothing to justify that warning voice which he had seemed to hear from the river among the hills. There was only the whisper of the wind among the big branches above him, and the continual shifting and interplay of the shadows on the white road and lazy cows, swelling with grass, had lain down in the neighboring field to chew their cuds. No, nothing could be less alarming than this, unless the rattle of approaching hoofbeats bore some unsuspected danger toward him.

In a moment the rider was in view, swinging around a bend in the road. But fear? It was only a girl of eighteen or twenty on a speedy bay mare, borne backward in the saddle a little by the rate of the gallop and laughing her delight at the boughs of the walnut trees and the glimpses of the deep blue sky beyond them.

And as her face grew out upon him, Macdonald turned cold indeed! For on the one hand he knew that he had never seen her or, at least, he had certainly never heard her voice, never heard her name; but as for her face, it was more familiar to him than his own. He had come into a ghostly land, with voices speaking from rivers and with roads on which familiar strangers journeyed.

She came straight on, and he searched her face with his stare. She was by no means like the girls he was familiar with. They rode astride like men in loosely flowing garments of khaki, but this one was clad in a tightly fitted jacket, with long tight sleeves, bunched up at the shoulders, and she was perched gracefully in a side-saddle, with the skirt of her riding habit sweeping well down past the stirrup.

When she saw him, she threw up a hand in greeting, and he heard her cry out in a high, sweet, tingling voice that went through and through him. The bay mare flung back and came to a halt with half a dozen stiff-legged jumps, then she busied herself touching noses with Sunset. But the girl in the side-saddle? She had thrown her hands to Macdonald, and she was laughing, but her eyes were filled with tears.

"Oh," she cried to him, "I have been waiting so long . . . so long! I have ridden here every day for you to come, and here you are at last. I thought my heart would break with the long waiting, Gordon, but now it's breaking with happiness!"

Was it from this that that voice from the river had bidden him turn back? His heart was thundering.

"Do I know you then?" he was asking her. "Have I really met you before?"

"Don't you remember?"

173

"I try to remember, but there's a door shut in my mind, and I can't open it."

"We have met in our dreams, Gordon. Don't you remember now?"

"I almost remember. But your name is just around the corner and away from me."

"I've never had a name . . . for you," she said. And then her face clouded. "But if I should tell you my name, it would spoil everything. You aren't going to ask me for that, dear?"

"How can a name spoil anything?"

"If I showed you my father's house, you would understand."

"If I should lose you, how could I trail you and find you again, if I did not know your name?"

"You could find the river, and the river will always bring you to me, you know. But we never can leave one another now! If we turn together and ride fast, they'll never overtake us . . . if we once get to the hills and ride down the valley road beside the river, just the way you came."

"I have never run away from any man or men!" he answered sternly. "How can I run away now? Who will follow?"

"My father and all his men. Have you forgotten that?"

Fear grew up in Macdonald, but at the same time there was a wild desire to ride on to the end of that road. And as for "father and all his men," he was consumed with a perverse eagerness to see them. It was from this, then, that the river had bidden him turn back. But on he went, with the girl riding close beside him, beseeching him to stop.

When they came to the great avenue of walnut trees, they entered a village and passed through it until they came into a deep garden and straight under the façade of a lofty house, one of the largest he had ever seen, he thought, with great wooden turrets and gables. To Macdonald it looked like a castle.

"Is this your father's house, where he lives with all his men?" he asked of the girl.

But no voice answered him and, when he turned, the girl was gone. He looked on all sides, but she was nowhere to be seen.

"They have stolen her away from me," he thought to himself. "They have taken her into the house and, if I follow her there, they will kill me; but if I do not follow her I shall never see her again." And it seemed to Macdonald that, if he never saw her again, it would be worse, far worse than death. For the sound of her voice he would have crossed a sea. And there was a soft slenderness to her hand, like the hand of a child, that took hold on his heart.

"If I follow her into the house," said Macdonald again to himself, "I am no better than a dead man; but if I do not follow her, I am worse than dead!"

So he marched resolutely up the winding path. He strode up the wide steps, but when he came before the door of the house, though he had not heard a sound of a footfall following him, a strong hand clutched him by the shoulder.

Swiftly he turned around, but there was nothing behind him save the empty air, and the grip of the hand held him by the shoulder, ground into the strength of his big muscles, and seemed biting him to the bone like a hand of fire.

Here Macdonald awoke. There was a hand indeed upon his shoulder, and over his bed a dim figure was leaning. Instantly he grappled with the other, found his throat, dashed him to the floor.

"For Lord's sake," groaned the voice of the other, "don't kill me . . . it's only Jenkins!"

V "In Quest of Trouble"

So real had been the dream, so vivid had been the sunshine which he had seen in it, so clear the flowers and the trees and the shrubs in that great garden and the looming house above him, that for a moment the black darkness in the room seemed to stifle the big man.

Macdonald recalled himself and raised the groveling form of Jenkins to his feet.

"A fool thing to wake a man up like that . . . in the middle of the night," he growled at Jenkins. "Wait till I light a lamp."

"Not a lamp, in the name of reason!" panted the gambler. "Somebody might be watching . . . somebody might guess. . . ."

"Guess what?"

"That you put me up to the work."

"What work?"

"Playing with Rory Moore and breaking him."

The whole story rolled back upon the mind of Macdonald, and for a moment the face of the girl in his dream was dim. "Ah, yes," he said. "And tell me what happened?"

"You seen just what would happen, Macdonald. Moore played like a crazy man. I won so fast it had me dizzy. Finally he was broke. He put up his watch; he put up everything he had."

"Even the ranch?"

"Nope, it seems that he made that over to his sister. It's in her name!"

"But he lost everything else?"

"Everything! And finally he put up Sunset. You'd have thought that he was staking his soul on them cards. And when he lost, he put his head between his hands and groaned like a sick kid."

"But you got the horse, Jenkins?"

"It's in the stable behind the hotel. I'm leaving the first thing in the morning. I'm going to tell them at the stable that I sold the hoss to you. Then I light out for Canada."

"Why that?"

"Rory Moore may find out what I am, that some folks think I don't always play square with the cards. And if he thinks that he's been cheated out of that hoss, he'll kill me, Macdonald! Why, he'd follow me around the world to sink a bullet into me."

"Shut up! You're talking like a woman, not a man. Be quiet, Jenkins. Go wherever you please, but let me have the horse. Good-bye."

"Will you shake hands and wish me luck, Macdonald?"

"You rat! You card-juggling rat! I've used you, and I'm done with you. You have the money, and I have the horse. Now get out and never come back!"

He could feel Jenkins shrinking away from him through the darkness, and from the door he heard the stealthy whisper of the gambler.

"I dunno that I'm any worse than you. You put me up to this game. I dunno that I'm any worse than you."

"Bah!" sneered the big man. "Get out!" Then the door shut quickly behind the other.

After he had gone, the strangeness of the dream returned upon Macdonald. He lighted a lamp and sat down with his face between his hands, but he found that his heart was still beating wildly, and the face and the form of the girl still stayed in his thoughts more vividly, so it seemed, than when he had first seen her in the vision. There was none of the usual mistiness of dreams about her. He could remember the very texture of the sleeve of her riding habit. He could remember the way a wisp of hair, blown loose from beneath her stiff black hat, fluttered and swayed across her cheek. He could remember how her bay mare had danced and sidled, coming back down the avenue of the walnut trees. And, above all, he still held the quality of her voice in his ear. How she had pleaded with him not to approach that house behind the garden! And how mysteriously she had disappeared, when at last he had called to her. What might have happened had he not persisted in going on? And, above all, what was it that made him persist? What was the pull and the lure which

179

drove him so irresistibly ahead?

At this he started up out of his chair with a stifled exclamation of disgust with himself. Of course anything was possible in a dream. There was no real existence except in his thoughts alone.

He stared around the room. It seemed to Macdonald that, if he could rest his eyes on some familiar daylight object, his nerves would quiet. But what his glance first encountered was the dark and faded portrait of an old gentleman with a white muffler — turned gray with age — around his throat, and one hand thrust pompously into the bosom of his coat. He smiled, and the smile was a grotesque caricature done in cracked paint. And the blue of his eyes was dim with time.

Daylight reality? There was more in one second of the dream than in an age of such pictures. And the whole room exuded a musty aroma of the past. Yonder dust, which lay in the corner, seemed to have lain there for a generation, and the footprint within it had been made by the foot of one long dead.

In vain Macdonald strove to rally from this obsession. In vain he told himself that this was no more than an old family mansion long used as a hotel — every room occupied many times in the course of each year. But the more he used his reason, the more it failed him.

The panic was growing momently in him,

and it was a strange sensation. Not on that day, when the five men had cornered him in an Australian desert and held him, more dead than living, in a group of rocks for forty-eight hours, without water — not even in the worst of those hours had he felt this clammy thing called fear. There was a weakness in his stomach and in his throat. He felt that if a knock were to come at his door, there would hardly be in his knees sufficient strength to answer it. Suppose that in this condition some enemy were to find him and reach for a gun?

He shuddered strongly at that thought. Then, driven by a peculiar curiosity, he forced himself to go to the mirror and to hold above his head with shaking hands the lamp. What he saw was like the face of another man. The pupils of his eyes were dilated. His lips were drawn. His bronzed cheeks had turned a sickly yellow, and his forehead was glistening with perspiration. He put down the lamp with a muffled oath, then glanced sharply over his shoulder to the window, for it seemed to him as though his eyes, a moment before, had been watching him from its black rectangle, with the high light from the lamp thrown across it, blurring the outer dark.

After this he consulted his watch. It was half past two, and at this hour he certainly could not start his day's journey. But the very thought of remaining in that room was unspeakably horrible to him.

He dressed at once. There was Sunset, at least, waiting for him in the stable. At that thought half of the nightmare fears left him. He hurried through the packing of his bed roll, then left the room and went down the stairs. On the desk in the deserted little lobby he left more than enough to pay his bill. Then he started out for the stable.

It was deserted like the lower floor of the big house. Even the stable, which the Moores had built behind their home, was lofty and mansion-like, finished at the top with sky-reaching gables and adorned at the upper rim of the roof with an elaborate cornice of carved wood, half of whose figures had cracked away with the passage of the years and the lack of paint.

As he stepped through the great arch of the central door, he found a single lamp burning behind a chimney black with smoke. This he took as a lantern and examined the horses in the stalls. There were only five kept there for the night. The rest were in the corrals behind the building, and in the first of these corrals he found Sunset.

The stallion had been placed by himself and, the moment the light from the lamp struck on him, he came straight for the bearer, his big eyes as bright as two burning disks, and the lamplight was quivering and running along the silk of his red flanks.

Macdonald uttered a faint exclamation of

delight. It was the first time in his wild life that he had secured anything through fraud. Treachery had never been one of his mental qualities. But, as the horse nosed at his shoulder and whinnied softly, as though they had been friends for many a year, his heart leaped. Every man, he had always felt, will commit one crime before his life was over, and this must be the crime of Macdonald. How much bloodshed, how many deaths could be laid to his score did not matter. He had risked his own life in taking the life of another. But here he had gone behind another man and cheated him with hired trickery!

It was very base. The whole soul of Macdonald revolted at the thought of Jenkins and the part he had played. But he would use Sunset as tenderly as any master could use him. That, at least, was certain.

In five minutes his saddle was on the back of the stallion, his roll was strapped to it, and he had vaulted into the stirrups and jogged out onto the main street of the town. There were no noises. The town slept the sleep of the mountains, black and stirless. The great stars were bright above him. And under him the stallion was dancing with eagerness to be off at full speed, dancing and playing lightly against the bit, but as smooth of action as running water.

He spoke gently, and Sunset was off into a breath-taking gallop, no pitch and pound, as of the range mustang, but a long and sweeping stride, as though the beat of invisible wings bore him up and floated him over the ground. They flashed out of town. Now the blackness of the plain lay before them, and Sunset was settling to his work. A horse? No, it was like sitting on the back of an eagle. The cold of the nightmare left him, and it seemed to Macdonald that, if he turned, he would see the girl of his vision cantering beside him, laughing up to him!

Now he touched Sunset with the spurs. It was half a mile before he could pull the startled horse out of a mad run and bring him into a canter again, with hand and voice soothing the stallion. By that time all thoughts of the dream were behind him. But for how long? When would she come again to make his heart ache with loneliness and to fill him again with the sad certainty of disaster toward which he was traveling?

One thing at least was necessary. He must find action — action which would employ him to the full. He must have battle such as he had never had before. He must fight against odds. He must plunge into danger as into cleansing waters, and these would wash the memory from his mind.

So at least it seemed to Macdonald, as he gnawed his lip and rode on into the night. And he cast around in his thoughts for an objective. It was no longer easy to find the danger which was the breath of his nostrils. Time had been when the shrug of a shoulder or a careless word would plunge him into battle. But that time had passed. His reputation had spread wide before him and men took far more from him than they would take from their ordinary fellows. Moreover, how many sheriffs had warned him solemnly that the next time there was a killing by him in their county, self-defense would be no defense, but he would be left to the mercy of the crowd?

He must find some ready-made trouble, and with that the inspiration came to him. Five years before in the town of Sudeth he had killed young Bill Gregory, and the Gregorys one and all had sworn that he would never live to spend another day in that town. What could be more perfect? He had only to ride into the town of Sudeth and take a room in the hotel. The next move would be up to the Gregorys. There were scores of them about the place, and they were not the type of men to forget past oaths.

VI "The Gregorys"

The tidings of his coming went out on wings, and that night the Gregorys assembled. In the course of two generations a large family had multiplied greatly and become almost a clan, of which the head was old Charles Gregory; and it was at his ranchhouse, a scant mile from the town of Sudeth, that the assembly gathered. Old or young, gray or dark, they packed into the big dining room. The elders sat. The younger men, the fighting van of the Gregory family, were ranged around the wall, smoking cigarettes until their faces were lost behind a haze, but speaking rarely or never. For it was felt in the Gregory family that age had its rights and its wisdom, and that young men may listen to them with profit.

Old Charles Gregory himself sat at the head of the board. Time had withered, but not faded, him. His arms and hands were shrunk like the arms and hands of a mummy, but his thin, bronzed cheek still held a healthful glow, and his eyes were as bright as the eyes of a youth. He opened the meeting with a little speech.

"There ain't no use saying why we've come together, folks," he said. "The hound has come back. It wasn't enough that we didn't follow him out and finish him off after he murdered poor Bill. That wasn't enough. We kept the law and stayed quiet. But being quiet only made him figure that he could walk right over us. So he's back here sitting easy at the hotel and waiting for us to do something. The question is: What are we going to do?"

The elders around the table neither stirred nor spoke, but there was a slight and uneasy shifting of feet around the wall and a dull jingling of spurs. Not a man there but was a man of action.

"None of you seem to have no ideas!" said Charles Gregory fiercely. "But first off I'd better tell you just what happened when Bill was killed. There's been a lot of talk about it since. There's been five years for talk to grow up, and talk grows faster than any weed on the range! I'll tell you the facts because, come my time of life, the longer ago a thing happens the clearer it is to me!"

He paused and closed his eyes. For the moment he looked like a weary mask of death. Now again his eyes looked out from the steep shadow of his brows, and he went on: "And you younger people listen close. You're going to hear the facts. It started over nothing, the way most shooting scrapes start. Bill comes riding into town one day and goes up on the verandah and sits down in a chair. Pretty soon Abe Sawyer comes up to him and says to him:

'You know who that chair belongs to?'

" 'I dunno,' says Bill.

" 'Gordon Macdonald has been sitting in it,' says Abe.

" 'Who's Gordon Macdonald?' says Bill.

" 'A nacheral born man-killer,' says Abe, 'and the worst man with a gun that ever was born.'

"Bill sits and thinks a minute.

" 'I don't know how much gunfighter he is,' says Bill, 'but he sure ain't got this chair mortgaged. If he happens to sit down in it in the morning, he ain't going to have it kept for him here all day!'

"Abe didn't say no more about it. He went off and sat down to watch, and pretty soon a big man comes out through the door of the hotel and taps Bill on the shoulder.

" 'Excuse me, partner,' he says, 'but this is my chair!'

"Bill answers without turning his head. 'D'you think that you can hold down a chair all day by just sitting in it once?'

" 'I was fixing my spurs,' says the big man, 'and I left one of 'em lying on each side of the chair. Ain't that enough to hold down a chair for a man for two minutes? Besides, there's other chairs out here on the porch, and you could have sat in one of them, couldn't you?'

"Bill looks down and he sees the spurs for the first time. He looks up to the face of Macdonald, and he said later that it was like looking up into the face of a lion. His nerve sort of faded out of him.

" 'Maybe you're right,' says he and gets up and takes another chair. But, while he's sitting in the other chair, he sees half a dozen of the gents that have watched the whole thing sort of looking at him and then at one another and smiling. A shiver runs up Bill's spine, and he starts asking himself if they think he's taken water. He's got half a mind to go over and pick a fight with Macdonald right there, to show that he has nerve enough to suit any man. But then he remembers that he's going to marry poor Jenny inside of a week, and he decides that he ain't got no right to fight a gunman.

"He goes on home. As soon as he sits down to the supper table in comes his cousin, Jack, over yonder . . . oh, Jack, it was a poor part you played that night! . . . and started joking with Bill because he'd give up his chair to Macdonald. Bill didn't say a word to nobody. But he gets up from the table and goes out and saddles a hoss and starts for Sudeth town. He runs down the street, jumps off'n his hoss, and dives into the hotel. There he looks up this Macdonald. He starts in cussing Macdonald, with his hand on the butt of his gun. He says that Macdonald must have started talking about him and calling him yaller. But Macdonald talks back to him plumb soft and says that he don't want no trouble, and that the matter about the chair don't mean noth-

189

ing. Pretty soon Bill got to thinking that *Macdonald* was yaller, I guess, from the soft way that Macdonald talks. Anyways he goes up and punches Macdonald on the jaw. Macdonald knocks him down. While Bill lies on the floor, he pulls his gun, and Macdonald waits till he sees the steel, then he pulls his own Colt like a flash and kills poor Bill."

Charles Gregory paused, looking down to his withered hands, clasped above the table. There was no sound in the room.

"That's the straight of that killing of Bill, and it sounds like Bill was simply a fool. But since then we've heard a lot about Macdonald, and we know that he's one of these gents that goes around hunting trouble, and when he gets into trouble he backs up and talks soft and tries to make the other gent lead at him, but the minute anything is started, Macdonald does all the finishing. He lives on murder! We've traced him a ways, and we've planted twenty dead men to his credit! Now, folks, this Macdonald is the man we told to get out of Sudeth and never come back, and here he is in town again. I seen the sheriff today. All he said was that he had a long trip to make and was leaving *pronto,* which was the same as saying that he knew that Macdonald was a plumb bad one, and that he wouldn't dislike having us wipe him out. Ain't I right? The only question is: How are we going to do it?"

There was a small, respectful pause at the

conclusion of this speech, and finally Henry Gregory, a wide-shouldered, gray-headed man, spoke from the farther end of the table. No one in that room was more respected by the others.

"I've had my storms," he said, "and I've done my fighting. But the older I get the more I figure that no good can come out of the muzzle of a Colt with a forty-five slug. And I say short and *pronto:* no more fighting! Let Macdonald stay. Poor Bill is dead. There ain't no doubt that it was no better than murder. There ain't no doubt that this Macdonald is a professional, and before we could get rid of him, a couple of our boys are sure to go down. I say: hands off of Macdonald."

"There'd be a lot of talk!" exclaimed half a dozen voices in a chorus.

"Nobody but a fool would accuse the Gregorys of being cowards," said Henry. "What fools say don't bother us none. We can let 'em chatter!"

Someone stepped forward from the wall of the room with a clank of spurs. It was the face of Jack Gregory that came out of the mist of smoke.

"Folks," he said, "I'd ought to wait until my elders have finished talking, maybe, but I got something to say that needs saying pretty bad. Grandfather Charles was sure right when he said that it was me joking Bill that sent him into town to fight. God knows that

I didn't mean no harm. Me and Bill was always pals, everybody knows. But it was me that got Bill killed, and I'll never live it down with myself! What I got to say is this. Let me go in and face the music. Let me meet Macdonald and try my luck. It's my business!"

There was a stern hum of dissent, and Mack Gregory, the father of Jack, turned and glanced gloomily at his son.

"No," said old Charles Gregory, speaking again, "we've passed our word that Macdonald should never come back to Sudeth, and he's done it. Right or wrong, we've passed our word. It ain't the business of Jack. It's the business of all of us! Speaking personal, I say that it would be suicide to send only one man. We need more! Macdonald is a lion!"

There was another growl of agreement.

"Are we going to let folks say that the Gregorys have to fight in twos?" protested Henry Gregory, but he was not heard.

In another moment they were busy preparing the lots and then making the draw. By weird chance it fell upon both the sons of the peacemaker, Henry Gregory. Steve and Joe were his only children, great-boned, silent fellows, as swarthy of skin as Indians and as terrible as twin wildcats in a fight. Certainly the choice could not have fallen upon two more formidable men.

"But it ain't right," protested Jack. "I sure ought to have a hand. If Steve and Joe are hurt, the blame of it will come back on me, and I can't stand it!"

"Shut up!" snarled his father. "You're playing the fool, son. Are you wiser than all the rest of us?"

So Jack was cried down, but his mind was not put at rest by all the talk. He heard it decided that the attack on Macdonald should be made in the morning. He heard the farewells, as the party broke up. And, witnessing all these things through a mist, all he saw clearly was the stern face of Henry Gregory, now wan with sorrow for his sons. He saw that, and it determined him on the spot. He waited until the assembly had scattered, then he took his horse, fell to the rear, and presently had turned down a path and started for the town of Sudeth.

VII "Between the Eyes"

In the meantime Macdonald had waited until the night. Yet it was not wasted time. In anticipation he was turning over the danger in his mind, as a connoisseur turns over the thought of the expected feast. He had put his head into the jaws of the lion, as he was well aware. How those jaws would close was the fascinating puzzle. They might attack him by surprise, or in a crowd. They might wait for the night, and then they would be truly terrible, or else they might strike boldly in the day, when he would have a better fighting chance.

Such surmises filled his mind all the late morning. In the early afternoon he fell asleep and, the instant he closed his eyes, he was once more traveling up the river in the mountains, with the voice forming out of the sounding current: "Turn back! Turn back! Turn back!" in endless reiteration. Once more he climbed to the headwaters of the stream; he crossed the divide; and he saw before him the same sunny plain, exactly as it had been before.

He wakened suddenly; and that afternoon he slept no more, but went down into the lobby of the hotel and then onto the verandah in front, where there would be other men around him.

The evening came, and still there was no sign of the coming of the Gregorys. But word was brought to him that the sheriff had left the town. And then new word came that the Gregorys were meeting that evening. For, wherever Macdonald went, though he had no friends and no companions, there was always a certain number of men, like the jackals who follow the king of beasts, ready to carry information to the great man, ready to cringe and cower before his greatness. He treated them, as they needed to be treated, with a boundless contempt; but on occasion they were invaluable to him. They were very necessary on this day, for instance, with their eager whispers to and fro. And it was one of these fellows who brought the word about Rory Moore.

"If anybody was to ask me where there was going to be trouble first," said this sneak of an informant, "I'd say it would come right here in Sudeth. And the second place it's going to come is to Rory Moore in his own town!"

"Rory Moore? Rory Moore?" asked Macdonald sharply. "What the devil do you know about him?"

"Nothing but what everybody will know pretty *pronto*. I ain't doing you no favor telling you this. Twenty men could tell it to you pretty soon. Rory Moore is telling folks around his home town that you stole his hoss, Sunset, from him!"

It brought a growl from Macdonald, and he dropped his cigarette to the floor and smashed it with his heel.

"I stole his hoss? It's a lie! I bought it from a man who won Sunset from him in a gambling game."

"It was a frame-up," said the informer. "Moore swears it was a frame-up. He says that he's found out that Jenkins, who won the hoss from him, was really a professional gambler, a crooked player whose real name is Vincent. Is that right, Macdonald?"

"Hang Jenkins and Moore both!" cried Macdonald. "Where does all this rot come from?"

"The telephones have been packed with it all morning. Seems that this fellow Vincent . . . was it really Vincent?"

"What if it were?"

"Nothing except that Vincent is an old hand. He was run out of Sudeth a couple of years back, and he's been tarred and feathered a couple of times for his dirty work with the cards. And one of these days they'll talk to him with a gun, they will! Anyway, it seems that this Jenkins, as he was calling himself, started right out of town after he'd cleaned Rory Moore up at the cards. But early the next morning Moore heard some talk about town that Jenkins was really Vincent, the crooked gambler. It took Moore about one second to see through everything, the way he'd lost the night before. He started on Jenkins's trail. By noon he'd run him down. He put a gun on Jenkins, and the hound got down and crawled and said he'd confess everything, if Moore would let him live.

"So Moore let him live, and Jenkins told him a crazy yarn. Said that you'd come to Jenkins the night before and found him broke. You offered to stake him to five hundred dollars, if he'd use it to clean out Moore and make him put up his horse at the end of the game. The horse was what you wanted. You'd tried to buy it and, when Moore wouldn't sell, you schemed to get Sunset this way. And the scheme worked, according to Jenkins. He got the money and hoss. He put the hoss in the stable, told you where it was, and then run for his life. And Moore swears that you rode out of town before morning, which shows that you were afraid to stay. Anyway, he got all his money back from Jenkins, and now he's hunting across country to find you and Sunset. I'm wondering if he'll have a hard time finding you?"

Here the speaker laughed hugely at the poor jest, but Macdonald found the story no laughing matter. If this story were out, if this story were proved — and who could doubt the confession of Jenkins, alias Vincent, the card shark? — then Macdonald would be established in the eyes of the men of the ranges not only as a man-slayer, but as a scheming rascal; and men who would never combine against one who merely took lives could immediately gather together to run to earth a crafty schemer. Decidedly it was tidings of the most serious import. Macdonald gritted his teeth, as he thought it over. If he could tear Vincent to small pieces and scatter the remnants to the dogs, there would be some satisfaction. But Vincent was a poor mongrel not worthy of a blow.

Meantime there was a pleasanter side to the story. Of all the men he had faced in the past half dozen years, there had been none to compare with Rory Moore in dash and spirit. He had not the slightest doubt that the young rancher was a warrior of parts. And a battle against him would be distinctly a pleasure worth a search of a thousand miles. If he came alive from this affair at Sudeth, he would be instantly back in Moore's home town and await him there in the hotel. What could be better than that? And in wiping out Moore, he would wipe out the person chiefly interested in telling that ugly tale about the crooked gambler's work.

It was evening, and he was back in the lobby before he came to all of those conclusions. And they were hardly formed, when his attention was sharply called by a silence which had fallen over the room. There was a soft and sudden shifting of positions. Macdonald, looking into a small mirror which was hanging on the wall in front of him — a little diamond-shaped affair meant to be a decoration — saw a big fellow striding through the door and into the room. He did not need more than one glance to make sure that this was a man come on desperate business. The pale, rather drawn face, the glaring eyes, the jaw set hard and thrust out a little, were all the features of a man on the verge of meeting death itself!

"Macdonald!" called the stranger.

As Macdonald rose slowly from his chair, he stretched his arms.

"Look out!" gasped the voice of the human jackal who had brought him so much news that day. "Look out! It's Jack Gregory, and he's a fighting fool!"

But Macdonald turned with glorious unconcern.

"Calling me?" he asked cheerfully.

"I'm calling you! Macdonald, I want to talk to you outside the hotel!"

Macdonald hesitated. One who dreaded Macdonald's speed and his accuracy with a gun often sought to equalize matters a little more by bringing him into the darkness. But, after all, he had fought a score of times in the light of the stars. He had made a point of doing as much target practice by night as by day, and the chances, which were heavy against any foe in the daylight, were even heavier against them in the dark. After that moment of delay he nodded and crossed the room to the other.

"I don't think I remember meeting you," he said.

"You don't," said the other. "My name is Jack Gregory!"

And, as he spoke, his body drew stiff and straight and his right hand trembled near to the butt of his gun. But such a killing was by no means in the mind of Macdonald. With the blandest of smiles he held out his hand.

"Very glad to meet you, Gregory," he said.

His hand was disregarded.

"I want to talk with you outside. Will you come?"

"Certainly."

They passed through the door and descended the steps. They stood in the street. Instantly the door of the hotel was packed with a blur of white faces, watching eagerly. Macdonald looked about him with infinite satisfaction. It was a moonless night, to be sure. The moon would not be up for another hour; but the sky was clear, and the stars were shining as clear as crystal. Certainly there was light enough for Macdonald to shoot almost as straight as by daylight, at such close range. But what was this Gregory saying?

"Macdonald," he said, "I've come to beg you to leave the town."

"*Beg* me to leave it?" asked Macdonald with

the slightest and most insulting emphasis.

"Just that," said the other.

"And if I don't go?"

"We fight!"

"I'm sorry to hear that," said Macdonald, and in the starshine he smiled evilly upon Jack Gregory. "But as for leaving," he continued, you must admit that this is a free country and a free town. Why should I leave, if you please?"

"Because," said Gregory, "my family has sworn that you cannot stay here."

"Interesting," said the mild, soft voice of the man-killer, "but unimportant, Gregory."

"Macdonald," pleaded the other, "it was some fool joking of mine that drove Bill Gregory, five years ago, to come in and have it out with you. I got his death on my conscience. Now some of the rest of the boys are going to try to get you out of town, but it ain't their business. It's mine. If you should kill them, their ghosts would haunt me! So I've come in to try to persuade you!"

"I'm listening," said Macdonald.

"Everybody on the range knows that you're a brave man, Macdonald. If you leave town, nobody'll think any the worse of you, and I'll let the folks know that I asked you to go and didn't drive you out by threats."

"Who'd believe you?" asked Macdonald grimly, as he saw the bent of the conversation. "You'd get a big reputation cheap. But what would I get?"

"A cold thousand. I've saved that much, and. . . ."

"You fool!"

"Listen to me! I'm not trying to insult you, but I'm trying to think of everything in the world to persuade you. If you don't want the money, forget that I mentioned it. But I'm desperate, Macdonald. I know that I can't stand up to you, but if you won't go by persuasion, I got to try my gun!"

It was a situation unique in the experience of Macdonald, and he hesitated. But what cause had he to love the world or trust or pity any man in it? From the very first his life had been a battle.

"If I gave way," he explained coldly, "I'd have twenty men ready to bully me wherever I went. The story would go around that you'd bluffed me, Gregory. I'd rather be dead than be shamed."

There was a groan from Gregory.

"You cold-hearted devil!" he cried. "If there's no other way, I'll try my luck!"

Gregory reached for his gun. Even then there was time for Macdonald to seem to protest — for the benefit of those who were jammed in the doorway of the hotel. He raised a hand in that protest, and he called loud enough for the spectators to hear: "Not that, Gregory!"

Macdonald saw the gun of the other flash. It was shooting at ten paces, and even a poor shot was not apt to miss him. He dropped his right hand on the butt of his gun, making it swing up, holster and all, for the end of the holster was not steadied against his thigh. At the same instant he pulled the trigger. Jack Gregory spun and dropped. He had been shot squarely between the eyes.

VIII "A Very Pleasant Party"

No doubt, when all was said and done, it was as fair a fight as had ever been seen in the town of Sudeth. There was no shadow of a doubt that Jack Gregory had pressed home the battle. There was no doubt that he had reached first for his gun, and that the odium of beginning the fight rested entirely on him. But, in spite of this, there was a roar of anger from the spectators when they saw him fall.

They were out through the doorway in a rush, and every man had a drawn gun in his hand. A moment before they had been watching as spectators at a game. Suddenly they realized that in this game the prize was death, and that Jack Gregory had received it — Jack Gregory whom every man there, perhaps, had known from his boyhood. His life was wasted, and yonder was the man of fame, the cool slayer, who had conquered again. And the horror of it took them suddenly by the throat.

One section of that little mob spilled out toward the body of Gregory, lying face down in the dust. The other section swarmed toward the slayer.

"Finish the murdering dog!" some one was crying.

"Hold him for the sheriff!" called another.

"And see him get free on self-defense?" was the answer. "No, we'll be our own law! Macdonald, put up your hands!"

There had been no chance to run. In that clear starlight with a dozen guns covering him, Macdonald knew that he could not get away. Therefore he stood his ground, and at the order he obediently thrust his arms above his head, not straining them high up, as men in fear will do, but holding them only a trifle above the height of his shoulders, standing at ease and facing the rush of the mob.

"He's dead!" cried voices from the rear. "Poor old Jack is dead. He'll never speak again. That murdering hound has sure got to pay for this!"

They joined the circle around Macdonald.

"Get iron on his wrists."

"No irons here. A rope will do. Where's a rope?"

"Here's one!"

"Your sheriff will hunt you down," said Macdonald.

"Do you think that a jury could be found in this country that would convict a man for helping to lynch you?" asked someone, and Macdonald felt the truth of the query.

"Put down your hands, one hand at a time," commanded the man with the rope. "Jab a gun into his middle a couple of you, and kill him if he tries to move!"

Macdonald smiled down upon them. Perhaps this was a little more than he had bargained for, but it was not at all unpleasant. The old tingling joy in peril, which he had found so early in his life and loved so long, was thrilling in him now. They had his life upon the triggers of a dozen guns and yet, if he could strike suddenly enough, their very numbers. . . .

He did not pause to complete that thought. He had been lowering his right hand slowly toward the rope, as though to show that he intended no sudden effort to escape. Now he jerked it down and knocked away two revolvers which had been thrust against his body. One of them exploded, and there was a yell of pain from a bystander through whose leg the big bullet plowed. At the same instant half a dozen pairs of arms reached for Macdonald, but he spun around. Their fingers slipped on the hard bulk of his muscles. And now he drove ahead, crouching low, as a football player charges a line. They tumbled away before him like snow before a snow plow. Who could fire, when the bullet, nine chances out of ten, would find lodgment in the body of a friend?

They poured after Macdonald, but two or three had lost their footing and gone down. They entangled some of those who followed. Now there was a sudden thinning of the mass before Macdonald. Two men stood before him.

He smote one on the side of his head, saw the head rebound, as though broken at the neck, and the man went down. His shoulder, as he rushed, crashed against the breast of the other, and the man fell with a gasp. There was an open way before Macdonald, and he went down it, like a racing deer with the sound of the hounds behind it.

With a sweep they followed but, before they had taken half a dozen steps, they saw he was stepping swiftly away from them, and the leaders stopped to shoot. But a fight, a scramble, a race, and the starlight, combined with the knowledge that one is shooting at a famous target, make a very poor effect upon the nerves. The shower of bullets flew wild. Macdonald ran on unscathed. He reached the corner of the hotel and whipped around it. He headed down the side of the building, then darted for the corrals, with the mob still in hot pursuit. But they lost at every fence, for he leaped them in stride, like the athlete that he was, and they had to pause to crawl between the rails or vault over.

He found Sunset at once. Onto his back he vaulted, and it seemed that the fine animal knew at once what was expected of him. A tap on the side of the neck turned him around, and a word started him away at a flying gallop. He took the fence with a wild leap that brought a yell of despair and rage from the pursuers and in another moment he was sunk in the outer blackness of the night.

They pursued him no more than one would attempt to overtake an arrow after seeing it leave the string. But Macdonald had not left to stay away that night. He galloped not half a mile, then returned and headed straight back to the hotel. Into it he ventured, stole up the back stairs, and got to his room. They had not touched his belongings. He packed them deliberately, returned down the stairs, went out to the shed and got his saddle and bridle, put them on Sunset, and was again ready for the journey.

As for the town of Sudeth, it passed through a sudden and violent transition. For two hours they raved against the cool-handed murderer and swore that they would run him to the earth, if it took them a life of labor to do the task. But at the end of the two hours, a committee went up to investigate the belongings of Macdonald and found them gone. On the plaster of the wall was written:

A very pleasant party.
Macdonald

When the others learned, there was a storm of wonder and then of appreciation. For they had heard enough to convince them that there was something almost supernal in the courage of a man who could return on the heels of the very mob which was hunting his life. There and then the townsmen lost their interest in the chase of Macdonald. That was left to the Gregorys, and the Gregorys solemnly took up the trail.

IX "Turn Back"

No seer was needed to tell Macdonald that the town of Sudeth was apt to lose its enthusiasm for war before long, but that the clan of Gregorys would never leave him until they had clashed at least a few more times. Nevertheless he had no desire to put a great distance between himself and his probable pursuers. There was first the little matter with Rory Moore which was to be settled. And he let Sunset run like a homing bird straight across the hills toward home.

They reached it nearly a day later, in the red time of sunset, with all the town as hushed and peaceful as a pictured place rather than a reality. He saw one old man smoking a pipe at the door of a shop. He heard in the weird distance one dog barking. But of living sights and sounds, these were the only two. The town might have died. It was like riding into the ghost of a place.

Of course it was easily explainable, Macdonald told himself. The people were simply at supper and, since they all kept the same hour for supper, they would all be off the streets at that time. And yet such a conclusion did not entirely satisfy him. There was a solemnity about this quiet, this utter silence, with the far off wailing of the dog, that warned him back like the voice of the river in his dream.

At the hotel he found the same sleepy atmosphere which he had noted before in the place. The hotel, in short, was not paying. For in spite of its size and the comfort of its arrangement, there was a forbidding atmosphere about the place which had held the trade away. Macdonald felt it again, as he stood in front of the desk in the hotel office and asked for a room. He would have given a good deal if he had not come to this hostelry where he had spent that terrible night so short a time before. He would have given a great deal if he had chosen, instead, the little shack which had been built at the farther end of the street, and which also went by the name of a hotel in the town.

But he could not withdraw, having come so far. He could not mumble and excuse and retreat. But his absent-mindedness, which was the curse of his life, having brought him on thus far, he must go on with the thing. He heard a cheerful promise that he should not only have a room, but that he should also have that very same room which he had occupied the last time he stayed there, the room which he had left so suddenly in the middle of the night.

And even from this proposal he could not dissent. He was kept quiet by the very violence of his feelings. How could he declare that the very last place on earth in which he wished to spend another night was the room where he had slept before? They might pin him down to the truth. They might discover — oh, monstrous joke to be roared at by the whole world — that Macdonald had run away from a dream like any brain-sick youth of fourteen years!

So he had to submit and was led upstairs to the room. When the door closed upon him, and he was left among its shadows, the old panic swept upon him. He could not stay there alone. Down the stairs he went again and out to the stable to look at Sunset. The stallion was digesting a liberal feed of grain and sweet-smelling hay. Half a dozen hungry chickens, roaming abroad in search of forage, were clustered around the outskirts of the pile of hay, scratching a quay into it and picking busily at the heads of grain. But the big stallion, when he had finished his grain and turned to the hay, made not the slightest objection to these small intruders. For he kept on steadily at his hay, merely cocking one sharp ear when the beak of a hen picked a little too close to that soft muzzle of his.

Macdonald hung over the fence of the corral, delighted, until the gathering of the shadows drove even those hungry chickens away from the hay and back to their roosting places.

"Yep," said a voice to the side, "that's a plumb

easy-going hoss, I'd tell a man!"

Macdonald looked askance with a scowl. It was by no means his habit to be so rapt in any observation that he allowed other men to stalk up beside him and take him by surprise. What he found was a little old man, very bent, so that his head was thrust far in front of his body, and he balanced himself with a round-headed cane on which his brown hands rested. He carried a short-stemmed pipe between his gums and puffed noisily at it. In a word he was like a figure out of a book, or off the stage.

"And who might you be?" asked the little man, and he had a quick, bird-like way of jerking his head toward the one to whom he was speaking, while he sucked on his pipe.

"Oh, I've just happened by," murmured Macdonald smoothly enough.

"You've heard that he's back again, I reckon," said the other. "You've come like me to have a look at Sunset before that Macdonald man rides him away ag'in. I disremember when I seen a finer hoss than Sunset!"

"Nor I!" exclaimed Macdonald, and at the sound of his deep voice the stallion looked up, swung halfway toward his new master, and then allowed the greed of a big appetite to draw him back toward his fodder. But the heart of Macdonald was beating with a great new tenderness.

"The hoss likes you!" piped the old man. "Well, I never seen a hoss yet that would waste a look on a bad man. All that makes me sorry is to think about Sunset being wasted on a man-killing, law-spoiling hound like that Macdonald."

"Is he as bad as that?" asked Macdonald slowly.

"He's worse," said the other with great venom, and he even removed his pipe from his mouth so that he might speak with more vehemence. Macdonald saw that the stem was wound with string to give a better grip to the old gums of the man. "He's a pile worse. There ain't nobody can say anything bad enough about him. What would you say about a gent that kills just for the sake of killing?

"Why," said Macdonald, "I think that depends on how he kills. Every man is a hunter, if you come down to that. They're all trying to kill one another, you know. But some are lucky, and some aren't so lucky. It depends, I say, on how he kills. If he takes as big a chance as the next man, what's so terribly wrong in that?"

"Suppose he killed with poison?"

"Do you mean to say that he does that?" cried Macdonald.

"Just as bad as that. He's such a good shot, and his nerves are so plumb steady, that he knows he ain't running no real risk when he faces another man. There ain't one chance in a hundred that he'll get so much as scratched. That's why I say he might as well use poison

214

for his killings. And to think that a hoss like Sunset. . . ."

But Macdonald heard no more. He had listened to too much already, as a matter of fact, and he climbed back to his room with a heavy heart. And on the way he fought over the truth about himself. It had not occurred to him to look at the matter from this new viewpoint. He had always felt that it was fair fighting. But now that he thought of it, how clearly he saw the new idea! His skill, he had to confess, was far greater than the skill of the average man. Just how much chance *did* the other fellow have, when matched against the practiced hand and the familiar gun of Macdonald?

He thought back to many of his conflicts. In the old days he had been often wounded. His body was still ripped and dotted with scars. Yes, he had been wounded almost as often as he had wounded others. Finally he had gone into a fight almost expecting to have his own body wounded, or the life shot out of him. But, as time went on, he learned new things, and among the rest he learned to practice with his weapons assiduously every day. How long had it been now, since an enemy had wounded him in fair fight, face to face? And what did that mean?

It meant that the old man standing by the corral had been right! He might as well have killed by poison.

He threw himself down upon his bed and,

staring up into the darkness, his mind filled with two thoughts — the girl of whom he had dreamed, and the men who had fallen before him in his life of fighting. And so fiercely did he concentrate that in another moment he was riding up a river among the mountains, a river whose voice gathered into human words: "Turn back! Turn back! Turn back!"

X "The Banquet of the Dead"

So sudden had been that sleep that even in his dream he was acutely conscious of something left behind him, of a change just made. One half of his mind was trying to turn back to what he had been, while the other half was listening to the shouting of the river. At length he gave all his attention to the road before him.

It was all as it had been before. He rode to the top of the divide, where the water dwindled to a little spring. He looked over the plain onto a great sweep of sunshine and shadow, with browsing cattle, and the faint sounds of their lowing was blown to him upon the height. And, as before, even while looking at that pleasant and warm scene, a chill of distress passed into the heart of Macdonald and a wild misgiving of something which was to come. For the voice which God or a demon had put into that river could not be wrong. This was the third time he had ridden up that river to its rising, and on this third time there was certain to be a revelation of the catastrophe.

Yet turn back he could not. A nameless eagerness filled him, far overbalancing his fear. And down the hill he swept and over the

217

meadow at the long-reaching gallop of the red stallion. So he came in due time to the same avenue of the walnut trees, under which he had passed before. And down that avenue he rode, with the growing dread which he had felt when he galloped there before, and yet with a wild desire to hear the beat of approaching hoofs and to see once more the girl riding around the sweep of the trees.

He reached that turn but she did not come. He went on more slowly. He came again to the town, all quiet under the sun. He came again to the garden. And he stood once more before the great castle of a house where, as he remembered, a hand had fallen upon his shoulders, and the girl had disappeared. Perhaps she would come to him again now!

Slowly he went up the steps, and the great house before him was wonderfully silent. There was a flutter of wings, as a bird darted under the roof of the porch, brushed close to his face, and darted out again. Then he knocked at the door. It was opened so quickly that it was obvious that his approach had been noted, and that there was someone ready to let him in.

Yet he saw no one inside the dark, high hall of the place. He stepped in and, the moment he did so, he discovered who had opened the door for him. It was a man whose hand was still on the knob, and he was standing flat against the wall. And the pale face was the face of Anthony Legrange, as he had been on that night eight years before, when he died in Cheyenne with a bullet from the gun of Macdonald through his heart. He had not altered by a single shade, save that he had been a gloomy man in those days, and now he was smiling, a calm smile of mockery and scorn, as though he had a knowledge before which Macdonald was as helpless as a child.

Macdonald reached hastily for his gun, but the smile of Anthony Legrange merely deepened and suddenly Macdonald knew that a gun would be of no avail to him in this house.

"Anthony," he said, "I thought that you were dead eight long years ago. But I'm a thousand times glad to see that I was wrong! A thousand times glad, old man!"

But the smile of Anthony merely deepened again. He closed the door and leaned his shoulders against it, facing Macdonald once more, as though he defied him to try to break out.

"Why," said Macdonald, frowning, "if you think that you've trapped me here, it makes no difference to me. Do you imagine that I'm afraid of you, Anthony? No, nor of a thousand like you!"

At once he turned his back on Anthony, stepped into the next room, and passed through this to a great dining hall. There he found a long table set, the longest table he had ever seen, and all around it men were seated, and before them food was placed. Some were eating, and some were drinking, and some were smoking, so that the air was blue with smoke. Yet, though Macdonald walked through a cloud of it, he smelled not the least taint of tobacco.

He noted, too, that though they seemed to be all laughing and talking, they were not making any sound, and the fall of knives and forks upon the plates made no sound. It was very strange, but stranger than anything they did were their faces. For there were men from a dozen nations, and everyone, he saw, was a man whom he had killed!

Yes, just before him sat young Jack Gregory, and with no mark of the mortal wound upon his forehead. And at the side of Gregory sat a great Negro, a giant of his kind, naked to the waist, just as he had been on that night, so many years before, when he had grappled with Macdonald in the fire room of the tramp freighter. That had been a grim battle. And it rushed back clean and clear upon the mind of Macdonald. He saw the Negro, blood streaming down his face, tear himself away. He saw the big fellow snatch up a great bar of iron used for trimming the fires. He saw himself catch up a lump of coal and with a true aim knock down the big stoker. He saw them grapple again, and his big hands had found a firm grip upon the throat of the black man.

And beside the Negro sat a hideous Malay,

with a split upper lip, rolling his wild eyes, as he talked. That was the human devil who had leaped upon him from behind in an alley in Bombay.

Yonder was the burly English mate who had striven to enforce obedience by the weight of his fists. They had grappled and gone over the rail together. Macdonald had come up, but the mate had sunk.

Sitting side by side, yellow of skin and dark of eyes, were the Arizona Kid and his two brothers. Macdonald had trailed them when he was a Ranger, and he had killed them all in one glorious and bloody battle. Now the Arizona Kid pointed him out, and his two brothers laughed in the face of their slayer. Indeed the whole table was laughing and pointing, until the perspiration rolled down the face of Macdonald.

He stepped to the table and struck upon it. The dishes jumped beneath the vibration of the stroke, but there was no jingling sound.

"You rattle-headed fools!" cried Macdonald. "Why do you laugh and point? I've sent you to damnation, every one of you, and I'd send you there again and think nothing of it! What are you doing here? What right have you in this place? I had no fear of you living. Do you think for an instant that I'll be afraid of you because you come back after death and gibber at me?"

The Negro giant leaned across toward him and extended a long, black arm, and along the naked skin the highlights glimmered. Macdonald could see the bull throat expand and quiver; he could see the chest of the monster rise; and he waited for the immense voice which, on a day, had been strong enough to stun the ears of men. But, instead, there ran forth only the faintest of faint whispers, hardly discernible.

"We're laughing at you, Macdonald, because we have gone to hell, every one of us, but a worse man than any one of us killed us. You saved us, Macdonald, with your gun, and that's why we laugh at you!"

"You lie!" thundered Macdonald. "Half of you were good men, and hell had no claim on that many of you. There's Jack Gregory at your side. What wrong had he ever done?"

He saw Jack Gregory convulsed with soundless laughter. Then he half rose and pointed an exultant arm at Macdonald.

"I was damned black until you saved me," he cried, and this time the sound that reached Macdonald was as faint as the ghost of an echo. "I'd forsworn myself to a girl that I got with a false marriage, and then I left her to take care of herself and her child. But I was killed by a worse man than I am, Macdonald, and that's why I laugh!"

Macdonald stood back from the table, sick at heart.

"What have I done, then?" he cried to them. "I've fought every man of you fairly, squarely, face to face! I took no advantage. I never struck a man that was down. I never shot a man that wasn't fighting back! I never harmed a man that asked for mercy. Why am I worse than you?"

But instead of answering, they fell into a hearty convulsion of that shadowy laughter, and Macdonald strode from the room. At the very threshold of the next apartment he was greeted by the delicate sweetness of flowers, and now he saw that they were banked everywhere about the room. There were flowers of every kind, little wild flowers and crimson roses and great smudges of violets. The air was alive with their fragrance. He could not decipher one scent from another, for all was a blended sweetness.

And with the fragrance went a profound silence. It was like that weighty quiet which lies in the high regions of the mountains, when no noise seemed strong enough to break it. For no matter how loud, the sound comes deadened upon the ear, and the thick silence rolls in swiftly behind it and drowns the echoes, as they come flocking from the distant peaks. Such was the quiet in that room, a bewildering and awful thing.

In the center of the apartment stood an open coffin on a flower-clad pedestal, and in that coffin lay the dead. The profile was clearly to be seen, and it was the face of Rory Moore — Rory Moore dead before he had been struck!

Rory Moore dead, and above him leaned the lady of the vision, still in her riding costume. Her lips trembled, and though no sound came from them, the tears streamed steadily down her face.

But that was not all Macdonald saw in that room of sorrow, for he made out that the face of the girl and the face of Rory Moore were wonderfully alike. They could not be more similar, save that what was drawn on a large and manly scale in Rory's dead face, was made small and exquisitely beautiful in the living face of the girl.

"It was not I!" cried Macdonald. "I swear to heaven that I have not touched him!"

At his voice she looked up. There was one glimpse for him of the horror and hatred in her eyes, and then with her raised eyes she shut out the sight of him.

And Macdonald wakened and found himself on his knees in the darkness of his room, with his arms stretched out before him, and his voice moaning vague words.

XI "The Note"

Instantly Macdonald hurried down to Sunset. He only paused to sweep his pack together before he was gone, and on the way he looked at the time. He noted with a shudder that it was half past two, the exact hour at which he had last left his chamber. Beyond a doubt a curse had fallen upon this house.

In the corral he roused the stallion with a word, and led him into the stable, and in the light of a lantern put on the saddle. While his swift fingers worked, he made up his mind. To leave the town would make it seem that he had lost his nerve at last, and that he dared not wait for the coming of Rory Moore. But let that be as it might. He must go nevertheless. For, if he met Rory Moore, nothing could keep him from killing the younger man, and kill Rory he must not. No, all the superstition in his strange soul urged him against it. He had received a warning, and that warning must be heeded.

Plunging into the darkness he headed away from the town, and he rode on until morning came. It was no sooner light than he camped by the way; by mid-morning his sleep was ended, and Sunset was rested; then he went on again. All that day he struck blindly ahead, and by nightfall he came into the heart of the mountains.

He had paid not the least heed to direction. He only knew that he was covering many miles, and that was sufficient. He went on from the second camp before the next day had well begun. By this time Rory Moore would have heard of his coming to the town, would have returned, found him gone, and would have published him abroad as a coward. But that was still a small thing in the mind of Macdonald. For the girl of his dreams was more to him now than all the rest of the living world. She had lived in his mind and in his very heart. She was never absent from him. And he found himself, a hundred times in the day, grown tense with waiting for her voice. And he found himself hurrying Sunset toward the rise of every hill in eagerness to see her coming.

It was just after he had camped to make coffee at noon and had gone on again that he found the place. He had come over a ridge, and journeying down to the sound of the waters he came suddenly upon the river up which he had ridden three times in his sleep.

There was no mistaking it. It was the very place. Yonder ran the swift brown waters, streaked with creamy foam. There hung the willow on the edge of the bank, with half of its roots exposed. And, above, the round hills tumbled away against the sky!

Macdonald covered his aching eyes with his hands. The devil had brought him at last to the road of his death. He had no more doubt of that than though he had seen it written across the sky in letters of gold. He had no more doubt of it than though a voice had whispered it at his ear.

With a groan he surrendered to that feeling of fate. He turned Sunset up the stream and rode slowly on. In a sort of mute agony he watched the happy head of Sunset tossing, with his sharp ears quivering forward. Ah, to be a mere joyous brute like the big horse, to be freed from all these tortures of the mind which went with manhood!

He passed among the hills and came again to the ridge. With a sick heart he looked down upon that landscape which he had three times seen in his dream — the bright sun falling — the spotting shadows from the trees and the far voices of the cattle. And who could struggle against such manifest destiny as this?

Riding down the slope he twisted over the undulating surface of the plain, and so he came at last to the place where that avenue of walnut trees should have been. But here he found, for the first time, a difference between the dream and the reality. For the trees were gone, nor was there any semblance of them standing on either side of the road, but only a few wretched shrubs here and there. He had passed down the road for a mile or more, when he saw a buggy approaching with an old man driving it. He hailed the driver and stopped him.

"Friend," said Macdonald, "I want to ask you a few questions about this country. Have you been living around here long?"

"Not more'n about fifty years," said the old man, laughing with some importance.

"And you've known this road all that time?"

"Yep."

"D' you mind telling me if there were ever walnut trees growing along the sides of it?"

The other started.

"How did you know that if you're a stranger in this here country, the way you say?"

But Macdonald rode to the side of the buggy and, leaning over, laid his hand on the shoulder of the other.

"In the name of God," he said solemnly, "tell me the truth! There *have* been walnut trees planted here?"

"There have!" gasped the other, overwhelmed by the question and the manner in which it was put to him.

"Then God have mercy on my soul!" groaned Macdonald, and spurred furiously down the road.

It was not long after this that he came upon the town itself, but he had hardly entered it before he began to recognize it, not as the thing he had seen in his dream — there was no silence here — but as a place where he had been before. Suddenly rounding a corner he came upon a blighting proof. For this was the town which he had left two days before. Fortune had led him in a circle. He had come back by a new approach, and yonder, straight before him, was the very hotel itself, big and towered like a castle. He looked closer at it, with all the freshness of the dream weighing upon him. Yes, this was the castle of his vision. It was only the town house of the Moore family.

He stretched out his arms and laughed in the sunshine. A thousand tons of dread seemed to have been removed from his mind. There were still other things to be explained. He must find where he had seen that row of walnut trees other than in the dream. He must find where he had seen the girl.

At least he was now startled out of that absent-mindedness which, as a rule, plagued him and closed his eyes to things which were most familiar around him. He would see whatever was to be seen. As for Rory Moore, let him take heed to himself, or one portion of that dream would at least come true.

He went again to the hotel, again he asked for a room, and again he was assigned to the same chamber. There needed no explanation of the frightened eyes which men turned upon him, as he crossed the lobby and went up the stairs. They knew he had come back to kill Rory Moore. Well, their knowledge was doubly right!

Once in that room where the dream had twice come to him, he looked sharply around him, and it was as though the scales had fallen from his eyes. He could see it all at a glance. Mystery? There was none at all! What he had half seen and left unnoted by his conscious mind, he was now keenly aware of, and here was all the substance of his dream.

Someone with no common touch had made those fading paintings which hung along the walls. There, a small sketch, was the narrow and rushing river streaking down from the ragged hills which rolled back against the sky. And here, too, was the sweeping bird's-eye view of the sunlit plain. But where was the girl?

He had only to turn to the opposite wall to see her, just as she had ridden into his dream, sitting lightly on the side saddle and riding around a curve down a long avenue of mighty walnut trees.

Here, then, had his dream gone out. But, as the first rush of relief left him, he was struck with a sharp little pang of grief. He had banished that dream and all that was in it. He had found the most simple of explanations. But what of the girl? By the fashion of that coat and the puffed shoulders, she was dead these many years, or else she had grown into middle age, something of her youth had died from her. She was dead, indeed, and he could never find her as he had seen her.

The door opened on the chambermaid with clean linen over her arm.

"Look here," said Macdonald to the old woman. "Have you ever known the girl in this picture?"

"Miss Mary Moore?" said the other. "Sure I knew her! Mind you, the man that painted that picture was her lover, and she died in a fall from that very same horse three days after that picture was painted. I mind it as well as if it was yesterday. I was a servant in this house then, and I've been here ever since!"

Macdonald dismissed her with a dollar bill and returned to his own gloomy thoughts. He had gone for two days in what he considered an exquisite torment. But now he began to wonder if the torment into which he was passing might not be worse after all. For there had lingered in his mind, all those hours, the hope that some day he would find her, just as she had been when she rode into his dream. And if all the terror of the dream were gone, all the beauty of it was gone, too.

There was a light rap at the door, and he bade the person enter. It was a dusty, barefoot boy, with a letter in his hand, and great frightened eyes fixed upon the face of Macdonald, as though the latter had been an evil spirit. He was gone the instant the big man took the envelope. Macdonald tore it open and found within it the shortest and the most eloquent of notes:

I am waiting for you, just in front of the blacksmith shop

Rory Moore

Methodically he tore the letter to bits. It was an old habit of his. Next, still out of force of habit, he took out his Colt and examined it from muzzle to the butt, polished by the years of use. Last of all he turned to the picture of Mary Moore. What he had seen in the dream was true enough. She was very like Rory. She might have posed as his sister.

XII "Not to Kill"

Like all events which grow in importance after
they happen, and which become a part of even
minor history, what happened that day was
remembered even to the most minute details.
And everyone of mature years in the town was
able to recall some part. At least they had seen
Macdonald issue from the hotel, dressed with
unusual care, a flaming red bandanna around
his throat, with the point hanging far down
between his shoulders, and a great sombrero
decorated with silver medallions upon his
head, and his boots shined until they were like
twin mirrors. One might have thought that he
was going to be the best man at a wedding,
the groom himself. But everyone knew that
he was going out to give battle and take a life,
or give his own. For the rumor had passed, as
swiftly as rumors do, through the length and
the breadth of the town that Rory Moore was
waiting in front of the blacksmith shop, and
that he had sent a message to the terrible
Macdonald.

So scores of eyes were watching as the big
man walked down the single street of the village. He had never seemed taller. He had never
seemed more sedate. He carried with him that

unconscious air of importance which goes with men who have seen or suffered much.

He paused at the corner, where the corral from the hotel bordered the street. There he leaned against the fence and called. And the big red stallion came running to the voice of his new master. A dozen men swore that they saw Macdonald pass his arms around the neck of the horse and put his head down beside the head of Sunset.

Then he went on again with as light a stride as ever. When the watchers thought of Rory Moore, their hearts shrank within them. For it seemed impossible that such a force as Macdonald could be stopped by any one man.

More than one hardy cowpuncher set his teeth at the thought and looked to his gun. If anything happened to Rory, it would take all the desperate nerve and skill of a Macdonald to get out of that town. For they had determined that, fair play or not, the time had come to finish this destroyer of men.

In the meantime Macdonald had passed the general merchandise store. He had come to the Perkins place, and there he paused to speak to an old Mexican beggar woman who came with a toothless whine to ask for money. They saw him take out a whole wad of rustling bills and drop it into her hand. The bills overflowed. She leaped upon them like an agile old beast of prey. When she straightened again, he was half a block away, and she poured out a shrill volley of blessings. Her borrowed English failed her, and to become truly eloquent she fell back upon the native Spanish and filled the air with it.

But her benefactor went on without a glance behind him.

"He's superstitious," said the beholders. "He's trying to get good luck for the meeting with Rory . . . and the devil take him and the old beggar!"

But now he had come in sight of the blacksmith shop. A cluster of men fell back. One or two lingered beside Rory Moore, begging him to the last minute not to throw away his life in vain. But he tore himself away from them and strode well out into the street, where the fierce white sun beat down upon him. Nearer drew Macdonald, and still his bearing was as casual and light as the bearing of any pleasure seeker.

"Macdonald!" cried Rory Moore suddenly in a wild, hoarse voice.

"Well, Rory," answered the smooth tones of the man-killer, "are you ready?"

"Yes, curse you, ready!"

"Then get your gun!"

And Rory, waiting for no second invitation, reached for the butt of his Colt. It was an odd contrast that lay between the two, as they faced one another, Rory crouched over and taut with eagerness, and the tall and careless form of Macdonald. And it seemed that the same carelessness was in the gesture with which he reached for his weapon. Yet such was the consummate speed of that motion that his gun was bare before the revolver of Rory Moore was out of the holster. His gun was bare, but there seemed to be some slip. Carelessness had been carried too far, for the gun flashed in his hand and dropped into the dust.

And Rory? His own weapon exploded. It knocked up a little fountain of dust at the feet of the giant. He fired again, and Macdonald collapsed backward, like a falling tower. The big sombrero dropped from his head, and he lay with his long red hair floating like blood across the dust.

And yet so incredible was it to all who watched that Macdonald should indeed have fallen, that there was a long pause before a yell of triumph rose from a hundred throats, and they closed around the big man, like wolves around a dead lion.

And when the wonder of it was faded a little, they picked up his gun, where it had fallen in the dust. They picked it up, they examined it, as one might have examined the sword of Achilles, after the arrow had struck his heel, and the venom had worked. They broke the gun open. But not a bullet fell out. And then they saw that it was empty, and that Macdonald had come so carelessly down that street not to kill, but to be killed!

It was a thunderstroke to the townsmen. It was as though the devil, being trailed into a corner, should turn into an angel and take flight for heaven!

"There ain't more'n one way of looking at it," said the sheriff, when he came into the town that evening on a foaming horse. "Macdonald didn't want to kill young Moore. But he had to face him, or be called a coward. And there you have it! He's been a hound all his life, but he's died like a hero!"

And that was the motive behind the monument which was built for Macdonald in that town. Although partly, perhaps, they simply wanted to identify themselves with that terrible and romantic figure.

But, while the turmoil of talk was sweeping up and down the town, two women were the first to think of striving to untangle the mysterious motives of Macdonald by something which he might have left behind him in his room — perhaps some letter to explain everything.

It was Mrs. Charles Moore who led the way, and with her went her niece, the sister of Rory. They found the room undisturbed, exactly as it had been when Macdonald left. But all they found was his rifle, his other revolver, his slicker, and his bed roll. There was nothing else except a few trifles. So they began to look around the room itself.

"And look yonder!" cried Mrs. Charles

Moore. "There's the place he dumped out the bullets from his gun . . . poor man . . . right underneath the picture of your poor dead Aunt Mary! And, child, child, how astonishingly you've grown to be like her! I've never seen such a likeness . . . just in the last year you've sprouted up and grown into the very shadow of her!"

"Oh," cried the girl, "how can you talk of such things!"

"What in the world . . . ," began the other.

"Here in this very room . . . and . . . here where he thought his last thoughts!"

"Heavens above, silly child, you're weeping for him!"

"But I saw him when they carried him in from the street," said Mary softly, with the tears running slowly down her face. "And even in death he seemed a greater man than any I'll ever see. And one great arm and hand was hanging down . . . I shall never forget!"

Partners

In the Golden Age of American fiction magazines, the decades between 1920 and 1940, many of the slick paper publications had a category known as the short short story. W. Somerset Maugham wrote several fine short shorts for *Cosmopolitan. Liberty Magazine* offered an annual prize of $1,000 above the standard payment for the best short short to appear in its pages, and there was one every week. In the 1930s Alan LeMay wrote numerous brilliant short shorts for *Collier's.* The short short at *The American Magazine* was called a "storiette" and in "Partners" in the issue dated January, 1938, Faust took up the challenge of this most demanding of all forms of fiction. During his lifetime Faust signed his own name to only ten stories. This was one of them.

Since the days of Anton Chekhov, who along with Edgar Allan Poe really pioneered the short short story, the structure has always been what Aristotle in the *Poetics* termed in Greek drama the *anagnorisis:* the shock of revelation. There is little time in a short short story for plot contrivances. The focus must be on one climatic moment in the life of a man or woman when all that went before and all that will follow, as in a sudden flash of summer lightning, stands painfully naked and starkly, quiveringly real. "Partners" records one such moment. What reaffirms that this is truly a *Western* story is to be found in the last line.

After September, no one takes Caldwell Pass because, although it is the shortest way west from Bisby, it is so high, so threatened with avalanches of snow and rubble. It has a bad name, also, for the northwest wind which, once it sights its way down the ravine, can blow frost even into the heart of a mountain sheep.

This was a December day, but Tucker was spending the early afternoon in Caldwell Pass, sitting behind a stone with his rifle across his knees. Once a bird shadow slid over him. As it moved beside the rock it touched Tucker with a finger of ice and forced him to shift his position. But he waited with the patience of a good hunter until he heard the footfall come down the pass toward him. Then he slid the rifle out into the crevice of the rock.

He waited till he could hear the man's breathing. Then he said, "Hands up, Jack!"

Huntingdon turned his back sharply. Seen from behind there was no trace of middle age about him. He looked as trim and powerful as a young athlete.

The echo in the ravine had fooled him. "Well, Harry?" he was saying.

"Keep your hands up. You'll get it straight through the back of the head if you don't," said Tucker to the big man.

He went out and laid the muzzle of the rifle against the base of Huntingdon's skull. He held the gun under his right arm and patted the clothes of his partner with his left hand. He found the fat lump which the wallet made, and drew it out. There was no weapon.

"All right, Jack. Turn around," he said.

Huntingdon turned. He was a bit white on each cheek, below the cheekbone. He kept on smiling.

"How much did you take?" asked Tucker, with his gun still threatening.

"I cleaned out the safe."

"You left me flat?"

"I left you the house, the office, and the good will," said Huntingdon.

"I had the house and the office and the good will before you came," said Tucker.

"You had a mortgage on the house; nobody ever came to your office; and where was the good will?" asked Huntingdon.

Tucker frowned. He had been telling himself that he was the mere executor of justice; but he might have known that the tongue of Huntingdon would turn this execution into murder.

"Kind of surprised to find me here, aren't you?" asked Tucker.

"I'm surprised . . . a little."

"Why, I've always seen through you," said Tucker. "I knew about you and Molly right from the first."

He laughed, without letting the laughter shake his body or the gun in his hands.

"You never knew a wrong thing between us," said Huntingdon.

"Maybe there wasn't anything wrong enough to get a divorce for," said Tucker.

"Molly's dead," said Huntingdon. "For God's sake, Harry . . . she's dead!"

Tucker licked his lips. It pleased him to see the pain in Huntingdon's eyes.

"There's more things than bedtime stories in the world," he persisted. "There's a sneaking into a man's life and taking his wife away from him. There's a holding together of eyes, when the hands don't touch. There's a way of just silently enduring the poor damned fool of a husband. There's . . . ! Oh, damn you! You rotten . . . !" He got out of breath and took a deep inhalation through his teeth. "I wish she could see you·here, with the stolen money!" said Tucker.

Huntingdon smiled. "I think you're going to kill me."

Tucker looked at that handsome face with a dreadful amazement; for he saw that his partner was not afraid.

"Before you put the bullet into me, though," said Huntingdon, "I want to speak about the money. I've worked for ten years for you.

Slaved. You called me a junior partner. But I was only a slave. At the end of that time, I had nothing."

"You know the kind of expenses . . . ," began Tucker.

"At the end of ten years," said Huntingdon, "I find eighteen hundred dollars in the safe, and I take it. It's the only way I'll ever get a share. I take the money and get out. I thought I was going ten thousand miles to have elbow-room between us. . . . But this way is about as good. It will put the greatest possible distance between us."

"Now, what in hell d'you mean by that?" asked Tucker.

"You couldn't understand."

"It's too high for me to understand? It's above me, maybe?" All at once Tucker screamed, "Take this, then! And this!"

He fired as he was shouting. And the rifle went crazy in his hands. It missed twice. The third bullet hit Huntingdon between the knee and the hip. He sank slowly to the ground. The blood came up in a welter of dark red. It soaked his trouser leg at once and began to trickle down over the rock.

"You're too high for me, are you?" yelled Tucker. "Well, what you think now . . . ? Another thing, damn you, and you listen hard to it. What you ever do with your life before you hooked up with me in the partnership? Just a bum. Just a rambling bum. Never did a thing. Isn't that true? Speak out!"

"It's true," said Huntingdon.

"Never a damn' bit of good to yourself or anybody else till you hooked up with me," said Tucker.

"That's true, also," said Huntingdon. He looked away from Tucker and smiled at the sky. "In a sense, I suppose, we needed each other; in a sense, perhaps we were ideal partners," he said.

Tucker began to laugh, and then a chill gust of wind stopped his breath, quickly, like a handstroke. It was not a mere breath of wind. It was the true northwester which had found the ravine and was sighting down it as down a gun barrel.

He withdrew himself from his passion and, looking about him, saw that the sun was about to set. It was more than time for him to start back home. In spite of his fleece-lined coat, his teeth would be chattering long before he got out of the pass. He turned with the rifle toward big Huntingdon. His face was blue with cold. Tucker had lifted the gun butt to his shoulder, but now he lowered it again.

"I've got to leave you, Jack," he said. "But it'll be thirty below in half an hour, with plenty of wind to drive the cold through you. You're going to have a few minutes to think things over, and then . . . you'll get sleepy!"

He saw Huntingdon's eyes widen; and then he was calm again.

"Good bye, then," said Huntingdon.

"Ah, to hell with you!" snarled Tucker.

He whirled, determined to run the entire distance down the pass in order to keep from freezing, but with his first springing step his feet shot from beneath him, because he had stepped in the blood that ran from Huntingdon. He came down heavily on his right knee, and heard the bone crunch like old wood.

For an instant the pain leaped out of the broken bone and ached behind his eyes; then he forgot all about it because he realized that he was about to die. The northwest wind pitched its song an octave higher, and right through the heavy, fleece-lined coat it laid its invisible hand on the naked flesh of Tucker.

Huntingdon's voice said, cheerfully, "If you finish me off now, and take my clothes, the warmth of them will do you less good than the warmth of my body. . . . But if we haul to the windward of that rock and lie down close together. . . . Sam Hillier comes through the pass tomorrow morning with his pack mules. We might last it out."

"Lie close together? You and me?" said Tucker, in a sort of horror. And then he saw that it was the only way.

Moving was bitterest agony, but both he and Huntingdon got to the shelter of the big rock, and the salvation from the wind was like a promise of heaven that they still might live. Tucker lay flat on his back, his teeth set with a scream working up higher and higher in his throat. The cut of the wind grew less and less. He opened his eyes and saw that Huntingdon was piling smaller rocks on each side of the boulder so that the icy eddyings of the gale might not get at them.

Afterward, Huntingdon lay down beside him, gathered him close.

"What chance is there?" asked Tucker. "What chance, Jack?"

"One in fifty," said Huntingdon. And then, as he felt the shudder pass through Tucker's body, he added, "Yes, or one in five. The thing to do is to keep on hoping, and talking."

"Ay, and we've things to talk about," said Tucker.

"We have," answered Huntingdon.

The warmth of Huntingdon's body began to strike through Tucker's clothes. He blessed God for it.

"But man, man," said Tucker, "what a fool you were to come up into Caldwell's Pass on a December day without a heavy coat! Take the fleece-lined thing off me and put it over us both. And hope, Jack. It's hope that keeps the heart warm!"

The Power of Prayer

It was time again for the annual Christmas number of *Western Story Magazine*. The magazine, founded in 1919, for some time now was published every Saturday rather than every Thursday. Faust was asked by Street & Smith in late 1922 to contribute two Christmas stories to magazines the company published, one to *Detective Story Magazine* — "A Christmas Encounter" (12/23/22) by Nicholas Silver — and the story that follows which he titled "The Power of Prayer." It appeared under the John Frederick byline in *Western Story Magazine* (12/23/22).

It is remarkable how often the word "prayer" appears in Faust's Western fiction — almost as often as the word "soul." Earlier that same year "Gun Gentlemen" by Max Brand had appeared in five parts in *Argosy/All-Story Weekly* (2/25/22–3/25/22) and later on in the decade Street & Smith's book publishing company would issue this serial as a novel under the same title, *Gun Gentlemen* (Chelsea House, 1928), but as by David Manning. Gerald Kern in "The Power of Prayer" embodies many of those same qualities of a figure found in several of Faust's Western stories, a gunman who is also a gentleman. Yet, beyond this apparent contradiction, Gerald's character has about it an element of the diabolical. Surely the figure of Shakespeare's Iago lingered in the shadows of Faust's imagination as he composed this tale, and perhaps no less that prototype of both Iago and Gerald Kern, the true and imperishable gentleman of darkness in the Book of Job.

I "When West Meets East"

One could not say that it was love of one's native country which brought Gerald home again. It would be more accurate to say that it was the only country where his presence did not create too much heat for comfort. In the past ten years, forty nations — no less — had been honored by the coming of Gerald and had felt themselves still more blessed, perhaps, by his departure unannounced. Into the history of forty nations he had written his name, and now he was come back to the land and the very region of his birth.

No matter if the police of Australia breathed deeply and ground their teeth at the thought of him; no matter if the sleuths of France spent spare hours pouring over photographs of that lean and handsome face, swearing to themselves that under any disguise he would now be recognized; no matter if an Arab sheik animated his cavalry by recounting the deeds of Gerald; no matter if a South American republic held up its million hands in thanksgiving that the firebrand had fallen upon another land; no matter were all these things and more, now that the ragged tops of the Rocky Mountains had swept past the train which bore him westward.

When he dismounted at a nameless town and drew a deep breath of the thin, pure, mountain air, he who had seen forty nations swore to himself that the land which bore him was the best of all.

He had been fourteen when he left the West. But sixteen years could by no means dim the memories of his childhood. For was not this the very land where he had learned to ride and to shoot? A picture of what he had been rushed upon his memory — a fire-eyed youngster with flaming red hair, riding anything on four feet on the range, fighting with hard-knuckled fists, man or boy, delving deep into the mysteries of guns, baffling his very brother with lies, the cunning depth of which were like the bottomless sea.

He smiled as he remembered. No one would know him now. The fire-red had altered to dark auburn. The gleam was banished from his eyes, saving on occasion! And the ragged urchin could never be seen in this dapper figure clad in whipcord riding breeches and mounted — oh, hardy gods of the Far West behold him! — in a flat English saddle.

But, for the once, an English saddle pleased him. Time was when he had made himself at home in a wild Tartar's saddle on a wild Tartar horse, emptying his carbine at the yelling pursuers — but that was another picture, and that was another day. For the present he was happier encased in a quiet and easy manner of soft-spoken gentility. It was the manner which this morning he had slipped into as another man slips into a coat. And for ten years, to do on the spur of the moment what the moment made him desire to do, had been religion with Gerald.

To be sure, when he came down to breakfast in that outfit and ate his bread and drank his coffee in the little dingy hotel dining room, people stared at him. But Gerald was not unaccustomed to being the cynosure of neighboring eyes.

Then he went forth to buy a horse, and the dealer, after a glance at those riding breeches, led forth a high-headed bay, with much profane commendation and a high price. But Gerald, in a voice as smooth as a hand running over silk, pointed out that the beast was bone-spavined and declined with thanks. And so he went on from horse to horse. But it seemed that his glance went through each beast like a sword of fire. One look, and he knew the worst that could be said of it. The horse dealer followed, sweating with discomfort, until Gerald pointed to a distant corral with a single dark-chestnut mare standing in it.

"That yonder," he said, "that one yonder, my friend, looks as though it might be for me."

The dealer glanced at the little English saddle which all this time Gerald carried over the crook of his arm.

"I'll saddle her for you in a minute," he said. "Yep. You picked the winner. I'd hate to see Sorrow go, but for a price I guess it could be fixed."

"Why is she called Sorrow?" said Gerald.

"Because she's got sad eyes," said the horse dealer and looked Gerald calmly in the face.

So the little English pad was placed on Sorrow, and she was led out, gentle-mannered as a lamb, until the rider dropped into his place. That jarring weight transformed Sorrow into a vivid semblance of dynamite exploding.

"She busted herself in sixteen directions all at once," said the horse dealer afterward. "And, when she went the sixteenth way, this fellow stopped follering. He sailed about a mile and landed on his head. I came over on the run. I sure thought his neck was broke. But he was on his feet before I got to him. And the light of fighting fire was in his eye. He up and jumped onto that mare in no time. Well, she sunfished and she bucked and she reared, and did she shake him this time? Not a bit of it! He stuck like a cactus bur. And after she'd tried her last trick, she realized she had an unbeatable master, and she quieted down like a pet kitten. He rode her away as if she had been raised by him and ridden by him for years."

Which was the truth. Sorrow stepped high and pretty, albeit obediently, back to the hotel. Here Gerald left her at the hitch rack while he threaded his way through the group of loungers on the porch and went in to freshen his appearance. In a few minutes he came downstairs whistling. On the front verandah he spoke to the first comer, and the first comer was Harkey, the big blacksmith.

"What is there to see around here?" he asked of Harkey. "Can you tell me of any points of interest?"

Harkey stared at him, and all he could see was the whipcord riding trousers and the tailor-made cigarette which drawled from a corner of Gerald's mouth.

"I dunno," said Harkey. "There ain't nothing that I've seen around here that would match up with you as a point of interest!"

And he laughed heartily at his good jest, and along the verandah the loungers took up the laughter in a long chorus.

"My friend," said Gerald gently, "you seem to me to be a trifle impertinent."

"The devil I do," said Harkey.

"But no doubt," said Gerald, "you can explain."

"Me?" said Harkey, and he balled his sooty fists.

"Yes," said Gerald, "you."

"I'll see you and ten of your kind in hell first," said Harkey.

"My dear fellow," said Gerald, "how terribly violent you are!"

And with that he stepped six inches forward with his left foot and struck with his left hand, swift as an arrow off the string, deadly as a barbed spear driven home. Vain were those thick muscles which cushioned the base of Harkey's jaw. The knuckles bit through them to the bone, and the shock, hammer-like, jarred his brain. The great knees of Harkey bent under him, benumbed. He slipped inert to the ground, his back against a supporting pillar, and Gerald turned to the rest.

"I have been asking," he said, "for the points of interest around the town. Can any of you tell me?"

They looked upon the fallen body of Harkey; they stared into the dead eyes of the giant; they regarded his sagging jaw; and they were inspired to speak. Yonder among the mountains, due north and a scant fifty miles away, where the Culver River had gouged for itself a trench, gold had been found, they said, not many months before. And in the town of Culver there would be points of interest, they said. Yes, there would be many points of interest for one who wished to see the West.

When his back was turned, they smiled to one another. No doubt this fellow was a man of some mark. There lay the body of Harkey, now showing the first quivering signs of life. And yonder was he of the whipcord riding breeches mounted upon famous Sorrow, famous Sorrow now dancing down the road with her first-found master. But in spite of these things, what would happen when Gerald reached Culver City, where the great men of the West were gathered? He might ride a horse as well as the next man. He might crush the slow-handed blacksmith with one cunning blow. But what would be his ventures among those men of might, those deadly warriors who fairly thought a gun out of the holsters and smote an enemy with an inescapable lightning flash?

Such were the thoughts of the wise men as they shifted their quids and rolled fresh cigarettes, but among them all there was not one guessed the truth, that the West was meeting the West as Greek meets Greek.

Even wiser men than they might have been baffled, seeing those daintily tailored trousers, those shop-made cigarettes each neatly monogrammed, and the high-stirruped, slippery saddle in which he sat. For who could have told that the same West which had fathered them in overalls and chaps and bandannas had fathered this returned prodigal also?

II "Gerald Goes to Culver City"

But Gerald knew. Ah, yes, Gerald knew, and the knowledge was as sweet to him as is the sight of a marked card to an expert gambler. Why had he roamed so long away from them? This, after all, was his country, in which he was to carve his destiny. Let Paris keep her laughing boulevards and Monte Carlo the blueness of her sea — these raw-headed mountains, these hard-handed men, spelled home to Gerald. What mattered it if, in his wallet, there was a scant fifty dollars, his all of worldly wealth, so long as there was a gun at his hip, smoke in his nostrils, and beneath him a horse that went as sweetly as a song?

Up the valley he wound and, topping the first range, he looked down on a pitching sea of peaks. Somewhere among them was gold. Yes, due north from him he would find gold, and wherever there was gold there was electric excitement thrilling in the air. Wherever there was gold, there were sure to be lovely women with clever tongues and brave men with hands of iron and other men with wits as keen as the glimmering edge of a Damascus blade. That was no meaningless simile to one who had learned saber play — and used it!

It was the dull time of the evening when he came in view of Culver City. The double-jacks and the single-jacks were no longer ringing in the valley. But up the valley road the teamster was still cursing his twelve mules to a faster walk, and up the valley road other men were coming on horseback or in old caravan wagons, a steady stream typical of that which flowed into Culver City all day and every day and never flowed out again. What became of them, then, since the city never grew beyond a certain size? That was an easy riddle. Superfluous life was needed. It was needed to be ground away in the mines which pock-marked with pools of shadow the valley here and there; it was needed still more to feed into the mill which ground out pleasure in the gaming halls and the dance halls in Culver City.

Gerald was new to mining camps. What he knew of the West was the West of the cow country, the boundless cattle ranges. But, with knowing one bit of the West, all the rest lies beyond an open door at the most. He who has burned the back of his neck in the sun and roped his cow and ridden out his blizzard, can claim knowledge of the open sesame which unlocks a thousand mysteries. So Gerald looked down upon the new scene with the feeling that he almost knew the men whom he would find strolling through the long, crooked street of Culver City.

And know them he did, though not out of his

knowledge of the West. He had seen all their faces before. He had seen them gather around the standard of that delightful revolution which had budded south of Panama and almost made him a famous man. He had seen them in politer garb around the gaming tables of the full forty nations. He had seen them hither and yon gathering like bees around honey wherever danger and hope went hand in hand.

But of course he had never seen one of them before. He was as safe under his true name in this little town as though he wore the most complicated alias and barbered disguise in Paris. And, ah, what a joy it was to be able to ride with eyes straightforward and no fear of who might come beside him or who from behind. Here in his own country, his home country, he was safe at last. He watched the yellow lights begin to burn out from the hollow as the evening thickened. And not a face on which those lights were now shining knew any ill of him!

He began to breathe more freely. He began to raise his head. Why not start life all anew? Hither and yon and here and there he had felt that life had pursued him through the world, and he had had no chance to settle down to labor and honesty. Now, however, he was quite free from controlling circumstance. He could carve his own destiny.

What if his capital were only honest resolution plus just a trifle more of capital than fifty dollars? Should he not spend one night at the gaming tables before he entered the sphere of the law-abiding, the law-reverent?

Sorrow had been going smoothly down the slope all this while. None like Sorrow to pick a way among the boulders, none like Sorrow to come through the rough going with never a shock and never a jar for her rider. And that day the mare had traveled farther into the land of knowledge than her rider had traveled into the mountains. She had learned that a human voice may be pleasantly low and steady; she had learned that a bit may be a helpful guide and not a torture instrument to tear her mouth; she had learned, for the mind of a man comes down the firm rein and telegraphs its thought into the brain of a horse. It was all very wonderful and all very strange.

A door slammed nearby. In the morning Sorrow would have leaped to the side first and turned to look afterward. But now she merely pricked her short, sharp ears. It was a girl singing in the door of a cabin, with the soft, yellow light of a lantern curving over arms which were bare to the elbow and glowing in her hair. Sorrow stopped short. In the old days of colthood and pasture and carelessness before she began the long battle against man, there had been even such a girl who would come to the pasture bars with a whistle which meant apples were waiting.

As for Gerald, he came on the view of the girl at that very moment when his thought was turning back toward the gaming tables and the necessary capital with which one might launch forth on a career of honesty.

"Good evening," he called.

"Hello," said the girl. "Tommy dear, is that you?"

Gerald frowned. Who was "Tommy dear?" At any rate, though at that moment she moved so that the light struck clearly along her profile, he decided that he did not wish to linger.

"No," he said dryly, "this is not Tommy."

A touch on the reins, and Sorrow fled swiftly down the valley toward the place where the lights thickened, and from which the noise was drifting up. So he came into Culver City at a gallop, with a singular anger filling him, a singular desire to find Tommy and discover what manner of man he might be.

In the meantime, he must have a room. He went to that strange and staggering building known as the hotel. In the barn behind it he put up Sorrow in a commodious stall and saw that she was well fed. Then he entered the hotel itself.

He had quite forgotten that his garb was not the ordinary costume for Culver City and its mines. The minute he stepped into the flare of the lanterns which lighted the lobby of the hotel, he was greeted with a murmur and then a half-stifled guffaw which warned him that he was an outlander to these fellows. And Gerald paused and looked about him.

Ordinarily, he would have passed on as though he were deaf. But now his mind was filled with the memory of those rounded arms of the girl at the cabin door, and how the lights had glimmered softly about her lips and chin, and how she had smiled as she called to him. Who was "Tommy dear?"

It made Gerald very angry. So he stopped just inside the door of the hotel and looked about him, letting his glance rest on every face, one by one. And every face was nothing to him but a blur, so great was his anger and so sharply was he still seeing the girl at the cabin door. He drew out a cigarette case. It was solidest gold. And a jeweler in Vienna had done the chasing which covered it. A millionaire had bought it for a huge sum. And the millionaire had given the case to Gerald for the sake of a little story which Gerald told on an evening — a little story hardly ten words long. From that gleaming case he extracted his monogrammed cigarette. He lighted his smoke. And then he shut the case and bestowed it in his coat pocket once more, while the laughter which had been spreading from a murmur to a chuckle, suddenly burst out in a roar from one man's throat.

It was Red Charlie. He stood in the center of the room. Above his head was the circular platform around which the four lanterns hung

— a platform some three or four feet wide and suspended by a single wire from the ceiling above. But Red Charlie laughed almost alone. The others preferred to swallow the major portion of their mirth for there was that about the dapper stranger which discouraged insult. The slow and methodical way in which he had looked from face to face, for instance, had been a point worth noting.

But Charlie could afford laughter. He had made his strike a week before, had sold his mine three days later, and he was now in the fourth stage of growing mellow. The more he laughed, the more heavy was the silence which spread through the room. And suddenly the laughter of Charlie went out, for there is a physical force in silence. It presses in upon the mind. And Charlie pulled himself together. The fumes of liquor were swept from his brain. He became cold sober in a trice, facing the slender figure of Gerald.

"I love a good joke," said the quiet voice of Gerald. "Won't someone tell me the point?"

There was no reply.

"I love a good joke," repeated Gerald. "And you, my friend, were laughing very loudly."

It was too pointed for escape. Red Charlie swelled himself to anger.

"There's only one point in sight," he said. "And you're it, stranger."

"Really?" said Gerald. "Then I'm sorry to say that, much as I enjoy a good jest, I detest being laughed at. But of course you are sorry for the slip?"

"Sorry?" said Red Charlie.

He blinked at the stranger and then grasped the butt of a gun. Had a life of labor been spent in vain? Had he not built a sufficient reputation? Was he to be challenged by every chance tenderfoot?

"Why, damn your eyes," exploded Charlie and whipped out his weapon.

Be it said for Charlie that he intended only to splinter the floor with his bullets so that he and his friends might enjoy the exquisite pleasure of seeing the stranger hop about for safety which existed only outside the door. In all his battles it could never be said that Charlie had turned a gun upon an unarmed man.

But now a weapon was conjured into the hand of the stranger. It winked out into view. It exploded. At the same instant the taut wire which held the platform and the lanterns snapped with a twanging sound. Down rushed platform and all and crashed upon the head of Red Charlie. Down went Charlie in a terrible mass of wreckage.

And Gerald walked on to write his name in the register. His back was turned when the platform was raised and Charlie was lifted to his feet. But as for Charlie, all thought of battle had left him. Mild and chastened of spirit, he stole softly through the door.

III "Tommy Dear"

Two things were pointed out afterward — first, that the oddly attired stranger who wrote the name of Gerald Kern on the register had not lingered to enjoy the comments of the bystanders; and, second, it was noted that the wire which he had cut with his bullet was no more than a glimmering ray of light, though he had severed it with a snap shot from the hip.

The second observation carried with it many corollaries. For instance, it was made plain that this dexterous gunfighter would maintain his personal dignity at all costs, but it was equally apparent that he did not wish to shed human blood. Otherwise, he would have made no scruple of shooting through the head a man who had already drawn a weapon. Furthermore, he had quelled a bully and done it in a fashion which would furnish Culver City with an undying jest, and Culver City appreciated a joke.

And when Gerald came downstairs that evening he found that the town was ready to receive him with open arms. Which developed this difficulty, that Gerald was by no means ready to be embraced. He kept the honest citizens of Culver City at arm's length. And so he came eventually to the gaming hall of Canton Douglas. A long residence in the Orient and an ability to chatter with the Chinese coolies accounted for the nickname. It might also have been held to account for the gaming passion in Douglas.

But he was famous for the honesty of his policy even more than for his love of chance. Gerald, the moment he stepped inside the doors of the place, recognized that he was in the domain of a gamester of the first magnitude. And he looked about him with a hungry eye.

Here was all that he could wish for. One glance assured him that the place was square. A second glance told him that the stakes were running mountain high, for these gamblers had dug their gold raw out of the ground, and they were willing to throw it away as though it were so much dirt. Gerald saw a thousand dollars won on the turn of a card and then turned his back resolutely on the place and faced the open door through which new patrons were streaming. The good resolve was still strong as iron in him. The clean life and the free life still beckoned him on! And, with a heart which rose high with the sense of his virtue, he had almost reached the door when he heard some one calling from the side.

"Hello, Tommy!" said the voice. "Here's your place. Better luck tonight!"

Gerald turned to see what this Tommy

might be, and he found a fellow in the late twenties, tall, strong, handsome, a veritable ideal of all that a man should be in outward appearance. But there was a promise of something more than mere good looks in him. There was a steadiness in his blue eyes that Gerald liked, and he had the frank and ready smile of one who has nothing to conceal from the world.

He knew in a thrice that this was the "Tommy dear" of the girl. And Gerald paused — paused to take out his cigarette case and begin another smoke. In reality, he was lingering to watch the other man more closely. And how could he linger so near without being invited?

"We need five to make up a good game," the dealer for Canton Douglas was saying. "Where's a fifth? You, Alex? Sit in, Hamilton? Then what about you, stranger?"

Four faces turned suddenly upon Gerald.

After all, he said to himself, he would make a point of not winning. He would make a point of rising from the table with exactly the same amount with which he sat down.

"I'll be very happy to sit in," said Gerald. He paused behind his chair. "My name is Kern, gentlemen," he said.

They blundered to their feet, gave their names, shook hands with him; as he touched each hand he knew by the awe in their eyes that they had heard the tale of the breaking of the wire in the hotel. Nay, they had heard even more, for the news of the riding of Sorrow and the encounter with Harkey had followed him as the wake follows the ship. After all, Harkey was a known man for the weight of his fists, and scientific boxing seems always miraculous to the uninitiated.

So Gerald sat down facing Tommy Vance, and the game began. As for the cards and the game itself, Gerald gave them only a tithe of his attention. They were younglings, these fellows. Not in years to be sure, but their experience compared with his was as that of the newborn babe to the seer of three score and ten. Even Canton Douglas's dealer was a child. In the course of three hands, Gerald knew them all. In the course of six hands, he could begin to tell within a shade of the truth what each man held, and automatically he regulated his betting in accordance. In spite of himself, he was winning, and twice he had to throw money away on worthless hands to keep his stack of chips down to modest pro-portions.

In the meantime, he was studying Tommy Vance. And what barbed every glance and every thought he gave to Tommy was the picture of the girl in the cabin door. It was odd how closely she lingered in his mind. The ring of her voice seemed always just around the corner in his memory. Through the shadow on her face, he still looked back to her smile. And why under heaven, he asked himself, did he dwell so much on her? There had been other women in the past ten years. There had been a score of them, and not one had really mattered. But when he paused on that dark hillside, it seemed that the door of his soul had been open and the girl had stepped inside.

So he watched every move of Tommy Vance, for every move of a man at a poker game means something. What better test of a man's generosity or steady nerve or careless good nature or venomous malice or envy or wild courage? And the more he saw of Tommy the more good there was in him, and the more dread grew like the falling of a shadow in Gerald.

Men who have seen much evil, and stained their hands with it, are still more sensitive to all that is good. They scent it afar. And all that Gerald saw of big Tom Vance was truest steel. He gambled like a boy playing tag, whole-heartedly, carelessly. When the strong cards were in his hand, how could he keep the mischievous light out of his blue eyes? And yet when his hand was strongest and one of the five had been driven to the wall, Gerald saw him push up the betting and then lay down his cards.

It was a small thing, but it meant much in the eyes of Gerald. He prided himself on his manner and his courtesy, but here was a gentleman by the grace of heaven, and by contrast Gerald felt small and low indeed!

Then Tommy Vance pushed back his chair.

"I've dropped enough to make it square for me to draw out, fellows?" he asked.

"You're not leaving, Tommy?" asked the dealer earnestly. "If you go, the snap is out of the game."

"There's another game for Tommy," and a hard-handed miner chuckled on Gerald's right. "She's waiting for you now, I guess. Is that right, Tommy?"

And Tommy flushed to the eyes, then laughed with a frankness and a happiness that sent a pang of pain through the heart of Gerald.

"She's waiting, Lord bless her," he said.

"Then hurry," said the dealer, "before another fellow steps in and takes up her time."

"Her time?" said Tommy, throwing up his head. "Her time? Boys, there ain't another like her. She's truer than steel and better than gold. She's. . . ."

He checked himself as though realizing that this was no place for pouring forth encomiums on the lady of his heart.

"This breaks up the game, and I'm leaving," said Gerald, rising in turn.

"Are you going up the hill?" said Tommy Vance eagerly.

"I'll walk a step or two with you," said Gerald.

They walked out together into the night, and as they passed down the hall Gerald felt many eyes drawn after him. Yes, it was very plain that all Culver City had heard of his adventures. But now they were out under the stars. Not even the stars which burn low over the wide horizon of the Sahara seemed as bright to Gerald as this heaven above his home mountains.

"Now that we're out here alone," said Vance, "I don't mind telling you what everybody else in Culver City is thinking . . . that was pretty neat the way you handled Red Charlie. That hound has been barking up every tree that held a fight in it. The town will be a pile quieter now that he's gone. Only, how in the name of the devil did you have the nerve to take a chance with that wire?"

"How in the same name," answered Gerald quietly, "were you induced to lay down that hand of yours which must have been a full house at least . . . that hand you bet on up to fifty dollars and then laid down to the fellow on my right?"

"Ah?" laughed Tommy Vance. "You knew that? Well, you must be able to look through the backs of the cards. It was a full house, right enough. Three queens on a pair of nines. It looked like money in the bank. But I saw that I'd break poor old Hampton. And that would have spoiled his fun for the evening."

"You're rich in happiness, then," said Gerald. "A good time for every one when you're so happy yourself, eh?"

"Yes," and Tom Vance nodded. "I feel as though my hands were full of gold . . . a treasure that can't be exhausted. And . . . well, I won't tire you out talking about a girl you've never seen! But Jack Parker brought her into the talk, you know," he apologized.

"I like to hear you," said Gerald. "It's an old story, perhaps. But what interests me is that every fellow always feels that he is writing chapter one of a new book. I remember hearing a man who was about to marry for the third time. By the Lord, he was as enthusiastic as you. It's the eternal illusion, I suppose. A man cannot help thinking, when he's in love, that a woman will be true and faithful . . . pure as the snow, true as steel. That's the way of it." And he chuckled softly.

It was entirely a forced laugh, and from the corner of his eye he was studying the effect of his talk upon Tommy Vance. He was studying him as the scientist studies the insect and its wriggling under the prick of the needle and the acid. And certainly Tommy Vance was hard hit. By his scowl and the outthrust of his lower jaw, Gerald gathered that his companion would have fought sooner than submit to such observations as these had they been made in other than the most casual and good-natured manner.

"You sort of figure," said Tommy Vance, "that women are pretty apt to . . . pretty apt to. . . ."

He was stuck for words.

"I hate to generalize on such a subject," said Gerald. "Every idiot talks wisely about women. But a man in love is a blind man. He wakens sometimes in a short period. Sometimes he stays blind until he dies. But I never see a pretty girl that I don't think of the spider, so full of wiles . . . and such instinctive wiles. She can't help smiling in a certain way which you and I both know. And that smile is like dynamite. It's a destructive force. Am I not right, Vance?"

So saying, he clapped his companion lightly on the shoulder, and Vance turned a wan smile upon him. It was delightful to be treated so familiarly by one who had so lately made himself a hero in the town. But still the brow of Tommy was clouded.

"Maybe there's something in what you say," he admitted. "But still, as far as Kate Maddern is concerned, I'd swear. . . ."

His voice stumbled away to nothing.

"Your lady?" said Gerald gaily, forcing his casual tone with the most perfect artistry. "Of course she's the exception. She would be true to you if there were an ocean and ten years between you!"

But here Tommy Vance came to an abrupt halt and faced Gerald, and the latter knew, with a leaping heart, that he was succeeding better than he had ever dreamed he could.

IV "Vance Makes a Bet"

Look here" said Vance, "of course I know you're talking about womenfolk in general, but every time you speak like that I keep seeing Kate's face, and it's uncomfortable."

Oh, jealous heart of a lover! Masked by the black of night, Gerald smiled with satisfaction. How fast the fish was rising to the bait!

"As I said before," said Gerald, "I haven't her in mind at all. She's all that you dream of her, of course."

"That's just talk . . . just words," said Tommy Vance. "Between you and me, you think she's most apt to be like the rest."

"If you wish to pin me down. . . ."

"Kern," said Vance, "if I was to go away tonight and never come back for twenty years, she'd still be waiting for me!"

"My dear fellow!"

"Well?"

"If you actually failed to keep your appointment with her?"

"Actually that."

"Well," said Gerald carelessly, "putting all due respect to your lady to the side so that we may speak freely. . . ."

"Go ahead," said Tommy Vance.

"Well, then, speaking on the basis of what I've seen and heard, I'd venture that if you go away tonight and don't come back for ten days. . . ."

"Well?" exclaimed Tommy.

"When you came back, you'd find a cold reception, Tommy."

"I could explain everything in five seconds."

"Suppose she'd grown lonely in the meantime? If she's a pretty girl and the town's full of young fellows with nothing to do in the evening . . . you understand, Vance."

There was a groan from Vance as the iron of doubt entered his spirit.

"It makes me sort of sick," he murmured. "How do I know what she'd do? But no, she'd never look at another gent!"

"How long have you been engaged?" asked Gerald.

"Oh, about a month."

"Have you been away from her for more than twelve hours during that time?"

"No," admitted Tommy reluctantly.

"My dear fellow, then you know that you're talking simply from guesswork."

Tommy was quiet, breathing hard. At length he said: "If she was to draw away from me simply because I missed seeing her one night and was away for ten days, why, I'd never speak to her again. I'd never want to see her again!"

But Gerald laughed.

"That's what they usually say," he declared. "But after the smoke has cleared away, they settle back to happiness again. They wear a scar, but they try to forget. They wish themselves back into a blind state. And so they marry. Ten years later they begin to remember. They hearken back to the old wounds, and then comes the crash! That's what wrecks a home. . . ."

He broke off and changed his tone before he went on: "But of course no man dares to test a woman before he makes her his wife. He tests a horse before he buys it; he tests gold before he mines for it; but he doesn't get a proof in the most important question of all! Pure blindness, Tom Vance!"

"Suppose . . . ," groaned Tommy Vance, his head lowered. He did not finish his sentence. He did not need to, for Gerald could tell the wretched suspicion which was beginning to grow in his companion.

"But you see there's never a chance for it," said Gerald. "There's a small, prophetic voice in a man which tells him that he dare not make the try. He knows well enough that, if the girl is ready to marry, she'll marry someone else, if she doesn't marry him. It's the home-making instinct in her that's forcing her ahead. That's all as clear as daylight, I think."

"Good Lord!" groaned Tommy. "Suppose I should be wrong!"

"Come, come," said Gerald. "I didn't mean

that you should take me seriously. I was merely talking about girls in general."

"I wish I'd never heard you speak," said Tommy bitterly.

"You'll forget what I've said by tomorrow . . . by the time she's smiled at you twice," said Gerald.

"Not if I live a hundred years," said Tommy. "And why not do it? As you say we test gold before we dig for it . . . and only ten days!"

He rubbed his hand across his forehead.

"You won't do it," said Gerald. "When it comes to the pinch, you won t be able to get away."

"What makes you so sure?" asked Tommy in anger.

He was boy enough to be furious at the thought that any one could see through him.

"Why, as I said before," went on Gerald, fighting hard to retain his calmness and keep his voice from showing unmistakable signs of his excitement, "as I said before, there's something inside of you which keeps whispering that I'm right!"

"By the Lord," groaned Tommy, "I won't admit it."

"No, like the rest you'll close your eyes to it."

"But if at the end of ten days. . . ."

"That's the point. If at the end of ten days, you came back and found her dancing with another man, smiling for him, laughing for him, working hard to make him happy, why. . . ."

"I'd kill him!" breathed Tommy Vance.

"Of course you would," said Gerald. "And that's another reason you must not go away. It might lead to a manslaughter."

Tommy tore open his shirt at the throat as though he were strangling, and yet the wind was humming down the valley, and the night air was chill and piercing. It was late November, and winter was already on the upper mountains, covering them with white hoods.

"You're so cussed sure!" said Tommy Vance.

"Of course."

"What gives you the right to talk so free and easy?"

"I'd wager a thousand dollars on it," said Gerald.

"The devil you would!"

"I'm not asking you to take up the bet," tempted Gerald.

"I could cover that amount."

"But a thousand dollars and a girl is a good deal to put up."

"Kern, I'll make the bet!"

"Have you lost your wits, Tom Vance?"

It was too wonderfully good to be true, but now he must drive the young fellow so far that he could not draw back.

"I mean every word of it," Tom said.

"I don't believe it! Think of what will go on in the girl's head, Tom. She's waiting for you now. She'd worry a good deal if she didn't hear from you till the morning and then got only a little bit of a note:

Dear Kate:
Have to be away on business. No time to explain. Back in ten days.
                    Tom

"A note like that, my boy, would make her wild with anger. A girl doesn't like to be treated lightly."

"But I," said Tommy Vance, "am going to send her just such a note."

"Tush! That's mere bravado even from you."

"Kern, is my word good for my money?"

"Good as gold."

"Then I'm gone tonight, and when I come back in ten days if she's . . . she's as much as cold to me, you win one thousand dollars!"

He turned away. Gerald caught him by the shoulder.

"Tom," he said, "I'm not going to let you do this. I'd feel the burden of the responsibility. And mind you, my friend, if the girl is not as strong as you think she is, and as constant, it is simply the working of Mother Nature in her. Will you try to see that?"

"I've come to my conclusion, Kern, let me go!"

"It's final?"

"Absolutely!"

"Ten whole days?"

"Ten whole days!"

"With never a word to her during all that time?"

"With never a word to her during all that time!"

The hand of Gerald dropped away. He stepped back with an almost solemn feeling of wonder passing over that crafty brain of his. How mysterious was the power of words which could enter the brain and so pervert the good sense of a man as the sense of Tommy Vance had been changed by his subtle suggestions!

"Well," said he when he could control his voice, "you're a brave fellow, Tom Vance!"

"Good night!" snapped Tommy over his shoulder.

"And good luck!" sang out Gerald.

He watched his late companion melt into the shadows, and then Gerald turned to saunter on his way. It was all like the working of a miracle. Without the lifting of his hand he had driven from Culver City the only man who stood between him and a pleasant visit with lovely Kate Maddern.

No matter if she were already engaged to another man. One curt note, and then ten days of silence could do much. Oh, it could do very much. Wounded pride was an excellent sedative for the most vital pangs of love. And silence and the leaden passing of time would help. Ten days to a lover were the ten eternities of another person.

Would it be very odd if she came to pay some attention to a stranger who was not altogether ungracious, whose manners were easy, whose voice was gentle, who could tell her many tales of many lands, and the story of whose manhood was even now ringing through Culver Valley — if such a man as this were near while Kate Maddern struggled with grief and pride and angry pique, would there not be a chance to win a thousand dollars from Tom Vance — and something more?

V "The Campaign Begins"

He went lazily on up the slope of the mountain. Behind him the town was wakening to a wilder life. And, staring back, he could see a thickening stream which poured in under the great light in front of Canton Douglas's place.

Yes, it would be very pleasant to sit at one of those tables and mine the gold out of the pockets of the men who were there with their wealth. But a game even more exciting was ahead of him. He turned up the hill again, walking lightly and swiftly now. Yonder was the cabin, with the door open and a spurt of yellow lamplight over the threshold and dripping down half a dozen stone steps.

He arrived at the path and turned up it, and in a moment she came whipping through the door and down the steps with a cloak flying behind her shoulders.

"Tommy, Tommy dear!" she was calling as she came dancing to him. Her arms flashed around his neck. She had kissed him twice before she realized her mistake. And then horror made her too numb to flee. She merely gasped and shrank away from him.

"I beg your pardon," said Gerald. "This is the

second time I've been mistaken for 'Tommy dear.' Do I look so much like him in the darkness?"

"What have I done!" breathed poor Kate.

She went up the steps backward, keeping her face to him as though she feared that he would spring in pursuit the moment she turned her back. But at the top step, near the door of the cabin, she paused.

"Who are you?" she queried from this post of vantage.

"My name is Gerald Kern," he said.

"Have you come to see Dad?"

"No."

"Are you one of the men from the next cabin?"

"No."

"Well?" inquired Kate tentatively.

"I came to see you," said Gerald.

"You came to see me? I don't remember. . . ."

"Ever meeting me?"

"Have I?"

"Never! So here I am, if you don't mind."

She hesitated. It was plain that she was interested. It was also plain that she was a little alarmed.

"I came down the hill this afternoon," he went on. "Rather, it was in the dark of the twilight, and some one called from the door of the cabin to 'Tommy dear.' "

"I'm so ashamed!" said Kate Maddern.

"You needn't be. It was very pleasant. It

brought me back up this mortal hill in the hope that you might let me talk to you for five minutes. To you and your father, you know."

"Oh, to me and to Dad."

There was a hint of laughter in her voice which told him that she understood well enough.

"I didn't know anyone who'd introduce me, you see."

"I think you manage very nicely all by yourself," said Kate Maddern.

"Thank you."

"You are just new to Culver City?"

"Yes. All new this evening."

"But you haven't come to dig gold . . . in such clothes as those."

"I'm only looking at the country, you know."

"And you don't know a single man here?"

"Only one I met at Canton Douglas's place."

"That terrible place! Who was it?"

"His name was Vance."

"Why, that's Tommy!"

"Your Tommy?"

"Of course! "

"Lord bless us!" said Gerald. "If I had known that it was he, I should never have let him go."

"Go where?"

"He's off to find a mine . . . or prospect a new ledge, I think."

"He left tonight?"

There was bewilderment and grief in her voice.

"Yes. I'm so sorry that I bring bad news. Shall I go back to find him?"

"Will you?"

"Of course. If I had guessed that he was your Tommy, I should have tried to dissuade him."

He turned away.

"Come back!" she called.

He faced her again.

"Don't go another step! I . . . I mustn't pursue him, you know."

"Just as you wish," he answered.

"But what a strange thing for Tommy Vance to do!"

"Wasn't it?"

"And to start prospecting in the middle of night. . . ."

"Very odd, of course. But all prospectors are apt to do queer things, aren't they?"

"Without saying a word to me about it!" And she stamped her foot.

"Hello?" called a voice beyond the cabin, and then a man turned the corner of the shack.

"Dad!"

"Well, honey?"

"What do you think of Tommy?"

"The same as ever. What do you think?"

"I think he's queer . . . very queer!"

"Trouble with him?"

"Dad, he was to come to see me tonight. It was extra specially important."

"And he didn't come?"

"He left town!"

"Terrible!" murmured her father and laughed.

"Dad, he's gone prospecting. Without a word to me."

"Leave Tom alone. He's a good boy. Hello, there!"

He had come gradually forward, and now he caught sight of Gerald, a dim form among the shadows.

"That's the man who has just told me about Tom."

"H'm!" growled Maddern. "Did Tommy ask you to bring us the news?" he asked of Gerald.

"No, Mr. Maddern."

"You know me, do you?"

"I know your name."

"Well, sir, you might have let Tom talk for himself."

"It was quite by accident that I told your daughter," he said.

"I don't believe it," said Maddern. "A pretty girl hears more bad news about young men from other young men than an editor of a paper. Oh, I was young, and I know how it goes. It was by accident you told her, eh?"

"Dad, you mustn't talk like that!"

"You don't need to steer me, honey. I'll talk my own way along. I've got along unhelped for fifty years. It was accident, eh?"

"It was," said Gerald.

"And that's a lie, young man."

"You are fifty, are you not?"

"And what of it?"

"You are old enough to know better than to talk to a stranger as you talk to me."

Maddern came swooping down the steps. There was no shadow of doubt that he was of a fighting stock and full of blood royal which hungered for battle.

"Dad!" cried the girl from above.

"Don't be alarmed," said Gerald. "Nothing will happen."

"What makes you so infernally sure of that?"

"A still small voice is speaking to me from inside," said Gerald.

And suddenly rage mastered him. It was the one defect in his nature that from time to time these overmastering impulses of fury would sweep across him. He lowered his voice to a whisper which could not reach the girl, but what he said to Maddern was: "You overbearing fool, step down the hill with me away from the girl, and I'll tell you some more about yourself."

To his amazement, Maddern chuckled.

"This lad has spirit," he said cheerfully. "Ain't you going to introduce me, Kate?"

"This is my father?" said Kate.

"I have gathered that," said Gerald.

"And, Dad, this is Gerald Kern, who was just. . . ."

"Gerald Kern?" shouted Maddern, leaping

back a full yard. "Are you the one that . . . come up here!"

He caught Gerald by the arm and literally dragged him up the stairs and into the shaft of light which streamed through the open door.

"It's him!" he thundered to the girl as he stood back from Gerald, a rosy-cheeked, white-haired man with an eye as bright as a blue lake among mountains of snow. "It's the one that kicked Red Charlie out of town. Oh, lad, that was a good job. Another day, and I'd've got myself killed trying to fight the hound. When he talked to me, it was like a spur digging me in the ribs. But Charlie's gone, and you're the man that started him running! Gimme your hand!" And he wrung the fingers of Gerald Kern with all his force.

This was pleasant enough, but in the background what was the girl doing? She was regarding the stranger with wonder which went from his odd riding boots to his riding trousers, thence up to his face. But anon her glance wandered toward the trail outside the house again, and the heart of Gerald sank. Truly, she was even more deeply smitten than he had dreaded to find her.

But William Maddern was taking him into his house and heart like a veritable lost brother.

"Come inside and sit down, man," went on Maddern. "Sit down and let me hear you talk. By Heaven, it did me good to hear the story.

I'd have given a month of life to see Red Charlie when the lanterns and the other truck landed on him. Kate, you can stand watch for Tommy."

Gerald was dragged inside the house. "Why should I watch?" said Kate.

"Make yourself busy," said Maddern. "We're going to have a talk."

"Am I too young to hear man-talk?" asked Kate angrily, standing at the door.

"Now there's the woman of it," said her father with a grin. "Lock a door, and she's sure to break her heart unless she can open it, even if she has all the rest of the house to play in. But if you're inside, you'll be sure to wish you were out to wait for Tommy Vance."

She tossed her head.

"Let him stay away," she said. "But not to have sent a single word, Dad!"

And Gerald bit his lip to keep from smiling. It was all working out as though charmed.

"When I was a youngster in Montana," began Maddern, "I remember a fellow in the logging camp as like Red Charlie as two peas in a pod. And when. . . ."

With one tenth of his mind, Gerald listened. With all the rest he dwelt on Kate. And she was all that he had hoped. The glimpse had been a true promise. Now for a season of careful diplomacy and unending effort.

Were not ten days long enough for a great campaign?

VI "Gerald Meets Cheyenne Curly"

But ten days were not enough! Not a day that he left unimproved. Not a day that he did not manage to see Kate Maddern. But still all was not as it should be. He felt the shadowy thought of big, handsome Tom Vance ever in her mind. It fell between them in every silence during their conversation.

Not that he himself was unwelcome, for she liked him at once and showed her liking with the most unaffected directness. But sometimes he felt that friendship is farther from love than the bitterest hate, even.

In the meantime, he had become a great man in Culver City. The sinews of war he provided by a short session every evening in Canton Douglas's place — a very short session, for it must never come to the ear of the girl that he was a professional gambler who drew his living from the cards. To her, and to the rest of Culver City, he was the ideal of the careless gentleman, rich, idle, with nothing to do except spend every day more happily than the days before it.

Neither was there any need for more battle

to establish his prowess. It was taken for granted on all hands that he was invincible. Men made way for him. They turned to him with deference. He was considered as one apart from the ordinary follies of lesser men. He was an umpire in case of dispute; he was a final authority. And the sheriff freely admitted that this stranger had lessened his labors by half. For quarrels and gun play did not flourish under the regime of Gerald Kern.

There was the case of Cheyenne Curly, for instance. Cheyenne had built him a repute which had endured upon a solid foundation for ten years. He was not one of these showy braggarts. He was a man who loved battle for its own sake. He had fought here and there and everywhere. If he could not lure men into an engagement with guns, he was willing to fall back upon knife play, in which he was an expert after the Mexican school; and if knives were too strong for the stomach of his companion, he would agree to a set-to with bare fists. Such was Cheyenne Curly. Men avoided him as they avoided a plague.

And in due time, stories of the strange dandy who was running Culver City drifted across the hills and came to the ear of the formidable Curly. It made him prick his ears like a grizzly scenting a worthy rival.

Before dawn he had made his pack and was on the trail of the new battle.

None who saw it could forget the evening on

which Cheyenne arrived in Culver City. He strode into Canton Douglas's place and held forth at the bar, bracing his back against a corner of the wall. There he waited until the enemy should arrive.

Canton Douglas himself left his establishment and went to give Gerald warning. He found that hero reading quietly in his room, reading the Bible and. . . .

But that story should be told in the words of Canton himself.

"I come up the hall wheezing and panting, and I bang on Gerald's door," he narrated. "Gerald sings out for me to come in. I jerk open the door, and there he sits done up as usual like he was just out of a bandbox.

" 'Hello,' says he, standing up and putting down the big book he was reading. 'I'm very glad to see you, Mr. Douglas. Sit down with me.'

" 'Mr. Kern,' says I, 'there's hell popping.'

" 'Let it pop,' says he. 'I love noise of kinds.'

" 'Cheyenne Curly's here looking for you,' says I.

" 'Indeed?' says he. 'I don't remember the gentleman?'

"I leaned ag'in the wall.

" 'He's a nacheral-born hell-cat,' says I. 'He don't live on nothing less'n fire. He's clawed up more gents than would fill this room. He'd walk ten miles and swim a river for the sake of a fight.'

"'And he has come here hunting trouble with me?' says Gerald.

"'He sure has,' says I.

"'But I'm a peaceable man and an upholder of the law, am I not?', says Gerald.

"'Which you sure are, Mr. Kern,' says I. 'When you play in my house, I know that there ain't going to be no gun fights or no loud talk. And that's the straight of it, too.'

"'Very well,' says he. 'Then, if you won't stay with me and try a few of these walnuts and some of this excellent home-made wine . . . if you insist on going back immediately . . . you may tell Mr. Cheyenne Curly that I am most pacifically disposed, and that I am more interested in my book than in the thought of his company.

"I let the words come through my head slow and sure. Didn't seem like I could really be hearing the man that had cleaned up Red Charlie. I backed up to the door, and then I got a sight of the book that he was reading. And . . . by the Lord, boys, it was the Bible! Wow! It near dropped me. I was slugged that hard by the sight of that book! Yep, it was an honest Injun Bible all roughed up along the edges with the gilt half tore off, it had been carried around so much and used so much.

"Well, sir, it didn't fit in with Gerald the way we knew him, so quick with a gun and so handy with a pack of cards. But, after all, it did fit in with him, because he always looked as cool and as easy as a preacher even when he was in a fight. It give me another look into the insides of him, and everything that I seen plumb puzzled me. Here he was reading a Bible, and the rest of us down yonder wondering whether he'd be alive five seconds after he'd met Cheyenne Curly! He seen me hanging there in the doorway, and he started to make talk with me. Always free and easy, Gerald is. He sure tries to make a gent comfortable all the time.

"He says to me: 'I get a good deal of enjoyment out of this old book. Do you read it much, Mr. Douglas?'

" 'Mr. Kern,' says I, 'I ain't much of a hand with religion. I try to treat every man as square as I can and as square as he treats me. That's about as much religion as I got time for.'

" 'Religion?' says he. 'Why, man, the Bible is simply a wonderful story book.'

"Yes, sir, them was his words. And think of a man that could read the Bible because of the stories in it! Speaking personal, there's too many 'ands' in it. They always stop me!

" 'Well,' says I to Gerald, 'I'll go down and tell Cheyenne that you're too busy to see him tonight. He'll have to call later.'

" 'Exactly,' says he. 'One can't be at the beck and call of every haphazard stranger, Mr. Douglas.'

" 'No, sir,' says I. 'But the trouble with Cheyenne is that he ain't got no politeness, and that when I tell him that, he's mighty liable to come a-tearing up here and knock down your door to get at you.'

"At that, Gerald lays down his book and shuts it over his finger to keep the place. He looks at me with a funny twinkle in his eye.

" 'Dear, dear,' says he, 'is this Cheyenne such a bad man as all that? Would he actually break down my door?'

" 'He would,' says I, 'and think nothing of it.'

" 'In that case,' says he, 'you might tell him that I am reading the story of Saul, and that when I have finished I may feel inclined to take the air. I may even come into your place, Mr. Douglas. Will you be good enough to tell him that?'

" 'Mr. Kern,' says I, 'I sure wish you luck. And if he gets you, there ain't a chance for him to get out of this town alive.'

"At that he jumps up, mad as can be.

" 'Sir,' says he, 'I hope I have misunderstood you. If there should be an altercation between me and another man, I know that the victor would never be touched by the mob.'

" 'All right,' says I and backed out the door feeling as though I'd stepped into a hornet's nest.

"I come downstairs and back to my place. There's Cheyenne Curly still standing at the bar with his back to the wall. He ain't drinking none. And all the half of the bar next to him is empty. The boys are doing their drinking in front of the other half. And Curly is waiting and waiting and not saying nothing to nobody, but his shiny little pig eyes are clamped on the door all the time.

"I go up to him and say: 'Curly, Gerald is plumb busy reading a book, but when he gets through with it he says that he's coming down to have a little talk to you.'

"Curly don't say nothing back. He just runs the tip of his tongue over the edge of his beard and grins to himself like I'd just promised him a Christmas dinner. Made my blood turn cold to look at him.

"Then we started in waiting . . . me and every other man in my place, and there was a clear path from the door to the place where Curly was standing at the bar. But outside that path nobody was afraid of getting hurt. When two like Gerald and Curly started the bullets flying, every slug would go where it was aimed.

"It wasn't more'n half an hour, but it seemed like half a year to all of us, before the swinging doors come open and in walks Gerald. He was done up extra special that night. He had a white silk handkerchief wrapped around his throat like he was afraid of the cold. His boots shined like two lanterns. And the gun he was carrying wasn't no place to be seen. Matter of fact, just where he aims to pack his gun we ain't been able to make out . . . he gets it out so slick and easy out of nowhere.

"I looked over to Curly. And there he was crouched a little and with his right hand glued to the butt of his gun, and he was trembling all over, he was so tensed up for a lightning-quick draw.

"But his hand hung on the gun. He didn't draw, and I wondered why.

"I looked down to Gerald. And by Heaven, sir, he wasn't facing Curly at all. He'd turned to one side and he was talking to young Hank Meyers. Yes, sir, with that wild cat all ready to jump at his throat, Gerald had turned his back on him, pretty near, and he was standing over by the table of Hank.

"Everything was as silent as the inside of a morgue. You could hear every word Gerald was saying. And his voice was like silk, it was so plumb easy.

" 'I haven't seen you since the last mail, Mr. Meyers,' he was saying. 'What is the word from your sick mother now?'

"Well, sir, hearing him talk like that sent a shiver through me. It wasn't nacheral or human, somehow, for a gent to be as calm and cool as that.

"Hank tried to talk back, but all he could do was work his lips. Finally, he managed to say that the last mail brought him a letter saying that his mother was a lot better. And Gerald drops a hand on Hank's shoulder.

" 'I'm very glad to hear the good news,' he says. 'I congratulate you on receiving it. I have a little engagement here, and when I'm through I'll come back to you and hear some more, if I may.'

"You could hear every word clear as a bell. He turns back again.

"Curly was still crouched, and now he yanks his gun half clear of the holster, but Gerald leans over and takes out a handkerchief and flicks it across the toe of his boot.

" 'Beastly lot of dust in the street,' he says.

"Well, sir, there was a sort of a groan in the room. We was all keyed up so high it was like a violin string breaking in the middle of a piece. I was shaking like a scared kid.

"But finally Gerald straightened and come right up toward Curly. I looked at Curly, expecting to see his gun jump. But there was nary a gun in his hand. Maybe he was waiting for Gerald to make the first move, I thought. And then I seen that Curly's eyes were glassy. His mouth was open, and his jaw was beginning to sag. And he was shaking from head to foot.

"I knew what had happened; that long waiting had busted his nerve wide open the same as it had busted the nerve of the rest of us.

"Up come Gerald straight to him.

" 'I understand,' says Gerald, 'that your name is Cheyenne Curly, and that you've come to see me. What is it you wish to say to me, sir?'

"Curly moved his jaw, but didn't say nothing.

I could hear the boys breathing hard. Speaking personal, I couldn't breathe at all.

" 'I was given to understand further,' says Gerald, 'that you intend to wipe up the ground with me.'

"Curly's hand moved at last. But it swung forward . . . empty! And I knew that there wasn't going to be no shooting that night. But it was like a nightmare, watching him sort of sag smaller and smaller. Straightened up he must have been about three inches taller'n Gerald. But with Gerald standing there so straight and quiet, he looked like a giant, and Curly looked like a sick boy with a funny beard on his face.

"Hypnotism? I dunno. It was sure queer.

"Pretty soon Curly manages to speak.

" 'I was just riding this way,' says Curly, his voice shaking. 'I ain't meaning any harm to you, Mr. Kern. No harm in the world to you, sir.'

"He starts forward. I felt sick inside. It ain't very pretty to see a brave man turned into a yaller dog like that. Halfway to the door Curly throws a look over his shoulder, and then he starts running like he'd seen a gun pointed at him. He went out through the door like a shot. And that was the end of Curly.

"But, speaking personal, you and me, I'd rather hook up with a pair of tornadoes than have to face Gerald with a gun!"

VII "Kate Rolls a Boulder"

There were other tales of that famous encounter between Gerald and Cheyenne Curly, that bloodless and horrible battle of nerve against nerve. And certainly the sequel was true, which related how terrible Curly sank low and lower until finally he became cook for a gang of laborers on the road, a despised cook who was kicked about by the feeblest Chinaman in the camp.

There was another aftermath. From that time on, men shunned an encounter with Gerald as though he carried a lightning flash in his eye. For who could tell, no matter how long his record of heroism, what would happen if he should encounter Gerald Kern in Culver City? Who could tell by what wizardry he accomplished his work of unnerving an antagonist? And was it not possible, as Canton Douglas had so often suggested, that there was a species of hypnotism about his way of looking a man squarely in the eye?

Even Kate Maddern was inclined to believe. And Kate was, of all people, the least likely to be drawn by blind enthusiasms. But she talked seriously to Gerald about it the next day.

301

It was a fortnight since Tommy Vance had disappeared, and Gerald himself was beginning to wonder at the absence of Tom. Was it possible that the young miner had determined to double the test to which he was subjecting himself? December was wearing away swiftly, and still he did not come. It troubled Gerald. It was incomprehensible to him, for he had not dreamed that there was so much metal in his rival. But perhaps it could be explained away as the result of some disaster of trail or camp which had overwhelmed Tommy Vance.

In fact, he became surer and surer as the days went by that Tom would never return — that somewhere among those hard-sided mountains lay his strong young body, perhaps buried deep beneath a snow slide or the thousand tons of an avalanche.

And yet there was no feeling of remorse in Gerald, even though it was he whose cunning suggestion had thrust Tom out of the camp. His creed was a simple one: "Get what you can from the world before the world gets what it can from you."

In his own life he had never encountered mercy, and for mercy he did not look in his dealings with others. He gave no quarter, because he expected none. And if, from time to time, the honest and happy face of Tom Vance rose before him, Tom Vance with his eyes shining with the thought of Kate — if that thought rose for a moment, it was quickly forgotten again. Did not an old maxim say that all was fair in love or in war?

And he loved Kate profoundly, beyond belief. He could no longer be alone. The thought of her followed him. It fell like a shadow across the page of the book he was reading. It whispered and stirred behind his chair. It laid a phantom hand upon his shoulder and breathed upon him in the wind.

Yet for all the vividness with which he kept the thought of her near him, she was always new. And on this bleak morning, as December grew old, it seemed to Gerald that it was a new girl who welcomed him at the door of her cabin.

He studied her curiously. All these days he had been waiting and waiting. There was something in her which kept certain words he was hungry to say locked behind his teeth. But this morning, with a bounding heart, he knew that there was a change.

He told her so in so many words.

"Something has happened," he said. "There's been some good news since I saw you yesterday. What is it, Kate ?"

"Didn't you see when you came up the steps?"

"Nothing," he said thoughtfully. "I saw nothing changed."

She brought him to the door again and threw it open. The strong wind, sharp with cold from the snows, struck them in the face and tugged her dress taut about her body.

"Don't you remember the boulder which used to be beside the door?" she inquired.

"I remember now," he said, looking down to the ragged hollow near the threshold, where the great stone had once lain.

"Now look down the hillside. Do you see that big wet brown stone among all the black ones?"

A hundred yards away, across the road and down the farther slope, he saw the stone she pointed out.

"I pried the boulder up this morning," she said. "All last night I lay awake thinking about it, but finally I made up my mind. This morning I pried it out of its bed, and it rolled down the mountain. It sprang across the road in one bound, and then it fell with a crashing and smashing away off yonder."

She closed the door. They turned back into the room, and Gerald sat down with her near the fire.

"Well," she cried at last, aren't you going to ask me what it all means?"

"I'd very much like to know," said Gerald.

"You're always the same," said Kate Maddern gloomily. "You keep behind a fence. You're like a garden behind a wall. One never knows what is going on inside. And it isn't fair, Gerald! It's like reading a book that has the last chapter torn out. One never has the ending of the yarn."

He smiled at her anger and said nothing.

"Well, the stone was in the way when we built the shack," she went on at last, still a little sulky. "Dad is very strong, and yet he couldn't budge it. He was about to blast it when Tom Vance came up from the mine. He laid hold of the stone . . . he's a perfect Hercules, you know . . . and he tugged until his shoulders creaked. He stirred it, but he couldn't lift it.

" 'It's no good,' Father said. 'You can't budge the stone, Tommy. Don't make a fool of your-self and break your back for nothing.'

"Tommy simply looked at him and at me. Then he jumped back, caught up the stone, and staggered away with it. He dropped it yonder, and when we built the house the stone was by the door."

She paused. Gerald had leaned forward, and she said the rest looking down to the floor.

"I've never been able to see that boulder," she said, "without thinking of Tommy. It meant as much to me as the sound of his voice, and it was just as clear. Can you understand what I mean?"

"Of course," said Gerald sadly. "Of course I can understand."

"But finally," she went on, "I made up my mind last night. Tommy was not coming back. Perhaps he had found some other girl. Per-haps he was tired of me, and he hadn't the words or the courage to tell me about it. So he simply faded away. And this morning I got up and pried out the stone and watched it roll away."

He could raise his eyes no higher than her throat, and there he saw the neck band of her blouse quiver ever so faintly with the hard beating of her heart.

"And after the boulder rolled away," said Gerald at last, "what did you do then?"

"What do you think I did?"

He looked up to her face. She was flushed with a strange excitement.

"You came back and lay on your bed and cried," said Gerald.

"Yes," she whispered. "I did."

"And then. . . ." continued Gerald.

He interrupted himself to draw out a cigarette, and he smoked a quarter of it in perfect silence before he completed his sentence.

"And then," he concluded, "you jumped out and wiped the tears out of your eyes and vowed that you were an idiot for wasting so much time on any man. Is that right?"

"My father saw me, then . . . and he told you all about it!"

"Not a word."

"But how do you know so well?"

"I make a game of guessing, you see."

She stared at him with a mixture of anger and wonder.

"I wonder," she said, "if there is something about you . . . something queer . . . and do you really see into the minds of people?"

"Not a bit," he assured her.

"Do you think I believe that?"

Her head canted a bit to one side, and she smiled at him so wistfully that his heart ached.

"Now that the boulder is gone, Kate, won't you be lonely?"

"On account of a stone? Of course not. And then I have you, Gerald, to keep the blues away, except when you fall into one of your terrible, terrible, endless silences. I almost hate you then."

"Why?"

"Because, when a man is silent too long, it makes a girl begin to feel that he knows all about her."

"And that would be dreadful?"

"Dreadful!" said Kate Maddern and laughed joyously. As though she invited the catastrophe!

"But I'm only a stuffed figure, I'm afraid," said Gerald. "You're like a little girl playing a game. You call me Gerald to my face, but you call me Tommy to yourself, and when you are talking to me you are thinking of him."

She flushed to the eyes.

"What a terrible thing to say!" cried Kate.

"Then it is true?"

"Not a word."

"Ah, Kate," said he, "I guessed it before, but that doesn't lessen the sting of knowing that my guess was right."

She sprang out of the chair.

"Do you imagine that I'm still dreaming about him?" she challenged him.

"I know you are."

"You're wrong. I won't be treated so lightly by any man!" She added: "Besides, I think I always cared for him more as a brother than a sweetheart. We were raised together, you know."

"Ah, yes," said Gerald.

"You're not believing me again?"

"I haven't said that."

"It's gospel truth! And I'll never care for him again. I really never want to see him again. I'm only furious when I think of all the sleep I've lost about his going away!"

How easy, now, to say the adroit and proper words. She had opened the way for him. That was plain. She had thrust the thought of Tom Vance away from her, and she wanted Gerald to fill the vacant room. And yet there was an imp of the perverse in him. He fought against its promptings, but he could not fight hard enough.

He found himself studying her shrewdly. Would it not be delightful to show her how truly weak she was — and make her in another moment weep at the very thought of Tom Vance? He spoke against his more sane, inner promptings.

VIII "Gerald's Blindness"

I'm going to tell you a true story," he said. "It will change your mind about Tommy, and it will make you hate me, among other things."

"Do you want me to do that?"

"I can't help telling you," said Gerald. "The devil seems to be in me this morning, making me undo all my hard work. But let's go back to that first evening when I passed you on the hillside."

"Of course I remember."

"I never told you why I came back. But naturally you guessed."

"Naturally," she said. "There aren't many girls in Culver City."

He raised his thin-fingered hand and brushed that thought away. He waved it into nothingness.

"I heard you call," he said, "and then I had a shadowy glimpse of your face in the lamplight. That was enough to catch me. Mind you, it doesn't take much . . . just the right touch, the right stir of the voice, a glimmer of the eyes, and a man is gone forever. I was riding on a bus in London once. A girl crossed the street and looked up to me with a smile. Not that she was smiling for me, you understand

". . . but there was an inner joyousness. . . ."

He paused to recall it. And Kate Maddern was still as a mouse, listening, her fingers interlaced.

"She was very beautiful," said Gerald. "And if there had been something more, I think I should have climbed off that bus and followed her. But something was lacking."

"A second look, perhaps," suggested the pagan heart of Kate.

He smiled at her.

"You miss my point," he said. "What I am trying to say is that men are sometimes carried away by shams. They think they have found the true thing, and they wake up to learn that their hands are full of fools' gold. But when the reality comes, it has an electric touch. And when I saw you and heard your voice, Kate, I knew that you were the end of the trail."

"Gerald," she said, "you are making love to me shamelessly."

"I am," said he and lighted another cigarette. "But to continue my story . . . unless it bores you?"

"I am fascinated! Of course I am!"

"Very well. That night I went into Canton Douglas's place, and almost at once I heard some one speak to Tommy. Of course I looked, and the moment I laid eyes on him I knew that this was the man you had called to. He was handsome, clean-eyed, young, strong. He was everything that a man should be. And I

310

managed it so that I should be asked to sit in at their game. I wanted to know more of Tommy Vance. I wanted to test the metal of my enemy."

"Enemy?"

"Because I knew that one of us had to win, and the other one had to lose."

She sat stiff and straight and watched him out of hostile eyes. Whatever kindliness she might feel for him now, might she not lose it if she learned the rest of his story? And yet he kept on. That imp of the perverse was still driving him as it had driven him, on a day, to lead his army of brown-skinned revolutionists into the jaws of death, tempting chance for the very sake of the long odds themselves.

"I watched Tommy Vance like a hawk," he went on. "I was hunting for weaknesses. I was hunting for something which would prove him to be unworthy of you. And if I had found it," — here he raised his head and met her startled glance squarely — "I should have brushed him from my path with no more care than I feel when my heel crushes a beetle. But as the game went on I saw that he was a fine fellow to the core, brave, generous, kind, and true as steel!"

He wrung those words of commendation from himself one by one.

"And I saw," he went on, "that as long as he was on the ground my case was hopeless."

He paused again.

"Well, in love and in war, Kate, men do bad things. I managed it so that I could leave the game when he did. He was walking up the hill to meet you, and I set myself to prevent him from coming to your cabin. I told myself that if I succeeded there was still a fighting chance for me. But if I failed I would pack up and leave town and forget you if I could, or at least try to obscure the memory of you with other faces and other countries. But luck helped me. There is a jealous string in every lover. I plucked at that until I had Tommy in agony."

"How horrible!" breathed Kate Maddern.

"Yes, wasn't it? But I was fighting for something better than life, and I took every weapon I could lay my hands on! He was a wide-eyed young optimist. But I planted the seed of eternal doubt in him. He began with an unquestioning faith in you. And before half an hour had passed, I had made a wager of a thousand dollars with him that if he left Culver City for a while and let you wonder why he had gone, when he returned he would find that you had forgotten him. Well, he made the wager, and he left the town that same night. And that's where he is now!"

"Oh, poor Tommy!" she cried. "And I've doubted him and hated him all these days, when all the time. . . ."

"When all the time he was simply making the test. But he was right, after all, and I was hopelessly wrong. At least, Kate, I've made a

312

good hard fight out of it. And the other day when I taught you how to manage Sorrow . . . just for an instant when you leaned and laughed down to me I thought my dream was to come true after all."

He rose from his chair and confronted her courteously.

"But to send him away by trickery . . . and all these days to let me think . . . oh, it was detestable!"

"It was detestable," he admitted gravely.

And, encountered by that calm confession, her fire of anger was smothered before it had gained headway. She began to regard him with a sort of blank fear.

"What is it that you do to people?" she asked suddenly, throwing out her hands in a gesture of helplessness. "There is Red Charlie, who stood as though his hands were chained while you shamed him. And there is poor Tommy, of whom you made a fool and sent away. And then there is Cheyenne Curly, whom you have turned from a brave man into a coward! Is it hypnotism?"

"Do you think it is?" he asked. "At least, they have seen the last of me around here."

He tossed his cigarette into the fireplace.

"Perhaps the devil inspires me to mischief, but the good angel who guards you, Kate, forced me to confess, and so all the evil I have done to Tommy is undone again. I'll leave tonight and trail him until I find him. I'll give him back to you as I found him. And, having been tried by fire, you'll go on loving each other to the end of time!"

He picked up his hat.

"You see that I retain one grace in a graceless life. I shall not ask you to forgive me, Kate."

"You are going . . . really?"

"Yes."

"To get Tommy?"

"Yes."

"For Heaven's sake, Gerald, don't do that!"

The hat dropped from his finger tips.

"What on earth do you mean?"

"I mean . . . nothing! Only, don't you see. . . ."

She had fallen deeper and deeper into a confusion of words from which she could not extricate herself. Now she looked around her as though searching for a place of retreat.

"Won't you understand?" she pleaded.

"Understand what?" asked Gerald huskily.

Then, as some wild glimmer of hope dawned on his brain, he sprang to her and drew her to the window so that the gray and pale light of the winter day beat remorselessly into her face.

"Kate!" he cried. "Speak to me!"

She had buried her face in the crook of her arm.

"Let me go!" whispered Kate.

Instantly, his hands fell away from her. And there she stood blindly swaying.

"Oh," she said, "it is hypnotism. And what

314

have you done to me? What have you done to me?"

"I've loved you, my dear, with all the strength that is in me!"

"Hush!"

"It is solemn truth."

She broke into inexplicable tears and dropped into a chair, and Gerald, white-faced, trembling as Cheyenne Curly had trembled in Canton's place, stood beside her.

"Tell me what I can do, Kate. Anything . . . and I'll do it. But it tortures me with fire to see you weep!"

"Only don't leave me," she whispered.

He was instantly on his knees beside her.

"I didn't know until you spoke of going," she sobbed. "And then it came over me in a wave. I had never really loved Tommy. He was simply a big brother. I was simply so used to him. You see that, Gerald?"

"I'm trying to see it, dear. But my mind is a blank. I can't make out what is happening, except that you are not hating me as I thought you would, Kate. Is that true?"

"Come closer!"

He leaned nearer her covered face. And suddenly she caught at him and pressed her face into the hollow of his shoulder.

"How can you be so blind!" she breathed. "Oh, don't you see, and haven't you seen almost from the first, that I have loved you, Gerald? And, oh, even when you tell all that

315

is worst in you, it only makes me care for you more and more. What have you done to me?"

"Kismet!" murmured Gerald and, raising his head high, he looked up to the raw-edged rafters and through them and beyond them to the hope of heaven.

IX "A Chance for a Kingdom"

An hour later, Gerald was riding Sorrow straight into the heart of a snow-laden wind, for some action he must have to work out the delirious joy which filled him, and which packed and crammed his body to a frenzy of recklessness. The very edge of the wind was nothing to him and, when the driven snow stung his lips, he laughed at it. For this was his home land, his native country, and all that it held was good to him, for was it not the land, also, which held Kate Maddern?

Lord bless her, and again, Lord bless her! He laughed to himself once more, and this time with tears in his eyes, to think how blind he had been to the truth. And he remembered how, with tears and with laughter, she had confessed that the rolling away of the boulder and the telling of that story to him had all been anxiously planned before in the hope that he would speak then, if ever.

"And I shall be good to her," said Gerald solemnly to himself. "I shall be worthy of her. Yes, I shall be very worthy of her, so far as a man may be! I shall make her a queen. I shall give her all the beauty of background which she needs. Her hand on velvet . . . a jewel at

317

her throat and another in her hair. . . ."

His thoughts darted away, every one winged. The energy which he had wasted here and there and everywhere he would now concentrate upon the grand effect. No matter for the wild failures which had marked his past. Was not even the young manhood of Napoleon filled with vain effort and foolish adventures? There was still time and to spare for the founding of an empire!

It was a glorious ride, and the flush of glory was still in his cheeks and bright in his eyes when he came back to the hotel. And there, in the window, he saw a great, rough wreath of evergreen. He studied it in amazement. It was not like Culver City to waste time and energy on such adornments when there was gold to be dug.

Of the proprietor, behind the stove inside, he asked his question.

"And you don't know?" asked the latter with a twinkle in his eye.

"Of what?" asked Gerald.

"It's Christmas, man! Tomorrow will be Christmas! And tonight will be Christmas Eve!"

Gerald stared at him, then laughed aloud with the joy of it. This surely was the hand of fate, which brought him for a present, on the eve of the day of giving, Kate Maddern and all her beauty and all her heart and soul, like a great empire!

He went up the stairs still laughing, with the voice of the proprietor coming dimly behind him: "There's a gentleman waiting in your room for you, Mr. Kern. He looked like I might tell him to go up and make himself to home. . . ."

The rest was lost and Gerald, kicking open the door of his room, looked across to no other than Louis Jerome Banti sitting in Gerald's chair and pouring over Gerald's own Bible. The act in which he was engaged shocked Gerald hardly less than the sight of Banti's face in this place. It was like seeing the devil busy over the word of God.

"In the name of heaven, Banti," he said, "how do you come here?"

"In the name of despair, Monsieur Lupri, what keeps you here?"

"Hush!" cautioned Gerald, raising his finger. "There are ears in the wall to hear that name."

"Are there not?" and Banti chuckled, rubbing his hands together. "Yes, ears in the stones to hear, and a tongue in the wind to give warning of it!"

They shook hands, and as their fingers touched a score of wild pictures slid through the memory of Gerald, fleeter than the motion picture flashes its impressions on the screen — a cold winter morning on a road in Provence, with the crackle of the exhaust thrown back to them from the hills as their machine fled among the naked vineyards —

and a night on the Bosphorus when they were stealing, with their launch full of desperadoes, toward the great hulk of the Turkish man-of-war — and a day in hot Smyrna when the. . . .

"Banti here . . . Banti of all men, and in this of all places."

"And you, my dear Gerald?"

"How did you find me? How on earth did you trail me?"

"How does one follow the path of fire? By the burned things it has touched."

"But I left you with the death sentence. . . ."

"Over my head, and three days of life before me."

"Yes, yes! I had done my best. . . ."

"And it was better than you knew. The poor girl loved you, Gerald. On my soul, I sorrowed for her when I heard her talk. But she it was who came to me at last. With her own hand she opened the doors for me. She guided me to the last threshold. She put a purse fat with gold in my pocket. She pointed out the way to escape, and she gave me the blessing of Allah and this little letter in French for you . . . for her beloved . . . her hero of fire and steel."

"Be still, Banti, in the name of heaven!"

He took the little wrinkled envelope. He tore open the end of it. Then, pausing, he lighted a match and touched it to the paper. The flame flared. The letter burned to red-hot ash, fluttered from his finger tips, and reached the floor as a crumbling and wrinkled sheet of

320

gray. A draft caught it and whirled it into nothingness.

"And that is the end?" quietly said Banti, who had watched all this from a little distance. "And yet there was an aroma in the words of that letter, I dare swear, that would have drawn the winged angels lower out of heaven to hear them!"

"It is better this way," said Gerald. "I burn the letter, and I send the fair thoughts back to the fair lady."

"And her fat papa," said Banti.

"And to her fat papa. And now . . . Banti, you have not changed. You are the same!"

"The very same," said Banti, and drew himself up proudly to the full of his height. He was a glorious figure of a man. And the cunning of his hand was second only to the cunning of his brain. Well did Gerald know it. Had he not, for three long months in wintry Moscow, dueled with this man a duel in the dark, a thousand shrewd strokes delivered and parried under cover of the darkness of polite intrigue? They had learned to read each other then, and they had learned to dread and respect each other, also. Victory in that battle had fallen to Gerald, but it was a Pyrrhic conquest.

"It is gold, then," said Banti. "It is gold that keeps you here?"

"No."

"A mystery, then?"

Gerald shrugged his shoulders.

"No matter. You will come with me?"

Gerald shook his head.

"No?" and Banti smiled. "But listen . . . there is a kingdom in the sea!"

"Damn the sea and its kingdoms," said Gerald. "This is my country. And here I stay!"

"There is a kingdom waiting in the sea," said Banti. "Ah, I laugh with the joy of it, monsieur, when I think! Gerald, dear fellow, we are rich men, great men. The task awaits us!"

"Banti, I shall not listen. And it is useless for you to talk."

"In two words, Gerald, what has happened to you?"

"I have a charm against your temptations. I have a flower to defy Circe, Louis."

"A woman?"

"My wife-to-be."

"She shall go with us, then. Where there is a king, may there not be a queen?"

"You are talking to the wind."

"You have not heard me yet."

"I don't wish to."

"You are afraid, then, in spite of your charm?"

"Talk if you must, and the devil take you."

"There is a kingdom in the sea . . . there is an island in the sea, Monsieur Caprice. Four great powers of Europe and Asia have reached for it . . . their hands met . . . and not a finger touched it. So, in mortal fear of one another, they withdrew. They made a compact. They erected the savage chief into a king. They erected the island into a kingdom in the sea, and they swore neutrality. But kings need wars for diversion and, since he could do no better, this amiable idiot of a fat man-eater began to fight with his own subjects. In a trice, a musical comedy set.

"Yonder stands the commerce of the world licking its chops at the sight of the spices of that island and the river dripping with un-mined gold and the mountains charged with iron ores and coal, the swamps foul with oil . . . but yonder is the king fighting his subjects. The island is split into halves. The king holds all the lowlands and the rich towns. The young cousin, with more brains in his little finger than in the whole sconce of the king, holds the uplands with a few hundred stout brigands and makes a living by inroad. Commerce is at a standstill. They kill a white man for the sake of his shoes. And the great, neutral nations and the great, neutral merchants stand about like a circle of lions and find one consolation . . . that no one is getting a piece of the dainty.

"But now, Gerald, enters a man of brains and money. He sees inspiration. He comes to me. He says: 'I give you money and a shipload of arms and a score of good men. Not too many, or my hand will be too apparent. I send you away. Your ship is wrecked . . . by unlucky chance . . . on the shore of the island. You go inland. You open communication with the young prince in the highlands. You offer him money and guns if he will give you the direction of his war. You, with your tact and your diplomacy, make a conquest of that young prince, who is man enough to appreciate a man. He takes you to his heart and into his councils. He turns over his army to you. The guns and the money are brought up. Your few white men are your bodyguard. You train the army of natives for a month. When they can strike the side of a mountain at fifty paces, you invade the domains of the king. In another month, you have routed him. You establish a new regime. You admit my money into your interior. And of the profits which come out of my ventures, one half goes to the kingdom . . . that is, to you . . . and the other half goes to me.'

"This, Gerald, is what the man of money and brains says to me. And I reply: 'This is all very well. If I were a Napoleon, I should undertake the task. I should agree to do all these things, ingratiate myself with the colored potentate, become ruler of him and his army, and conquer the kingdom. But I am not Napoleon. I am, however, one of his marshals. In a word, I know the man. Give me only six months to bring him to you!'

"That, Gerald, was my reply, and here I am. Pack up your luggage. Pay your bills . . . I

have ten thousand, and half of it is yours . . .
and come with me at once. We can reach a
train by tomorrow morning!"

He stopped, panting with the effort, and he
found that Gerald was twining his hands together and then tearing them apart and staring down at the floor. But at last he raised his
head.

"No," he said, "I cannot."

"In the name of heaven, Gerald! It is all as
I have said! All that is needed to turn the
dream into real gold is your matchless hand,
your brain!"

"No again. A month ago, I should have gone
with you. Today, not if you offered me England
and its empire! Banti, you waste words!"

Banti was pale with despair, but he had
learned long years before that words are
sometimes worse than wasted. He maintained
a long silence.

"Gerald," he said at last, "if I may see the
lady, my long trip will not have been wasted!"

X "The Gathering of the Storm"

Footfalls stormed up the stairs, clumped down the hall, and a heavy hand beat on the door.

"Come!" said Gerald as Banti discreetly turned his face to the window.

The door was thrown open by Canton himself.

"Kern," he said, "there's some devilish bad luck! Young Vance. . . ." He stopped as he caught sight of Banti.

"This is my friend, Mr. George Ormonde," said Gerald. "And this is my friend, Canton Douglas."

Gravely, having received a glance, Banti advanced, bowed, and shook hands.

"You may say anything you wish," said Gerald, "before Mr. Ormonde."

"It's Vance come back raving and crazy," said Canton. "He's been out, and he struck it rich ... rich as the very devil. He came back, went to see Kate Maddern, and then came down to town like a lion. I dunno what happened between them two. Maybe you know that better than me. But Vance calls you all kinds of names and says that he'll prove 'em on you when he meets you. He's been in my place, saying that he'll come there again at eight tonight, and that he expects to find you there."

"Very well," said Gerald. "I'll meet him."

Was it not better, once and for all, to have the matter ended and poor Tommy Vance out of the way?

"It's got to be that?" said Canton sadly. "But Tommy's white, Kern. Ain't there any other way?"

"There would have been," said Gerald, "if the fool had come in private to me. But now that he's challenged me before the town, can I do anything but meet him?"

"It don't look like there's no way," and Canton sighed. "But it's a mighty big shame."

"It is," said Gerald. "He's a fine fellow. I've no desire to meet him with a gun."

"Suppose he were to be arrested and locked up till he got over this. . . ."

"Do you think he ever will get over it?" asked Gerald.

Canton hung his head.

"It's a mess," he muttered. "I dunno what to think . . . except that it's the devil."

"Go back and tell the boys that I'll be there," said Gerald, and Canton left the room sadly.

Banti sat down again, whistling softly to himself.

"I suppose this man Vance is the former lover?" he asked.

"He is," said Gerald.

"He will depart from this sorrowful world tonight, then?"

"He will," said Gerald.

"And then," said Banti, "I shall take you and the lady of your heart away with me."

Gerald paused in his walking, then frowned upon Banti.

"Louis," he said, "let me make this clear to you: I would give up a kingdom rather than take a chance which might harm her. Carry her into an adventure like that? I had rather be burned alive."

"Really?" said Banti, arching his brows. "But, my dear Gerald, if you marry the lady, do you think that you will be able to trust yourself thereafter?"

"Louis, you have never seen her."

"To be sure. But marriage is a great blunder of good resolutions. They vanish like the rainbow under the sun. One never comes to the pot of gold. Consider yourself. Here in the full flush of a new love, Gerald, when I paint the picture of that kingdom which is waiting for you in the sea, I notice that your eyes roll and your lip twitches and your hand jumps as though you were already in the fight. And in your heart of hearts you are already down yonder in the fight, scheming, plotting, learning a Negro tongue, working your way into Negro hearts, drilling a savage army. Tush! I can see the pull on you. It almost shakes you even now. You are on the verge of saying that you will take the wife with you. But after marriage, Gerald, when time dulls the gold

. . . what then, *monsieur?*"

"Then there will be no devil named Banti bringing temptations."

"I? I am only one weak ship bringing a single cargo to port. But you, Gerald! What of you? Your own mind is the fruitful hatchery of strange schemes. The love of adventure is born in the blood. It is in yours. The time will come, lad, the time will come. The good Lord watches! He will whisper into your ear of some strange land . . . by the pole . . . an oasis in the desert . . . a shrine in Persia . . . and you must be gone. The tiger cannot be tamed. It may be wounded. It may be subdued by pain and kept quiet for the moment. But when it is healed, when you are past the first pangs of love, what then, Gerald?"

"Curse you and your tongue, Louis. I'll hear no more of this!"

"You love her, do you not?"

"Like a part of heaven . . . like all of heaven . . . and she is all of it that I shall ever see."

"If there is such a thing as punishment for sin, why, yes, Gerald, she is all of it that you will see. But, if you love her, you care for her happiness more than for yours."

"A thousand times!"

"Then give her up!"

"Ah?"

"I say give her up. Come. You are capable of noble action. This will be one of them. Step out of her life while you may. Step out before you break her heart."

"Banti. . . ."

"I shall not come back."

"No, no! I have to thrash this out with you!"

"Talk it over with yourself. You are a better judge than I!"

"Banti, stay for five minutes!"

"I shall be waiting . . . at eight o'clock . . . on the edge of the town. I shall have a horse. Bring your own. And we will ride all night into the lowlands. Remember!"

"Banti, for the sake of our friendship. . . ."

"*Adieu!*"

The door closed in the face of Gerald. He leaned against it until a tumult of new thoughts rushed into his brain — things which he should have said. He tore the door open, but Banti was already out of sight, and Gerald turned slowly back into the room.

XI "Tom Writes a letter"

Night came early on that Christmas Eve. The steep shadow dropped from the western peaks over the little town, and by four o'clock it was dusk, with a wild wind screaming about the hotel. It shook the crazy building. It blew a vagary of drafts through the cracks in the floor, through the cracks in the walls. But through it all Gerald lay forward on his bed with his hands over his face.

There had never been a torment like this before. Not that march across the desert when the mirage floated before them with its blue, cool promise of water — not that moment earlier in this same day when he had told the truth to Kate — nothing compared with that long time of loneliness.

If Banti had been there, if one human being had been near to argue with and convince and thereby convince himself — but there was no one, and the solitude was a terrible judge hearing his thoughts one by one and spurning them away.

He looked at his watch suddenly and saw that it was seven o'clock. In a single hour he must face poor Tom Vance in Canton Douglas's place and kill him. There would be

331

no chance to shoot for the hip or the shoulder, for Tom Vance would himself shoot to kill his treacherous enemy, and it was life or death for Gerald.

Not that he doubted the outcome. He had met sterner men than Tom Vance and killed them. And he would drop Tom with the suddenness of mercy.

And yet his soul rebelled against it. Rather any other man he had ever met than this fellow whom he had so wronged. But suppose he could meet him and talk with him, man to man, for ten minutes, might not something be done?

He hurried out into the night, filled with the blind hope. Through the slowly falling sleet — for the wind had fallen to a whisper — he went up the street to the cabin of Tom Vance far at the end. He could look past it up the hillside to the glimmer of light in the cabin of old Maddern. In that house were the only people in the town who did not know, for the story would be kept from their ears surely.

With his hand raised to knock at the door, he hesitated. To walk in suddenly on Tom might be merely to bring to a quick head the passion which was in the young miner. There might well be a reaching for guns — and then the tragedy even earlier than he had dreaded to meet it.

Full of that thought, he went around the shack to the window on the farther side. It was sheltered by a projection of the roof and was clear of snow or frost; he could look through to the interior. There was Tom Vance not the distance of an arm's reach away!

Gerald shrank back. Then, recalling that the light inside would blind the man within to all that stood beyond the window, he came closer again. And he saw the pen scrawl slowly across the paper, hesitate, and then go on again, a painful effort.

It wasn't hard to make it out. The lantern light fell strongly upon the page, and the stub pen blotted the paper with heavy, black lines. So he read the letter with ease:

Dearest Kate:

If this comes to you, I shall be dead as you read it, and Kern shall have killed me. I have challenged him. We are to meet tonight at Douglas's place, and there will be only one ending. I know what he can do. He can almost think with a six-shooter. And, though I am a good shot, I cannot stand up to such a marksman. But I shall do my best.

I don't want you to think of me as a man who has thrown himself away as a sacrifice. I know that the chances are against me, ten to one, but the tenth chance is worth playing for. With the help of heaven, I shall kill him!

You may think that I am a hound for

fighting with a man you have said you love. But once you told me that you loved me, and I believed you. And I still believe that you cared for me as much as you care for him now. But there is some sort of fascination about him. The boys have told me when they begged me to take back my challenge or else fail to appear at Canton's tonight.

They have told me how he broke down the nerve of Curly. They had sworn that no one can stand up against him.

And wouldn't it be odd if a man who can break the nerve of trained fighters couldn't win over a girl just as he pleased?

That is why I'm taking the tenth chance. Not that you'll ever care for me afterwards, but because at least I'll have cleared the road for some other good man more worthy of you than either Kern or me.

I know that he is not your kind of man. He's a stranger. He talks in a new way. He thinks in a new way. He acts as no one in the mountains acts. He has a manner of fixing his eye on a person and paralyzing the mind and making one think the thoughts he wishes to put into one's head. And that's what he has done with you.

You half admitted it when you told me that you no longer cared for me because of him. When I asked you if you really loved him, you looked past me — a queer, far-away look. You seemed half afraid to answer. You would love him some day, you told me, more than you could ever love any other man.

But I think that you will never come to that day. Kate, take this letter as my warning. I am dying for the privilege of telling you what I think in honesty. And I swear to you that you can never be happy with him.

Where has he been? What has he done? Who knows his past?

Have you ever thought of asking him those questions? Has he ever spoken to you about friends of his? No, and I think he never will. One thing at least I know. I know that he is a man who has been hunted. He has a quick, sharp way of looking at new faces that come near him. Sometimes, when people pass behind him, he shivers a little. And, when he is not speaking, his mouth is set, and his teeth are locked together. He looks in repose as though he were making up his mind to do some desperate act.

I saw all these things that one evening I was with him. And I knew then that danger — hours and days and months of deadly danger — had given him those characteristics.

So, in the name of heaven, Kate, learn more about his past before you marry him. And remember this — that a man who is capable of cheating and betraying another man as he cheated and betrayed me is capable of no really good thing.

I know that you will hate me when you have read this letter. Warnings are never welcome. But because I love you, Kate, I cannot help writing. Good bye, my dear.

Tom

So the letter came slowly to its end, and Gerald stepped back into the blanketing night and the soft whisper of the wind.

Who was it that said that truth sits upon the lips of dying men? He could not remember, but he knew the truth of all the words which Tom had written. And it was new to Gerald. Yes, the power with which he had been able to break down the wills of strong men might surely be strong enough to break down the will of a young girl. And had she, indeed, come to care for him chiefly because he was strange? He was recalled to a dozen times when he had found her looking at him half in terror, looking at him and past him as though she were seeing the future and trembling at what she saw.

Sick at heart, he came slowly back to the window. In the farther corner Tom was strapping on cartridge belt and the heavy Colt hanging in the holster. He took up a broad-brimmed, felt hat and placed it carefully on his head. Over his shoulders he threw a slicker. Next he drew out the revolver and went carefully over its action.

When he was assured that all was in working order, he dropped the gun back into its leather sheath and marched to the door.

"The fool!" muttered Gerald. "To go twenty minutes ahead of time and then stand the strain of waiting!"

But Tom was not yet ready to leave. He turned again. He hesitated with a strange, half-sad, half-bewildered look. Presently, he dropped to his knees beside his bunk. He clasped his thick, brown hands together. He raised his head, and Gerald watched the moving of his lips in prayer — words which came slowly, a long-forgotten lesson, learned at his mother's knee, was brought back to him and delivered him from the evil he would have done.

XII "What Women Hate Most"

Assembled Culver City was packed into Canton Douglas's place, and yet not a dollar's worth of business had been done, except at the bar. And when the door finally opened, at three minutes before the great clock at the end of the hall showed eight, all heads jerked around and watched Tommy Vance step in.

It was noted that he was quite pale, and that his lips were compressed hard — a bad sign of the condition of his nerves. But he bore himself stiffly erect. He looked quietly over the crowd, made sure that the man he wanted was not yet come, and walked with deliberation to a seat near the clock, pulling up a chair well apart from the others. There he sat and crossed his legs and waited.

"Just like the time that Cheyenne Curly . . . ," muttered someone.

"Except that it's different," said another. "Curly was a skunk. And Tom Vance is as white as they make 'em."

"He is," agreed another. "It's a shame that they got to have this trouble. Women sure get at the bottom of all the mischief."

"And Christmas Eve, too!"

"Is it? God damn me if I hadn't forgot that

it was the twenty-fourth! Tomorrow's Christmas?"

"It sure is."

"There'll be no Christmas for poor Tom Vance this year."

"Why not? Maybe he'll have the luck against Kern."

"Luck? There ain't any luck against Kern. He's like fate. You can't get away from him. When his eye takes hold of you, you just feel that you're gone, that's all."

"There's a considerable talk about this Kern," said a grizzle-haired old-timer who was proud of being able to remember the early frontier and the men of those hardy days. "But what's he done? He scared out two low-lived bullies. And any white man that don't get scared can beat an ignorant hound that don't know nothing but picking trouble. This here will be different. This boy Vance is clean. He'll make a different kind of fight."

"If his nerve holds. Look here! He can't hardly roll a cigarette!"

Tom had ventured on this task and was dribbling tobacco wastefully over the floor. Finally, the paper tore across. He crumpled it, dropped it, and drew out the makings again.

"There you are," said the gray-haired observer. "There's the right nerve for you. He's going to try again. He'll do better this time, too. Look!"

The second cigarette was deftly and smoothly manufactured, lighted, and a cloud of smoke puffed from Tom's lips.

"That ain't nerve," said Canton himself, who was near. "That's the way a gent will act when he's facing a death sentence. He ain't got any hope. All he wants to do is to die game without showing no white feather. But why don't Kern show up? It's past time!"

Here eight o'clock began striking, the brazen chimes booming loudly through the hushed room, and when the last sound echoed away to a murmur every man leaned forward, expecting to see the door fly open. The cigarette fell from the numbed fingers of Tom Vance. But the door did not stir. And slowly the crowd settled back.

"He's waiting so's he can break Tom's nerve just the way he busted Cheyenne Curly's."

"It's a mighty poor thing to do," said Canton with heat. "I don't mind saying that it's downright low to play that sort of game with poor Tom that ain't got a chance in a hundred, anyway."

They waited five minutes, ten minutes, and the scowls of the miners grew blacker and blacker. The trick of Gerald was patent to all, and it enraged them.

"Hey, Jerry!" called Canton suddenly to one of the men who was making a pretense at continuing a card game. "Run over to the hotel, will you? Tell Gerald that his friend is waiting for him plumb anxious, will you? And tell him that he's a mile overdue!"

There was a growl of assent from a hundred throats, and Jerry went off reluctantly on an errand which might prove dangerous unless the message were phrased tenderly enough. In three minutes he came back, and he came with a rush that knocked the swinging door wide.

"Boys!" he shouted as he came to a halt, "I looked up in his room. He ain't there, and his things are gone. I run down and looked into the stable. And Sorrow wasn't there. And nobody ain't seen nothing of Kern nowhere!"

"By heaven!" roared the old-timer of the gray hair, rising from his place. "I sort of suspicioned it! He didn't like this game. He knew he had different kind of meat to chew this time! He's been bluffed out! He's quit cold, the yaller dog!"

Tumult instantly reigned in Canton's place. Out poured the hundred searchers. They swarmed through the town, but they found no trace of Gerald Kern.

"Up yonder!" called an inspired voice at last, pointing to the light in the window of the Maddern cabin. "I'll bet a thousand that he's up there sitting pretty and talking to his girl. Let's take a look!"

And up the slope they went with a willing rush. They reached the door. It was opened by Maddern, with Kate behind him.

"Where's Kern?" they demanded.

"Not here," they were told. "And what's up, boys?"

"The hound has run out on Tom Vance. He's showed yaller! He's quit without daring to show his face!"

"No, no!" cried Kate.

"Here's a hundred of us to swear to it," said Canton Douglas furiously.

And Kate raised her hands to her face.

It was hard going over the mountains. Though the wagons had beaten out a trail, it was deep with snow, and the two horsemen let their mounts labor on, giving them what aid they could to guide them until the clouds were brushed from the sky and the stars looked down to show them the way. A little later, they reached the last of the ridges. Below them spread the lowlands and a safer and an easier trail to follow.

Here they drew rein, and Gerald looked back.

"Cher ami," said Banti, "no halting by the way. The small waiting makes the great heart ache. Forward, comrade!"

"Hush, Louis. It is my last look!"

"Ah, my friend, it will be far better when you have your first look at your kingdom yonder over the sea."

"But this is my country," he said. "And this is the last time that I shall see it."

So the silence grew, while Banti gnawed his lip with anxiety.

"It is my torment if you linger here," he said gently, at last.

"Louis," murmured his friend, "what is it that a woman detests most in a man?"

"A close string drawn on the pocketbook."

"We are not in France," said Gerald with a touch of scorn. "Tell me again."

"Long silences at the table," said Banti. "They drive the poor dears mad. Yes, a silent husband is even worse than a pinched wallet."

"Still wrong," said Gerald. "What a woman hates most of all in a man is cowardice. A woman ceases to love a man who runs away from danger."

"Eh?"

"Because that is rot at the heart of the tree."

"Perhaps you are right. But what of that?"

"Nothing," said Gerald. "Let us ride on again."

They passed on down the slope. And the steady trot of the horses covered the weary miles one by one. As for Banti, he whistled; he sang; he told wild tales of a dozen lands, and all without drawing a word from his companion until, as they drew near to a town, he said:

"What is in your head now, Gerald? Tell me the thought which has stopped that restless tongue of yours so long?"

"I shall tell you," said Gerald, "though it will

343

mean nothing to you. I have been thinking of Christmas Day, Louis, and the power of prayer."

Louis considered a moment.

"Ah, yes," he said at last. "I had forgotten. But this is Christmas, and on this day one goes back to the silly thoughts of one's childhood. Is it not so?"

Acknowledgments

The Black Rider" by George Owen Baxter was first published in *Western Story Magazine* (1/3/25). Copyright © 1925 by Street & Smith Publications, Inc. Copyright © renewed 1952 by Dorothy Faust. Acknowledgment is made to Condé Nast Publications, Inc., for their cooperation. Reprinted by arrangement with Golden West Literary Agency. All rights reserved.

"The Dream of Macdonald" was first published under the title "'Sunset' Wins" by George Owen Baxter in *Western Story Magazine* (4/7/23). Copyright © 1923 by Street & Smith Publications, Inc. Copyright © renewed 1951 by Dorothy Faust. Copyright © 1996 for restored material by Jane Faust Easton and Adriana Faust Bianchi. Acknowledgment is made to Condé Nast Publications, Inc., for their cooperation. Reprinted by arrangement with Golden West Literary Agency. All rights reserved.

"Partners" by Frederick Faust was first published in *The American Magazine* (1/38). Copyright © 1938 by Crowell Publishing Corporation. Copyright © renewed 1966 by Jane Faust Easton, John Frederick Faust, and Ju-